SWEET INTENSITY

A DARK MAFIA ROMANCE

RUTHLESS OBSESSION

BOOK SIX

ZOE BLAKE

CONTENTS

CHAPTER 1

BRYNN

*H*is dark gaze locked on me the moment I entered the room.

My steps faltered as fear closed my throat.

I didn't have to know who the man was to know he was someone to be feared.

It wasn't just the fact that he was significantly taller and bigger than most of the men in the reception room of the Four Monks Private Club, or the sinister tattoos that peeked out above his tuxedo jacket collar and on the top of his hands, although those things certainly helped.

No, it was the way everyone seemed to keep a respectful distance around him despite the crowded room.

Even those who dared to approach him in conversation did so hesitantly, and not before doing this awkward dance of bowing their head and pausing, as if waiting for permission to speak.

Only powerful men with authority and obscene amounts of money, enough to make them someone to be feared, commanded that kind of fidelity.

My heart pounded in my chest.

I lowered my head and focused on the brightly polished emerald marble floor, tracing the shimmering gold veins with my eyes, in an attempt to calm my frazzled nerves.

This was a mistake.

A huge mistake.

I shouldn't be here.

I should never have agreed to this stupid scheme.

I swallowed past the paranoia that made my mouth dry.

I couldn't believe I was actually in the reception hall of the infamous Four Monks Private Club.

This was so far from my world I might as well have been waltzing into Buckingham Palace, yet even I knew about the Four Monks Club.

You'd have to live under a rock in Chicago to not know about its reputation for ties to the Russian mafia and its powerful influence over not just local, but national politics and financial affairs because of its elite membership.

Rumor was it was called the Four Monks because the owners were named after Russian monks who had all been tortured to death.

I shivered and held my clutch purse more tightly over my stomach to cover the slight damp mark from where I had scrubbed off a smudge of white deodorant in the taxi over here.

I really didn't belong here, among these uber-rich and famous people.

Especially knowing why I am here.

My toes scrunched in my too-big borrowed high heels, praying I didn't trip and fall on my face.

God, I wished I was home right now on my sofa watching some ridiculous reality TV show, still only dreaming of attending an event like this one day, because the reality of actually attending one was stomach-churning.

Hiding behind a wave of my long, dark hair, I hazarded a glance in the man's direction again and gave a start.

He was *still* staring intently at me.

I desperately wanted to look away, to break the contact, but it was as if I was mesmerized.

My elbows pressed against my ribcage to stop my arms from shaking.

He knows.

Somehow he knows what I'm here to do.

There was a man trying to talk to him, and he either didn't seem to notice or didn't care.

The man ignored all those around him and just gazed at me with a cool arrogance that was seriously off-putting.

Maybe I was wrong?

How can he possibly know why I'm here or about our plan?

I didn't even know about the scheme until a few hours ago.

Again, I chastised myself for being guilted into agreeing to it.

If I survived this night not being thrown into jail, *or worse*, I would never complain about my boring life ever again.

I had to be wrong.

Why would a man like *him* stare at someone like *me*?

He had to be looking at something, or someone, behind me. Right?

I mean, he was rich, not to mention handsome in that tuxedoed James Bond villain meets dirty sexy cage fighter sort of way.

Older, distinguished, rich-as-fuck men like him stared at gorgeous haute couture models and European hotel heiresses.

They wouldn't stare at a twenty-something broke-ass cosmetologist wearing a slightly too small, off-the-rack dress.

I yanked on the too short hem of my black cocktail dress.

My curves made the dress more form-fitting than I liked, making me very self-conscious. Unfortunately, my hem tug pulled the dress too far down in the front, exposing the top curves of my breasts and the scalloped edge of my black lace bra.

With a gasp, I covered my chest as I pulled on the neckline, adjusting it.

As my cheeks warmed with embarrassed heat, I tortured myself with another reluctant glance in the man's direction.

Of course, the man had seen the entire humiliating, uncouth display, further proof I didn't belong among this cultured crowd.

And so had the person talking to him.

His leer and the crude way he licked his lips and gestured in my direction gave him away.

What happened next sent a shockwave throughout the reception room.

The man turned and grabbed the person leering at me by the throat, and lifted him off the floor.

My hand flew to my mouth.

There were several gasps from women in the crowd, but other than that, no one said a word…and no one moved to help the man being attacked.

Someone within earshot of me chuckled. "Stupid fuck. That will teach him to piss off Antonius Ivenchenko."

Antonius Ivenchenko.

So that was his name … and he was Russian … as if the man could get any freaking scarier.

The spectator's companion then said, "Everyone knows the four monks have short fuses and to steer clear of them. You would never catch me talking to one of them. Not worth risking my membership to the club."

The four monks?

He is one of the infamous four monks?

The room spun.

Antonius Ivenchenko, the man staring at me, was one of the owners of the private club I had just agreed to help rob.

CHAPTER 2

BRYNN

I opened my lips as if to speak, but closed them.

What on earth would I say?

Please don't kill that man for staring at my boobs?

For starters, I was across a room filled with over two hundred people.

No, not people, witnesses.

Attempted murder witnesses.

Was it possible the owners of the Four Monks were so powerful that one of them could literally strangle a man to death in front of a room full of people and get away with it?

I was fairly certain there were at least several aldermen here and at least one state senator in attendance.

Thankfully, security appeared.

Antonius released his grip and the man fell to the floor in an inelegant heap.

Far from accusing Antonius of trying to kill him, the man actually rose up on his knees and clutched at Antonius' tuxedo pants.

He started to beg him for forgiveness and was still begging when security grabbed him under the arms and dragged him away.

Antonius lifted his arm and barely gestured with his two fingers.

A smaller man in a tailcoat tuxedo and a gold waistcoat who seemed to be some sort of floor manager came rushing over.

Antonius nodded in my direction.

Uh oh.

This must be what drowning in ice-cold water felt like, to suddenly feel numb and overwhelmed, to want to move and thrash about and escape but be too terrified.

My limbs felt heavy and weighted down.

All the sounds around me were just loud rushing water.

Just then an elegant older woman, with her silver hair arranged in a French twist, distracted the assembled guests. "Good evening, ladies and gentlemen, the card tables are now open, please enjoy."

She swept her left arm out as, on cue, three arched, double oak doors opened in unison.

Inside was a stunning two-story ballroom decorated with crystal chandeliers, gold and cream damask wallpaper over deep cherry wood wainscoting, and plush cobalt blue velvet high-backed chairs surrounding oval green felt poker tables evenly spaced throughout the room, each with a tailcoat tuxedoed dealer standing at attention.

Bile rose in the back of my throat at the sight of it.

I was going to be sick.

"I can't do this," I whispered.

Yuri, my friend's boyfriend, and the person who dragged me into this mess, leaned in closer. "What did you say?"

I sucked my lips between my teeth, trying to quell the nervous nausea.

"I'm sorry, Yuri. I wanted to help you and Heather, but this is all too much! I didn't sign up for *this*!"

I gestured low with my hand, not wanting to draw any more attention to us.

Thank God, Antonius' attention was at least on the swarm of guests eagerly filing into the poker room.

Yuri wiped his hand over his mouth. He then leaned in close and hissed, "You promised, Brynn."

My shoulders hunched as I lowered my head, anxious at his rising anger.

I didn't know Yuri that well.

Hell, I barely knew Heather when it really came down to it.

The only reason why I had even agreed to this stupid scheme was because Heather was my co-worker and eight months pregnant.

This was just supposed to be a little harmless misadventure while doing a favor for a pseudo-friend … but it had turned into a freaking nightmare.

My right arm around my waist. "You said it was a *casual* poker game with some friends of friends and that you only needed to win a couple hundred bucks to cover rent so you two didn't get evicted," I accused.

He shifted from one foot to the other as he looked at the people moving past us, clearly eager to get inside and choose his seat. "Yeah, so?"

Gesturing with my head, I whispered through clenched teeth, "This isn't a fucking casual poker game, Yuri! This is the fucking Four Monks Club! I heard someone say the buy-in is fifty grand on some tables."

A *just for rent* poker game with some friends was on a rickety card table surrounded by a couple of metal folding chairs and covered in a faded piece of thin green felt with the fold marks still down the middle.

It took place in a cluttered garage that smelled like gasoline and dusty cardboard. And the refreshments were cans of lukewarm cheap beer served out of a scuffed-up cooler filled with watery ice and a bowl of slightly stale pretzels.

It was not a stunning nineteenth-century multi-million-dollar private club housed in two converted townhouses located on Astor Street in the exclusive Gold Coast neighborhood of Chicago.

With drinks served by gorgeous women in long cocktail dresses wearing black diamond chokers, carrying sterling silver trays with crystal martini glasses.

The members currently chatting warmly with one another and taking their seats were the who's who of the powerful elite of not just Chicago, but Washington, D.C., and Hollywood.

And Yuri thought I was going to help scam these people out of their money!

My fingernails dug into the cheap patent leather of my clutch.

I needed to get the fuck out of here.

Yuri rubbed the back of his neck. "I've got it handled. Someone's staking me. Now come on. I need to make sure I sit in the seventh seat of the seventh table and eat seven olives before we start."

I blinked.

Ignoring the ridiculous superstitious nonsense gamblers were notorious for, I held back. "Staking you? Yuri, listen to me. This is insane!"

I lowered my voice. "Even I know the Four Monks Private Club is affiliated —" I stopped and looked around.

Antonius seemed to be in a heated conversation

with three other equally large, super scary-looking men in tuxedos with tattoos, probably the other three 'monks.'

At least his attention was not on me.

I turned so my back was facing them and mouthed, "With the Russian mafia."

Yuri was also Russian but not big, scary Russian, more like scrawny, twitchy Russian.

He should definitely have known this club had a sinister reputation.

Yuri's eyes twitched.

See … twitchy.

He rubbed his neck again. "Brynn, you promised Heather you'd do this for us."

This was pretending to be Yuri's companion for the night, and if necessary, handing him one of the playing cards that were hidden in a special pocket along the side hem of the dress Heather insisted I wear.

It was called a *card switch*.

Apparently, Heather had done it for him in the past, but being eight months pregnant, she was drawing too much attention and couldn't pull off the sleight of hand required.

I guessed Yuri couldn't hold the cards himself because he had been caught card switching before.

So now he worked with a partner so he wasn't busted with extra cards on him.

And it was totally *cheating*.

Stealing really.

The only reason why I had agreed to be part of it was because he and Heather had laid a huge guilt trip on me about how they were broke and she was pregnant and they were about to be put out on the street and how it would only be one harmless hand of poker for a few hundred, just enough to cover their rent shortfall.

I made him swear he would only gamble enough for rent.

Just enough for rent.

Fifty fucking grand buy-in at a private club owned by the Russian mafia was not a just-for-rent-money poker game.

I shook my head. "I'm sorry. I didn't sign up for this."

Pivoting on my too big heels, I turned to leave.

He grabbed my upper arm. "You can't leave. Look, we lied to you. It's not rent. I'm in the hole for a lot of money to a lot of bad people. I'm in real trouble. They're going to kill me if I don't pay them back soon. This game is my only chance. Just one hand, please, Brynn, I'm begging you."

I wasn't sure why, but I looked over my shoulder at Antonius Ivenchenko.

He was no longer speaking with his partners.

There was a dark scowl on his face as he looked from me to Yuri then down at Yuri's hand on my arm.

My eyes widened as Antonius separated from them and stepped toward us.

The very real possibility that I would end the evening explaining to Heather how I got her baby daddy killed by a big scary Russian, possibly mafia dude, flashed across my mind.

Turning toward the ballroom entrance, against my better judgment, I gave in as I allowed him to pull me inside, losing us in the crowd.

"Fine. One hand."

WITHIN TWENTY MINUTES, it became painfully obvious why Yuri owed people money and had to resort to cheating to pay them back.

I barely knew how to play the game, and even I could tell he was a terrible poker player.

The current hand had a staggering seventy-five-thousand-dollar pot.

It was dizzying to watch the other men and one woman around the table just casually toss in the custom-made poker chips worth thousands of dollars, with the embossed Four Monks logo made of real gold leaf, or so I overheard one of the players say, as if it were no big deal.

Finally the moment I had been dreading came ….

Yuri reached down and flicked the side of my thigh with his finger.

That was the signal.

One flick meant he wanted an ace.

Two meant he wanted a queen.

Three a king.

He flicked my thigh twice.

I had been standing next to Yuri's chair pretending to watch the game, and not to be searching the room for any sign of Antonius Ivenchenko.

So far, I hadn't seen him, which somehow made me even more nervous than when he had been openly staring at me.

The moment I felt the signal, I froze.

I stared at the stacks of chips in the center of the table.

It was so much money—seventy-five thousand dollars—that I was about to help Yuri *steal*.

That it didn't seem to matter to these people was no excuse; it was still cheating, stealing.

It was still wrong.

If we were caught, it was a felony … or worse.

At least I thought it was, I wasn't sure.

I wasn't even sure if poker was legal.

I didn't even know why I was worried.

If we were caught cheating at the freaking Russian mafia owned Four Monks, I seriously doubted they were going to call the freaking cops.

Oh, God.

My stomach turned.

I was seriously in over my head.

Yuri flicked my thigh again.

This time more insistently.

The players around the table shifted in their seats.

A few of them made comments to Yuri to decide.

Yuri cleared his throat and looked up at me.

His eyes were pleading as he said to the table, but looked at me. "Sorry, I was distracted thinking about my *pregnant* girlfriend waiting for me at home."

Low blow, asshole.

Tightening my stomach to stop the nervous butterflies, I unclenched my right hand and slowly lowered my arm to the hidden pocket where he and Heather had stashed the queen of hearts.

Just as my fingertips touched the edge of the playing card, strong fingers clamped down on my wrist.

A hard body pressed against mine from behind, as an arm wrapped securely around my waist, trapping me.

Antonius Ivenchenko leaned down and growled in my ear, "You're in big trouble, little one."

CHAPTER 3

BRYNN

*W*as it possible to die from fear?

If he hadn't been holding me upright, I would have crumpled straight to the floor.

Fear made my teeth chatter. "Please," I rasped.

I couldn't think of anything else to say.

My brain was frozen in terrified shock.

I didn't have to turn around to know who held me.

I knew.

It was him.

Antonius Ivenchenko.

I had been right to be suspicious of him.

I had no idea how he could possibly have known what we were up to, but somehow he had known.

We were caught … and now we would pay.

I couldn't believe I was about to die, and all

because I got guilted into helping someone I barely knew cheat at a stupid fucking card game.

It wouldn't matter that I hadn't actually handed Yuri a card.

Somehow, I suspected that in this world, those types of distinctions weren't important.

I flinched as Antonius shifted his stance.

He released my wrist and reached for Yuri's cards. "He folds."

Antonius then tossed the cards onto the table, snatched Yuri by his shoulder and yanked him to a standing position.

Yuri wiped his mouth before gesturing at the table. "Dammit, Uncle Anton, I would have had pocket queens!"

Wait ... Uncle Anton?

What was going on here?

Had I been set up?

One of the other scary Russian monks approached.

Anton nodded. "Mac, you got him?"

Mac laid a heavy hand on Yuri's other shoulder. "Yeah." He raised his chin. "You want me to handle her, too?"

Anton's arm tightened around my waist.

His breath brushed the curls near my ear when he spoke. "No, I have something *special* for this one."

I stared unblinking at Yuri so hard my eyes

watered as I foolishly expected him to speak up for me.

Yuri reached for his vodka and slammed it before tossing the empty glass back on the table. "Fuck this place."

He then turned and stormed off.

My mouth dropped open as I blinked several times. My dry eyeballs burned as I glared at his scrawny retreating back.

The man named Mac followed, but not before gesturing to a tuxedoed floor manager who swooped in holding an expensive bottle of champagne as several women, their diamond chokers sparkling in the chandelier light, surrounded the poker table and dropped crystal flutes at each place setting.

It was all a smooth choreographed dance.

Soon the low conversational hum of the room returned to its former ebb as the quartet on the stage at the far end of the ballroom continued to play, accompanied by the soft click-clack of the heavy clay poker chips hitting the center of pots.

The table Yuri had been playing at continued with their game as if nothing had been amiss.

Anton tightened his grip on my hip. "Come."

I resisted, trying to root my feet to the floor, wondering if I dared to cry out for help.

Then I remembered how this same jaded crowd watched a man almost get strangled to death before their very eyes and none of them so much as raised a pinky finger to stop it.

And that man was probably one of their own.

Not a poor interloper like me.

For the first time, I forced myself to turn and look at Anton.

The top of my head barely reached above his shoulder.

This close, the harsh angles of his face were even more fierce and intimidating.

His salt and pepper hair gave him an air of distinction, although he was probably no more than in his early forties, but to look into his dark gray eyes, you'd think he was a hundred.

I swallowed. "Are you going to kill me?"

He raised one eyebrow as his gaze moved to my lips then back to my eyes. "Are you going to be a good girl and come quietly?"

I nodded.

He then winked.

Actually winked.

The gesture gave him a roguish sort of charm... for a super scary murdering mafia billionaire.

He pulled me closer to his side. "Then I think we can spare your life."

My eyebrows rose as I hugged my clutch to my chest. "I'm sorry. I don't mean to be difficult, but I can't tell if you're being sarcastic or serious."

He gestured with his hand. *"Nemnogo togo i drugogo."*

What the fuck?

He responds in Russian? Really?

Anton kept the flat of his palm firmly on my lower back as he shepherded me through the winding rows of poker tables.

Although the poker room wasn't overly warm, there was a rush of cool, fresh air as we crossed the threshold after two porters rushed to open the tall oak doors that led into the entry hall.

I glanced to the left, seeing a glimpse of Astor Street through the intricate etched glass windows of the entrance doors to the private club.

My toes scrunched inside my high heels in readiness.

Maybe … if I kicked my heels off …?

A gruff voice whispered harshly in my ear. "You'd never make it."

I stiffened.

Anton stretched out his right arm. "This way, *moya ocharovatel'naya malen'kaya vorovka.*"

I clenched my jaw.

More Russian.

Despite being impossibly afraid and in mortal danger, I was also cranky.

Yuri had promised to feed me and hadn't.

I was tired and hungry.

My toes were cramping from trying to keep from stumbling in these stupid high heels, and I wanted nothing more than to burn this dress.

I twisted my hips, pulling out of Anton's grasp.

Crossing my arms over my middle, I took a deep breath and pushed it out in a frustrated huff as my lower lip protruded into a pout.

In full temper tantrum mode, I even attempted to stomp my foot, but failed spectacularly when my ankle rolled and my foot slipped out of the heel.

After an awkward side trip, I kicked off the other heel and adjusted my arms to place my fisted hands on my hips to look more in control. As if it was *totally* my plan to suddenly put myself at an even more significant height disadvantage by taking off my four-inch heels.

Anton turned and crossed his arms over his chest to glower down at me.

I looked like a mouse trying to face off against a bear.

I tightened my lips. "Stop speaking Russian. It's not fair!"

Internally, I face-palmed myself. It was as if I was checking off a mental list of how to appear like an immature toddler in front of this man.

Throw a tantrum. Check.

Stomp your foot. Check.

Pout. Check.

Complain that it's not fair. Check.

The small lines around his eyes creased. "You realize, *moya ocharovatel'naya malen'kaya vorovka*," he repeated with emphasis, "that you are currently on *my* private property and that I happen to *be* Russian and that this is in fact a *Russian* private club?"

Not wanting to give in, I thrust out my chin. "I'm aware. That doesn't mean you don't have to be a gentleman about it. It's not seemly to speak another language in front of a lady."

I didn't have the faintest idea if that was true, but it sounded like something that would be in an etiquette book.

Putting on my best dowager duchess impression from *Downton Abbey*, I thrust out my chin.

Faking it got me into this mess, maybe it would get me out of it.

If they thought I was the daughter of someone important, someone with power, then they couldn't hurt me.

Anton stepped forward, towering over me.

I had wanted to stand my ground, but I buckled and stepped backward.

He stepped forward.

I moved back, until I connected with the wall.

He placed a forearm high over my head.

He was so large, he completely blocked my view of the entry hall behind him.

I couldn't even see if there was anyone walking by to offer help, not that I held out much hope that they would.

He placed a hand under my chin and raised my head to stare up … way up … at him.

His eyes were an unusual color, a dark stormy gray with jagged flecks of obsidian, like a thunderstorm with black lightning.

He then bowed his head slightly. "You are correct, my apologies."

Holy shit! Did he actually just apologize to me?

Be cool. Be cool.

I cleared my throat and schooled my features.

Thinning my lips to keep my expression suitably stern, and hopefully rich-person-looking, I said, "Apology accepted… just don't let it happen again."

His mouth quirked up at the corner, but swiftly stiffened into a straight line as his brow wrinkled. "Understood."

His thumb caressed my lower lip. "Would you like to know what I said in Russian … *my lady*?"

My stomach flip-flopped.

It was hard to tell whether it was from the sensual way he was touching me, or from the mixed signals of his tone.

Again, I couldn't tell if he was being serious or sarcastic.

Only a complete fool would miss the sinister energy radiating off the man.

And yet, whenever he spoke, there seemed to be a dark-humored charm to everything he said.

But that was the problem with dark humor … few people found anything charming about the dark and twisted macabre.

Deciding I had no choice but to play along with the game, I nodded, then licked my lips, tasting the salt from his skin. "Yes, please."

His gaze focused on my mouth.

I resisted the urge to self-consciously lick my lips again, not wanting to be accused of encouraging him.

He cupped my jaw more firmly and pushed down, opening my lips.

His thumb then brushed my lower lip again as he stared at my open mouth. His eyes widened slightly as his lips curled back, baring the sharp edge of his teeth.

I wasn't sure if he was going to kiss me or … I wasn't sure what … but I knew the intensity with which he stared at my mouth was terrifying.

The dark lightning in his eyes seemed to catch fire.

When he finally spoke, it was as if he was chewing on rocks, as his Russian accent thickened. "I called you … *my adorable little thief*."

He didn't have to hold my mouth open then, because in that moment, I gasped, opening it wider on my own.

So much for blustering my way out of this mess.

He pushed back from the wall and grabbed my hand.

"Come, let me show you how we punish naughty little thieves."

CHAPTER 4

ANTON

I grabbed her high heels and took her small hand in mine, making an effort not to squeeze it too hard as I led her across the hall.

Everything about her seemed adorably small … which only increased my anger.

What the fuck was someone as innocent and sweet as she seemed to be, doing with a scumbag like Mac's nephew?

He wasn't fooling me trying to curry favor with that Uncle Anton crap. He had always been a fuckup. Losing his mother last year had only made things worse.

He had been abusing Mac's sympathies, but to listen to Yuri, you'd think he was a snot-nosed kid who'd just lost his mommy instead of a grown-assed man.

Tonight had been the final straw.

The Four Monks was not the place for his cheap street hustling tricks.

He could have gotten someone killed.

I cast a glance over my shoulder at the beautiful woman trailing nervously in my wake.

Fuck, she was beautiful.

With her pale heart-shaped face and her long waves of honey-brown hair, she looked like a living doll.

The moment she walked into the club, I knew she didn't belong.

Her eyes were too big and bright as she took in her surroundings, not jaded and bored.

Then there was the way she self-consciously tried to hide her spectacular figure instead of strutting around like a preening peacock like the rest of the guests.

But when I saw who she was with an irrational, seething anger had taken hold.

Not just because the last time I saw Yuri he was with a woman who was heavily pregnant and it was my understanding he was the father. A true man honored his responsibilities.

But because a piece of shit like Yuri did not have the stones to protect an obviously inexperienced innocent little doll like her among a crowd of heathens like the members of the Four Monks.

I became determined to keep an eye on her …

until truth be told … I had finished with my obligations that night.

My plan had been to separate her from Yuri, which I didn't anticipate was going to be a problem, and take her for my own.

Then I saw Yuri signal to her ….

I had spent too many years in poker gaming halls not to know what that signal meant.

In that moment, I decided to put my plan into play sooner than expected.

But the end result was still the same.

Yuri was out … she was now mine.

I pushed on a hidden panel in the mahogany wainscoting just off to the right of a gilded framed Turner masterpiece depicting a turbulent sea.

The secret panel swung open revealing a wide black-and-white marble-tiled hallway with more mahogany wainscot paneling along the bottom wall and rich hunter green damask cloth wallpaper above.

Then I pulled her along until we passed several doors, stopping at the third one. I entered the nine-digit electronic code and pressed my thumb onto the keypad.

The deadbolt slid back and I turned the brass doorknob on the heavy oak door and swung it open.

One of the perks of having millions to convert two nineteenth-century townhouses into a luxury private club with a penthouse above for my living quarters was a spacious traditional executive office with wall-to-wall custom bookcases, priceless artwork, full lounging seating, and a hand carved black marble fireplace, all completely soundproof, of course.

It came in handy for my various business interests.

Stepping to the side, I gestured with a wave of my arm. "Ladies first."

She turned a wide-eyed face up to me, looked into the darkened room, then back at me.

She shook her head and took a step back. "I think I shall decline your kind offer."

I smirked. "Nice try."

I gave her cute ass a swat.

She cried out and hopped forward, crossing the threshold.

Stepping in behind her, I purposefully let the door slam shut behind me. It automatically locked with a resounding click.

She turned with a start.

I stood still, crossing my arms over my chest.

She bent to the side in an attempt to look around me at the shut door. Then she straightened and stared up at me.

She swallowed. "Did that door just lock?"

I nodded.

She licked her lips.

Fuck. The things I plan to do to that cute mouth.

My cock swelled against my thigh inside my tuxedo trousers.

She pulled her lower lip between her teeth. "I don't suppose you'd agree to open it again?"

I raised one eyebrow. "What do you think?"

She nodded as she swiped at a single tear that slipped down her cheek. "Look, I'm really sorry. I know what we did... or almost did... was wrong, but I was doing it for the right reasons, you have to believe me."

I tossed her shoes aside and crossed deeper into my private office. Shrugging out of my tuxedo jacket, I tossed it over one of the leather oxblood chairs placed in front of the large, carved executive desk.

Then I turned and sat on the edge of the desk and unhooked one platinum and black diamond cuff link, then the other.

Slowly rolling up one cuff, I studied her. "First, let's start with your name."

She grasped her black clutch purse to her stomach. "Are you going to call the police?"

"Do I look like the kind of man who calls the police?"

"You look like the kind of man people call the police on." She slapped her palm over her mouth.

Her next words were muffled. "I'm so sorry! I can't believe I said that out loud. I'm sorry. I'm really nervous."

She was adorable.

31

I rolled up my other cuff, exposing even more of my Russian prison ink, which I'm sure added to her fairly accurate criminal impression of me. "It's fine, little one. Now… your name."

She scrunched her brow as she raised a placating hand. "I'm trying really hard not to offend you… but I don't think I should tell you my name."

I nodded. "That's fair."

Her shoulders lowered as she visibly breathed a sigh of relief. Her grip loosened on her purse.

I leaned over, stretched out my arm, and easily snatched the purse from her open grasp.

"Hey," she cried out.

I held the purse over my head as she tried to lunge for it.

Her body brushed against the full length of mine, coming into contact with my already hard cock.

I watched her closely.

Her head dipped low as she looked to where our hips pressed together before her shocked gaze shot up to clash with my amused one.

She staggered backward, breaking the pleasurable contact.

With a chuckle, I flipped open her purse and pulled out her wallet, noticing there was no cash inside. I frowned. "Why is there no money in here?"

I scrutinized the contents.

A wallet and lipstick and keys. No cellphone. Strange.

Also a Metra card, which meant she didn't have a car and relied on dangerous public transportation, a fact I didn't like.

A single debit card, but no credit cards.

No ready cash and an Illinois State identification card, which meant that not only did she not have a car, but no one had taken the time to teach her how to drive, which spoke to possibly losing her parents at an early age.

My youth was misspent as an *aristokrat s sognutymi pal'tsami* — an aristocrat with bent fingers, or pickpocket. I had learned to become an amateur profiler just through the contents of a person's wallet or purse.

Brynn Caitlin Moore.

A Welsh proper name and a Scottish surname, interesting, not that that meant much for an American.

The name suited her. It was soft and feminine.

I looked at her age and smirked.

Twenty-two.

I was twice her age.

Usually, I didn't go for the younger ones.

Too much trouble.

But there was something different about Brynn.

She wasn't just young ... she seemed vulnerable and alone.

She clearly needed someone's protection.

Perhaps an older man with money, power, and

influence, who could make her life easier and more … pleasurable.

Someone like me.

She placed the leather chair between us, as if it would save her from me. "I have my debit card," she answered defensively, but rushed to amend. "But there's less than five hundred dollars in my account so please don't take it. I have to pay rent by the end of the week."

Her vulnerabilities were stacking up.

A beautiful young woman with….

No car.

No money.

No ring on her hand.

If she was with Yuri, the piece of shit had abandoned her.

So under no man's protection.

The address on her identification was in a rundown part of the city, on a street known for old apartment buildings with no security features to speak of.

All of which made her easy prey for any man with illicit intentions … a man like me.

I tucked her identification back in her wallet and placed it in her purse. I then leaned back, pulled out the center drawer of my desk, tossed her purse inside, and pushed it closed.

Brynn made a slight squeaky sound the moment the drawer slammed shut.

I turned back to face her.

My gaze roamed over her, from the top of her head to the tips of her pale pink painted toes.

She shifted under my scrutiny, twisting her fingers nervously.

When I finally spoke, my voice was harsh. "Take off your dress."

The blunt command took her by surprise.

She started, then blinked several times. "What?"

I straightened and took a step toward her. "You heard me."

Her shoulders hitched up as she crossed her forearms over her chest and backed up.

Her voice rose an octave. "Is this one of those times you're being sarcastic, not serious?"

I glanced down at the hard length of my cock straining against the fabric of my trousers, then captured her gaze. "What do you think?"

I knew what was coming the moment her pretty lips opened to inhale a deep breath.

She pivoted on her heel and dove for the locked door.

Wrenching on the doorknob, she slammed her open palm repeatedly against the door. "Help! Help! Help!"

I pressed my body against her, reveling in the feel of the curve of her ass as it pressed against my cock. Capturing her wrist around the cluster of cheap bead bracelets, I kissed the bright red skin of her palm.

As I pushed her silky hair over her shoulder, away from her ear, running my lips along the delicate whirl, I whispered, "Tsk, tsk, tsk, *moya malen'kaya vorovka*, you should be more careful. You are going to hurt yourself and for no purpose. That door is two inches of solid oak. No one is hearing your screams."

A shiver of fear racked her body. "Please don't hurt me."

I pulled her soft earlobe between my teeth before saying, "That will be difficult, since you need to be punished."

She whimpered. "Punished?"

I flipped her around and pinned both her wrists against the door over her head with one hand. "You insult me, Brynn. Did you honestly think I would allow you to waltz into my club and steal from my members without there being any consequences?"

Her thick black eyelashes clumped and spiked as her golden-brown eyes filled with tears. She sniffed. "But I didn't steal anything!"

"Only because you were caught."

Her gaze shifted to the side as she sniffed again.

Her full bottom lip pushed out in an adorable pout.

I was fast learning this was a sign she was about to become ill-advisedly stubborn.

"How do you even know I was going to steal? I mean, just because your nephew, Yuri, steals—"

"He's not my nephew. He's the nephew of a friend.

He just calls me Uncle because I've known him since he was a child."

"Well, just because Yuri steals doesn't mean I do!"

"So, if I prove that you were his partner in a poker card switching scheme, you will be a good girl and take your punishment?"

She lowered her head as she bit her lip.

I ran my knuckle down her cheek before cupping her chin and raising her gaze to mine. "Yes or no, Brynn?"

She took a deep breath. "Fine. Yes."

"Yes, what?"

She tried to avoid my gaze. "Yes, if you prove that I was Yuri's partner … I'll … I'll take my … my … punishment …."

"Like a…."

She pouted. "Like a good girl."

With a smirk, I flicked my wrist and held two queens and two aces in front of her face between two of my fingers.

Her eyes widened.

She tugged on her arms.

I released her wrists.

Her hands immediately went to the hidden pockets in her dress.

The playing cards were, of course, gone.

She stared at me. "How? When? I didn't even feel you touch me."

I winked. "That will be the last time you utter that sentence."

Her eyes widened as she slid away from the door and circled around me.

Since she couldn't leave through the door, she had no choice but to move deeper into my office.

I crossed my arms over my chest. "A deal's a deal, Brynn. Take off the dress."

"What are you going to do?"

My eyes narrowed. "Take off the dress. If I have to ask you one more time, I'm ripping it off," I warned.

With a gasp, she reached behind her and unzipped the ill-fitting cocktail dress.

I made a mental note to make room in my schedule this week to take Brynn shopping along Michigan Avenue. I would show her what designers I liked best on her gorgeous body and what type of lingerie to purchase to please me.

That cheap dress wasn't worthy of her.

Looking at the thick band of crystal bead bracelets around her left wrist, I imagined replacing them with diamonds.

She held the unzipped dress over her chest as she swiped a tear from her cheek. "Please…."

I raised an eyebrow. "Would you rather I change my mind and call the police and have you arrested?"

"No! Please don't do that!"

"Then take your punishment like a good girl. Drop the dress."

She obeyed and let the dress fall to the floor.

She then crossed her forearms over her chest again.

I gestured with my head. "Walk over to my desk."

Although it wasn't the high-quality handmade lace and silk I would be purchasing for her, I appreciated the matching black lace and pale pink satin bra and panty set she was wearing.

The delicate, yet modest scallop-edged lace paired with the pastel satin gave it an elegant, sensual appeal that a more daring, sexually overt set would have lacked.

She moved stiffly, in small side steps, careful not to turn her back to me.

As she did so, I opened a door that was nestled among the floor-to-ceiling bookshelves. Inside was a spacious walk-in closet.

Dangling from a brass hook on the back of the door was a heavy, worn brown leather belt that I wore with my work jeans.

Part of my success was due to the fact that I didn't spend all my days in suits.

I lifted the belt off the hook and folded it in half.

I turned to face Brynn.

Stretching the belt between my fists, I commanded, "Now bend over the desk."

CHAPTER 5

BRYNN

I was too busy staring at the thick leather belt suspended between his massive, tattooed fists to hear what he'd said.

Anton tilted his head to the side as he attempted to catch my eye. "Brynn? Babygirl? Trust me when I say you're going to have to start learning to obey me the first time, because I'm not going to have the patience to keep repeating myself like this, after tonight."

After tonight?

After tonight implied he would see me again after this.

There was no *after tonight*.

If I had the money or resources I would move to another city *after tonight*.

Hell, I'd move to another planet if it were possible, *after tonight*.

Shifting my right thigh over my left, I crossed my legs and bending at the middle, trying to curl myself into a standing ball as I pushed my long hair over my shoulders to try to cover my chest.

I gestured with my chin. "What are you going to do with that belt?"

He crossed to me in two swift strides and placed the folded end of the belt under my chin, then lifted my gaze. "Tell me, *moya malen'kaya vorovka*, how would a daddy punish a little girl who put herself in danger by stealing from a big, bad man?"

"Are you the daddy or the big, bad man?" I slapped my hand over my mouth.

Oh, my God.

What the fuck is wrong with me?

Why did I ask him that?

All my life, I'd been told my lack of a filter would get me in trouble.

Silly me, for thinking it meant getting detention in school or maybe losing a friend for saying the wrong thing … not getting spanked by a tall, tattooed Russian *daddy*.

The lines around his eyes appeared again.

It was the only way I could kind of tell he was smiling … sort of.

"You really are the most adorable little doll. I definitely think I will keep you."

I shook my head as I pulled on my hair to make sure it was still covering my boobs. "You see! There you go again! You're being sarcastic, but it sounds like you're actually serious."

My nerves were shot.

I was never leaving my apartment ever again except to go to work.

Tonight had been all the adventure and excitement I ever wanted for the rest of my life. From now on my life would be popcorn and TV movies on my sofa.

And maybe a cat.

Fuck wishing my life had more passion and drama. It was definitely overrated.

He pushed the hair on my left shoulder back. "I'm always serious."

Before I could argue, he cupped my jaw and rubbed his thumb over my lips. "Enough stalling. Do as you're told. Now."

Fresh tears blurred my vision. My lower lip trembled as my arms and legs stiffened.

My head swam with so many contradictory emotions it made me dizzy.

On one hand, Anton gave off a very masculine, protective vibe, one that I was unaccustomed to, having not really grown up with a father.

On the other, he scared the crap out of me.

Again, the whole tall Russian with a bunch of sinister tattoos and owner of a mafia gambling club thing didn't help.

My jaw locked as I tried to force the words. "I can't," I rasped. "I'm afraid."

He leaned down and tenderly kissed the center of my forehead.

I closed my eyes and leaned into the comfort he offered.

Then he growled softly, "You should be ... I'm not going to be gentle."

My eyes sprang open as I leapt backward. "I'll scream."

"You wouldn't be the first person to do so in this office, but I've already told you, no one will come help you."

I circled around the desk. "So, is this what you do? Prey on young women who come to your club? You take them back to your office to have your wicked, evil way with them?"

He followed. "Actually, you're the first. I was referring to the men who try to steal or cheat the club."

I continued to circle around the desk as I gestured to the belt. "Do you punish the men by making them strip down so you can spank them with a belt too?"

He lifted one shoulder in a casual shrug as he kept his steady dark gaze on me. "No ... I just kill them."

This time I didn't need to ask if he was being sarcastic.

Lowering my head, I shuffled my bare feet along

the soft wool carpet to the end of the desk and placed my palms on the cool, polished surface.

Pressing my stomach against the edge, I bent forward until my cheek rested on the desktop.

His form was just a watery blur as I watched him move to stand behind me.

"Pull down your panties."

I swallowed past the lump in my throat. "Do I have to?"

"Yes."

I reached back stiffly and pulled on the waistband of my panties until they rested at the tops of my thighs just below my ass.

When his warm hand pressed against my lower back, my body jumped.

"Were you never disciplined as a child?"

I thought of my fragmented childhood.

Not a topic I liked discussing, but I also instinctively knew that he wasn't going to accept a lie or half-truth. "Not really."

He moved his hand in an oddly soothing circular pattern over the top curve of my ass. "Perhaps if you had been, you wouldn't have been tempted to try something so dangerous and stupid as trying to cheat a high-stakes poker game. Now what do you say?"

I curled my right hand into a fist that I pressed against my lips. "I'm sorry."

"Daddy."

"What?"

He pressed his fingertips into my left ass cheek, squeezing so hard, I lifted up on my toes. "Say I'm sorry, *Daddy*," he growled.

I clenched my inner thighs, shocked at the strange, unexpected thrill his command gave me.

Internally I cringed.

Between getting caught trying to steal and practically admitting I had a feral childhood, I screamed *girl with Daddy issues.*

As if he had read my mind, Anton leaned over me and said, "You liked that, didn't you, little one."

He moved his hand to between my legs.

I tried to cross them, but couldn't stop his fingers slipping over my pussy lips.

My wet pussy.

My cheeks flamed as I squeezed my eyes closed.

Anton chuckled soft and low as his fingertip pressed against my clit. "So my babygirl has a daddy kink?"

I groaned. "I don't have a daddy—"

My words were bit off with a moan as he pushed a single, thick finger deep inside of me.

Oh, God.

"Tsk, tsk, tsk. Stealing and lying. I can see a lot of punishments coming your way, babygirl."

He pulled his finger free.

I felt oddly empty.

He straightened to his full height over me. "Now let's see how you handle pain."

That was my only warning.

The first strike of his belt was like pure fire.

The heavy leather belt struck across the center of both ass cheeks.

I cried out as I bolted upright.

Anton was quick to press my torso back down onto his desk.

He lashed me again with his belt.

"Ow! This hurts!"

"It's a punishment, my little thief."

He whipped me with his belt several more times.

"Please, it hurts so much!"

Each lash was worse than the last.

My skin was on fire.

It was like a thousand hot pinpricks. As if someone was pinching and twisting my flesh over and over and over again.

There was a pause between lashes and I clenched my cheeks in dreaded anticipation.

He rubbed his palm over the top curve of my ass. "Unclench your bottom. That only makes it worse."

I did my best to obey. "How much longer?" I sniffed as the tears fell down my cheeks.

"Have you learned your lesson?"

"Yes," I sobbed as I pressed my fists against my closed eyes.

My ass throbbed with hot pain.

I was certain I wouldn't be able to sit for a week after this.

"What is the lesson?"

I sucked in a shaking breath. "It was wrong to agree to help Yuri cheat at cards—"

Anton leaned back. "Good girl—"

If only I had stopped there … damn my no filter.

"—even if I thought I was helping a friend and didn't really go through with it."

He cursed low under his breath in Russian.

He fisted my hair at the base of my skull and wrenched me upright to bring his face close to mine.

His upper lip curled back as he snarled, "What did you just say to me?"

I raised my hands up in a feeble attempt to ward him off. "Nothing!"

His hard gaze traveled over my face to rest on my mouth. "It seems I've been punishing the wrong end."

My eyes widened.

He stroked my bottom lip. "This mouth of yours is what keeps getting you in trouble. This is what I need to punish."

I tried to shake my head but his grip prevented me. I didn't even want to think of what he meant by punishing my mouth, but somehow I didn't think he meant with a bar of soap.

Fresh tears coursed down my cheeks. "I didn't mean it. Please, I really am sorry!"

"I'm doing this for your own good."

Without warning, he lifted me as if I weighed nothing and laid me on my back on the desk.

I gave a cry of pain as my sore ass hit the hard surface.

I looked up at his towering frame as he glowered down at me.

From this angle he looked even more ferocious.

Before I could attempt to get up and escape, he placed one restraining hand on my stomach as he used his other hand to lower his zipper.

He reached into his trousers and pulled out his hard cock.

"I'm not putting that thing in my mouth!" I cried out.

On top of having very little experience with boys because of my irregular teenage years, I had even less sucking cock.

Let alone *python* cocks.

"It's not going in your mouth. It's going down your throat."

"The hell it is!"

I tried to rise again as I kicked out my legs.

He wrapped his hands around my throat, stilling me. "Bend your knees. Place your feet on the edge of my desk."

It was a little awkward, because my panties were still tangled around the tops of my thighs, but I did as I was told.

"Now push back with your heels and slide your body along my desk, until your head drapes all the way off the edge."

As I did so, he positioned himself behind me with his legs spread.

The moment my head dipped low, he lifted his cock so the heavy, thick shaft was perpendicular to my mouth.

I tucked my lips between my teeth as tears blurred my vision. It was a strange sensation since they couldn't fall down onto my cheeks, but pooled into my lashes.

His thumbs caressed my jaw. "Open your mouth, baby."

I shook my head, feeling the weight of my hair as it pulled on my scalp as it moved.

I heard the scrape of the metal buckle of his belt against the desktop as he picked it up. Then the heavy leather settled between my legs.

I closed my thighs, but not in time.

"Do you feel where my belt is?"

"Uh. Huh." I kept my lips tightly between my teeth, not risking opening my mouth to answer.

"Well, if you don't open your mouth like a good girl and take your punishment, I'm going to whip your delicate pussy even harder than I whipped your bottom."

I was so shocked I opened my mouth and gasped.

He pushed the head of his cock past my lips.

My first instinct was to bite down.

"Don't you dare," he warned.

I whimpered as he pushed in deeper.

The head of his cock was so big, it flattened my tongue against the bottom of my mouth.

I raised my hands and reached over my shoulders to push against his thighs.

"Relax your throat."

Relax my throat? I didn't even know how to do that.

He thrust in further.

I gagged.

He pulled back but then pushed in again. "Good girl. Open your throat for Daddy. Show me how sorry you are."

Spittle formed in the corners of my mouth as I struggled to do as I was told.

He shifted his cock back and forth, each time pushing it a little further down my throat.

And each time I gagged, my throat muscles seemed to get weaker and looser.

His hand moved from my stomach to between my legs.

I smashed my legs together.

He thrust his cock to the back of my throat. "Open your legs."

My hips bucked at the sudden pain.

The movement pushed my head lower, which allowed him to push past my final gag reflex deep into my throat.

My lips were stretched wide around the base of his shaft. I had to breathe through my nose.

My open palms slammed against the desktop as I tried to scream around his cock.

Still he wouldn't relent.

He kept his cock buried in my throat, not moving. "Open your legs," he ground out.

I swung my knees open.

Only then did he pull his cock back, pulling it free from my mouth.

I sucked in a gulp of air.

That was all I was allowed, before he pushed the head past my lips again.

This time, he pushed two fingers between my pussy lips at the same time.

I was mortified at how wet I was.

If his cock wasn't in my mouth, I would have screamed that it meant nothing.

The tip of his middle finger circled my clit, applying just the right amount of pressure.

He increased the pace and pressure as he slowly and methodically forced his cock deep down my throat. He didn't fuck my mouth like you saw in porn meant for men.

It was like he wanted me to feel every inch of his cock as it slipped past my lips and over my tongue. Like he wanted me to *taste* him.

He would drive it long and deep and then wait, letting my throat clench around him, until my lungs screamed for air, before he would gently pull back.

He matched these movements with the movement of his fingers on my pussy.

It was a constant ebb and flow of pressure and pace, of feeling lightheaded and breathless, almost as if I were floating.

Finally, I couldn't take any more.

My body jerked as my hips bucked.

Holy shit, I was coming.

In that moment, he pushed two fingers inside of me as he thrust his cock deep down my throat.

I felt owned.

Claimed.

Filled.

Taken.

Possessed.

My body was no longer under my control.

I came so hard it was almost painful.

My abdomen muscles cramped and released.

Jesus Christ, what was it like to actually have *sex* with a man like this?

I was determined *never* to find out.

CHAPTER 6

ANTON

Knowing my sweet innocent was inexperienced, I didn't want her to choke on my come.

After relishing the sight of her release, I pulled free of her mouth and swept her into my arms.

I carried her over to the sofa in front of the fireplace and sat, placing her on her stomach to my side. Then I stroked her hair; twisting a handful at the base of her skull, I lifted her head up, until her eyes locked with mine.

I fisted my shaft. "Have you learned your lesson?"

Her big, beautiful eyes filled with tears. "Yes," she whispered.

"Good girl, your punishment is almost over."

"Almost?" she whimpered.

"Let's see if you've learned to put that pretty

mouth to better use than getting you in trouble," I said with one eyebrow raised.

She looked down at my still hard cock.

Her lower lip trembled. "Please, my throat is so sore."

I let go of her hair and raised my hand.

With my open palm, I spanked her bare ass, which was exposed as her panties were still twisted around her thighs.

She cried out and swung her arm back to cover her ass.

"Move your hand," I barked.

She was so stunned, she obeyed.

I spanked her ass several more times.

A few swats for each cheek. "I see you still haven't learned your lesson."

She lowered her head to my thigh as she started to cry. "I'm sorry."

"Now what do you say?"

"I don't know what you want me to say."

I remained silent.

She bit her lip. After another moment, she whispered, "I'm sorry I was a bad girl who tried to cheat at cards, please … please put your cock in my mouth … *Daddy*."

Damn.

I had said the daddy kink thing just to get a rise out of her.

See what her boundaries were … but *holy fuck.*

It was fast becoming my thing now.

I didn't usually go for younger women, so the daddy thing had never been a bedroom game I'd played.

But fuck if it wasn't hot as hell seeing this sweet innocent little doll's mouth saying *Daddy* with her cock-swollen lips right after I'd just spanked her ass red.

It was all I could do not to cover her face with come right then and there.

If it wasn't for a desire to watch her swallow my come, knowing it was sliding down her throat and deep in her stomach, I would have.

I cupped the back of her head and guided her to my cock. "Good girl."

I fisted the base as she opened her mouth.

After the head and the first two inches slipped in, she hesitated.

I applied pressure to the back of her head.

After earlier, I already knew what her limitations were … at least for now. They would get even better with practice … and I had every intention of giving her plenty of opportunities to practice.

Her whimpers sent vibrations down my cock as she pressed her hands against my thighs.

Switching my grip on the back of her head to my right hand, I swept my left hand over the curve of her back to give her punished ass a quick squeeze.

Her body trembled in response.

I then pushed my hand between her thighs.

Letting her raise her head up on my cock to take a breath before pushing her back down, I timed it perfectly to push my fingers inside of her.

At that same moment, I used her own arousal to tease her tight asshole with the pad of my thumb.

She shimmied her hips, trying to avoid the invasive touch.

Fuck, my little doll was going to be such a fun toy to play with.

Just the thought of fucking her tight little asshole was enough to make me come.

Grinding my teeth, I breathed heavily through my clenched jaw, sweat breaking out on my brow as my balls tightened. I pulsed my fingers in her pussy, thrusting in and out, determined to bring her to orgasm a second time before I came.

The moment I saw her ass cheeks clench as her hips rose, I pressed my right hand down on the back of her head, forcing my cock deeper into her mouth and roared my release, shooting my hot come deep down her throat.

She coughed as her body bucked.

My come streamed back down my cock as I allowed her to pull her head back and breathe.

She wiped the back of her hand across her mouth as her eyes watered and she gasped in gulps of air.

I pushed her hair back from her shoulders so she didn't get my sticky come in her curls.

I then ran the backs of my knuckles down her cheeks. "You're almost done, babygirl."

Her lower lip puffed out in a pout. "Please don't spank me anymore."

"I won't … unless you do something to deserve it."

Her relief was short-lived.

I leaned back. "You still need to lick my cock clean."

Her gaze fell on my cock and the thick come that coated my still semi-hard shaft. "Can I just wipe it off?"

I ran the pad of my thumb over her lower lip and spoke softly with patience. My tone belied my words. "You were supposed to swallow it all, but you didn't. Now you can be a good girl, and clean up your mess or I can use it as lube and fuck your tight asshole, but I thought you'd had enough punishment for one night. Your choice."

With a sigh she lowered her head.

I stopped her. "Get on the floor, down on your knees."

She slipped off the sofa and prostrated herself before me on her knees between my spread legs.

My cock hardened at the beautifully submissive pose.

Her small hand wrapped around the base of my cock; her fingertips didn't even touch.

Fuck, I was already determined to keep her for

my own pleasure for a while, but with a view like this, I might not let her leave this room.

She opened her mouth and her cute pink tongue poked out.

The tip stroked my shaft, licking the come from the base to the tip.

A groan rumbled from deep inside my chest.

She looked up at me with innocent uncertain eyes.

I stroked her hair and pushed a lock behind her ear.

With that encouragement, she continued to lick the come off my cock with her tongue.

She was young for my usual taste, but not *that* young.

Especially by American standards, it was odd she wasn't more experienced.

She was twenty-two and yet she was obviously spectacularly innocent.

I could tell by the way she sucked my cock and how tight her pussy was, not to mention her tiny asshole.

I had no idea what events had conspired for this sweet doll to escape the average idiot American male, but thank God for miracles.

Fortunately, Russian men knew how to claim a treasure when they found it.

When she was done, I caressed her hair, pushing

it away from her cheek as I gently pushed her head down against my inner thigh. "Open your mouth."

It was a final test.

I was pleased that this time, she opened her mouth without hesitation.

I knew this obedience was not likely to last and probably had more to do with how I had worn her out with multiple spankings and orgasms, but I would take it just the same.

I guided my semi-erect cock to her mouth.

Her wide eyes pleaded with me.

I stroked her hair. "Shhh, babygirl. Just rest your head against my thigh and suck on my cock. I won't push it down your throat any more tonight."

She laid her hand along my thigh and closed her eyes as her body relaxed, all while keeping my cock snug between her lips.

I leaned my head back against the sofa and closed my eyes as well, while I kept my hand gently resting on the top of her head.

This was another first for me.

I didn't know what made me even think to do this, just that I didn't want to leave the warmth of her sweet mouth just yet.

Not to be crass, but usually once I blew my load, that was it with a woman.

Not tonight. Not with her.

There was something … soothing about just

sitting there with her innocently on her knees before me, her mouth on my cock.

Like a dirty little sleeping angel.

Did I say a new wardrobe and some diamonds?

Hell … I was going to buy this sweet thing a fucking car and house.

After several more minutes, I decided it was time for another first.

I was going to take her upstairs to my penthouse. I usually had a strict policy of no women in my private home.

I lived a very dangerous lifestyle and controlled extremely sensitive business information of countless criminal enterprises around the world. That kind of life didn't exactly lend itself to allowing my latest piece on the side up in my bedroom. My company had luxury real estate holdings around the city that usually suited my purpose.

It didn't feel right for Brynn.

Everything about her had felt different.

This would be too.

"Come, babygirl."

She pulled her mouth off my cock.

I already missed her warmth.

"Where are you taking me?"

"You're tired. I'm taking you upstairs to my bed."

Not seeming to hear me, she looked over her shoulder at the antique mantel clock over the fireplace. "Oh, my God! It's almost midnight! The

Metra gets really dodgy once the bars start letting out."

She stood and pulled her panties up as she stumbled over to her cocktail dress. Shaking the wrinkled mess out, she placed one foot in, then the other as she shimmied it up over her hips.

I stood and tucked my cock back in my trousers as I zipped them up. "You don't honestly think I'm going to let you ride the motherfucking Metra, do you?"

She barely looked up as she struggled to zip up her dress. "It's fine. I do it all the time."

After quelling the rage that burned in my chest at the thought of her riding those dangerous cesspool trains alone at night, I clenched my fist at my side. "It's not happening, babygirl."

"I can't afford to take a taxi home. It's too far. It will cost a fortune."

I said through clenched teeth, "You're not going home."

She stared at me with wide eyes. "You promised you weren't going to call the police if I was a good girl and … and let you"—she swallowed—"let you punish me instead. I kept up my end of the deal."

I ran a hand through my hair. "I'm not calling the police. I live in the penthouse over the club. I'm taking you upstairs with me."

She straightened her shoulders. Tossing her tangled hair over her shoulders, she pushed her chin out. "Thank you, but I believe I shall decline your kind offer."

I raised a single eyebrow. So we were back to this nonsense. "It wasn't exactly an *offer*."

She crossed the room and put on her high heels. "All the same, I *respectfully* decline."

Even with the extra height, I still towered over her as I crossed my arms over my chest. "And I *respectfully* decline your declination."

She huffed. "That's not even a word."

"It is so," I charged back.

"Well, it doesn't matter because you can't decline my decline. I took my punishment, now you have to let me go. Those are the rules! Now can I please have my purse?" she asked as she held out her open palm.

"I make the rules here, not you."

"You're a bully!" She stomped her foot as she stuck out her tongue.

My God, it is like arguing with a child.

Maybe I needed to rethink this younger woman thing.

I threw up my hand. "Fine! I'll take you home."

I stormed over to my desk, yanked open the drawer, and grabbed her purse.

After handing it to her, I stalked over to my closet and threw open the door. After disappearing into it for a few minutes, I emerged with a soft cashmere sweater and tossed it to her.

She caught it and looked at me. "What am I supposed to do with this?"

"Put it on."

She shook it out. It looked like a small cobalt blue blanket as she held it in front of her small frame. "It's too big."

Biting back a retort, I crossed the room in two strides and swiped it from her grasp.

Opening up the sweater, I pulled it over her head, disregarding her objections.

As her head popped out through the neck, I growled, "That's the point. I don't want you prancing around in that ridiculous dress. It's too small and tight."

She pushed her hands through the sleeves as she pulled the hem of the sweater down, which reached far below the hem of the dress, not that that was difficult.

"I only wore it because of the stupid hidden pockets," she grumbled.

"Don't remind me," I groused back as I tossed on a wool overcoat and grabbed my Range Rover keys.

* * *

AFTER TELLING me a different address to what was on her license, because she had apparently moved, I drove her to a slightly nicer neighborhood, but still not up to my standards.

After a brief argument when I wouldn't allow her to just hop out of the car and enter the building alone, I escorted her to the apartment door.

She cast a nervous glance over her shoulder at me before reaching along the upper doorframe and extracting the door key.

"What the fuck, Brynn?"

"Um … I don't like having my house key with me in case my purse gets stolen."

I rubbed my eyes. "So you leave your key in the most obvious place imaginable so any thief, rapist, shifty landlord, or ex-boyfriend could gain access to your place at any time?"

She put the key in the doorknob and unlocked the door while tossing over her shoulder, "Well, when you put it like that, of course it's going to sound bad."

Just the doorknob, no deadbolt or additional lock.

I shook my head. "You're killing me here, Brynn."

She slipped inside and tried to close the door.

I grabbed it. Pulling it open, I thankfully spied a deadbolt.

I pointed to it. "Lock this."

She rolled her eyes. "Fine."

"I mean it. I'm standing right here until I hear it slide into place."

"Okay, I will."

I looked at my watch. "I have a morning meeting tomorrow, so I will pick you up afterwards at ten a.m. Be ready. You don't need to pack anything."

She frowned. "Wait. Pack? Why?"

"Because I'll take you shopping first."

"I'm confused. Why are we meeting and why are you taking me shopping?"

"I'll take you to set up the lines of credit at all the shops. After that you can go yourself. I'll make reservations for us at Le Colonial for dinner. Do you like Asian food?"

She blinked. "What is happening?"

I leaned in and kissed her on the forehead. "You're tired. Get some sleep. Remember, ten a.m. sharp. Be ready."

She backed up and I closed the door.

I waited a few moments and then called through the door, "Lock it, Brynn."

After a few seconds, I heard the deadbolt slide into place.

As I drove back to the Four Monks, I realized I never kissed her.

I adjusted my grip on the steering wheel. Something to look forward to tomorrow. In fact, I had a great deal to look forward to.

Although I couldn't cancel my morning meeting, third world dictators could be annoyingly squirrely about that sort of thing, I would clear my schedule for the rest of the day so I could spend it with Brynn… in my bed.

Tonight was just a taste of her charms.

I was looking forward to feasting tomorrow.

CHAPTER 7

BRYNN

I peeked through the curtains waiting for the black luxury Range Rover to drive away.

The moment I saw Anton emerge from the building, I ducked below the windowsill behind a cream gauze curtain, even though I was two stories up, his back was turned, and it was dark.

That was the powerful stranglehold this man had on my nerves in the short time I'd known him.

I didn't realize I was even holding my breath, until I released it when his Range Rover finally drove out of view.

Slumping down on the floor, I leaned against the wall, stretched out my legs and let the too-big high heels fall off.

I wiggled my toes and just stared straight ahead for I don't know how long.

Across from me was a floor-length mirror tacked up on the wall behind the front door, next to the coat closet. The perfect position for a final look before leaving for work.

I tilted my head to the side and stared at my reflection as if I were looking at a stranger's image through a shop window.

My hair was a tangled, teased-out mess. My eye makeup had a rather sexy, if unintentionally smoky-eye effect from the black eyeliner and mascara smeared from all the tears.

And my lips looked like I had achieved the perfect bee-stung, Botoxed Hollywood pout. They were a bright, dark pink, swollen and puffy. And my complexion was a strange combination of haunted pale and flushed.

I looked like an impeccable throwback to the ninety's heroin-chic now that I thought about it.

I had even nailed the far off, hit by a bus, hazy gaze.

Which was precisely how I felt … that, or like one of those poor victims of a natural disaster you saw interviewed on the news the morning after.

They always had this slightly stunned look on their face like they weren't really sure what had just happened … but they were absolutely certain they were *fucked*.

I opened my mouth and shifted my jaw from left to right.

Then I lifted my hand to trace my lower lip with my fingertips.

It was like I could still feel the press of his cock inside my mouth.

Nothing about tonight should have been a turn-on … and yet … *damn*.

I mean, the man had that raw masculine arrogance that only an older man with power and money could pull off.

A guy my age wouldn't have been able to get away with half the shit Anton had tonight, no matter how much money he had.

But fuck … a tall, dark, handsome man like Anton?

In a tuxedo? With the tattoos and the growly voice ordering me to bend over his desk while he fisted a fucking leather belt?

Fuccccckkkkkkk.

I crossed my legs as my insides warmed all over again.

It was no surprise a girl like me with my background had Daddy issues, fucking news at eleven, but I'd never thought I'd meet a man who'd actually bring them to spine-tingling reality like that.

It wasn't right. It wasn't normal.

That sort of stuff needed to stay in dark and twisty romance novels tucked under my bed in a box marked 'old sweaters,' where it belonged.

Men like Anton were not meant for *real* life … and definitely not for *my life*.

With fresh resolve, I got to my feet.

Just in case, I peeked out of the curtains to make sure he was really, *really* gone.

As I did, I glanced down at the various potted plants on the sill. Picking up the small copper pitcher, I shook it to see if it still had enough water in it before tilting it under the glossy green leaves, being careful not to spill onto the wood-stained sill.

I then refilled the pitcher several times and watered the rest of the plants around the condo.

Making sure I hadn't disturbed anything in the neatly decorated space, I picked up the spare key and moved toward the front door.

At least something good had come out of tonight. I wouldn't need to swing by the Carmichaels to water their plants on my way to work tomorrow. It was just one of the countless odd jobs I did to scrape by as I tried to save up money to rent my own chair at a nicer salon.

They weren't due back from their business trip to New York for at least another three days so I wasn't worried about them finding out about me using their place as a cover.

Anton would probably come by tomorrow, *if he came by*, see that I wasn't here, and move on.

I locked the door and braced myself for the cold, sketchy ride home on the Metra.

* * *

I SHOVED my purse into the tiny half locker in the break room of the Third Base Salon.

Checking the mirror on the door, I fixed my high ponytail and adjusted my pink lip gloss before tugging on the insanely misogynistic tiny shorts I was forced to wear as part of my work uniform.

Third Base Salon was a baseball-themed men's salon.

All the hairdressers were women and were forced to wear ponytails and hyper-sexualized, low-cut baseball T-shirts and Daisy Duke denim shorts. Treatments were all baseball themed and the entire place had televisions with nonstop sports.

And that was nothing compared to how we were forced to greet each customer.

I hated everything about it with a burning, white-hot passion.

The only problem was the tips were insanely high, way more than I would make at a regular mid-level salon at this point in my career.

And I was saving every penny, plus doing side jobs like house sitting and dog walking, to save up enough money to rent my own booth at one of the swankier salons downtown.

The problem was they could cost as much as one thousand dollars a week and it could take several months to establish a regular clientele.

So I knew I had to have at least fifteen thousand saved at a minimum.

So far I had two thousand, three hundred and twenty-three dollars and six cents.

I would have more if … I sighed.

There was no point in thinking about it. He'd taken the money and left, like he always did. He'd done it to my mom and now he'd done it to me.

Lesson learned.

I had lied to Anton last night.

I had learned the hard way, another lesson after watching my mother, that saving money was way more important than a new pair of shoes or going out for a drink with friends.

Probably why I was so susceptible to Heather and Yuri's persuasion to help them out last night.

It had been at least six months since I had done something other than work.

Hell, I hadn't even been on a date since … well … since what had happened in high school.

No one wants to date the crazy chick.

I adjusted my bracelets and fluffed my ponytail one more time.

It was fine by me.

Boys were a distraction.

I needed to focus on work and saving money, securing my future.

I stepped back just in time as my locker door slammed shut.

Heather was standing in its place.

She was wearing the same uniform as me, and the same size she had worn eight months ago. So the cheap material of the T-shirt was practically see-through the way it stretched over her pregnancy-enlarged breasts and her protruding belly. Her ass cheeks hung below the already short denim booty shorts.

Her slightly overdrawn eyebrows frowned into artificial peaks. "What. The. Fuck. Brynny?"

She punctuated each word with a swipe of her extremely long artificial gel nails, painted a glowing neon blue.

I hated that nickname.

It made me sound like a poodle.

I was not going to be cowed. "I should be saying the same thing to you, Heather. Your piece of shit baby daddy ghosted, leaving me holding the bag."

"He said you pussied out and cost us ten grand!" She caressed her belly. "You know how badly we need that money, Brynny."

"First off, he's lying to you. There was seventy-five grand in the pot, not ten. And it wasn't my fault! You two made it sound like we were going to be taking a couple hundred bucks off a couple of dads playing poker in a garage, not the—" I looked around and lowered my voice. "Fucking mob!"

She narrowed her eyes. "Seventy-five? Are you lying to me?"

I threw up my hands. "What possible reason would I have to lie to you, Heather? I'm not the degenerate gambler in this equation. I'm just the idiot who was trying to do you a favor! I won't be making that mistake again."

She waved her hands in front of her face, making her bracelets and rings jangle. "Oh, God, I'm sorry, Brynny. You're right. I'm a terrible friend."

I rolled my eyes as I leaned in and hugged her. "You're not a terrible friend, Heather."

You just have terrible taste in men.

She wiped under her eye with her knuckle to clean up her eyeliner from the nonexistent tears she didn't just cry. "So what happened to you? Yuri said his uncle dragged you off?"

My cheeks flamed as I lowered my head. "He's not his uncle."

"What?"

I waved it off.

I didn't want her to know that I'd had any kind of conversation with Anton.

I didn't want her to know anything about what had transpired between me and Anton last night.

I was still trying to process it myself. More than likely I was just going to bury it into a little dark fantasy box deep inside of me, that I only pulled out on lonely nights when I was home alone and had too many glasses of cheap wine.

I shrugged. "He just yelled at me and told me to

get out and never come back. Listen, Heather, are you aware of Yuri's debts and the real reason why he was there last night?"

She looked away. "Yuri said this sort of thing happens to professional gamblers all the time. It's not his fault. He was playing in this sketchy game and the dealer took a rake so he came up short to the guy that staked him. So he played a little too hot the next game and went on credit and got into a hole and he's just having a hard time climbing out."

She sounded like some gangster's moll from an old black-and-white film.

I took her hand. "I'm just worried about you. That was a pretty intense crowd there last night and it sounds like Yuri might get himself *and you* into some dangerous trouble if he doesn't stop."

Before she could respond, Nigel, our boss, strolled in. "Hey! Your shift started two minutes ago! Chop! Chop!"

Heather yelled and threw a hairbrush at him. "Out of the girls' break room, perv!"

He ducked. "Hey! Watch it, or I'll take you off tomorrow's schedule!"

She smirked as she put her hands on her hips. "I'd like to see you try! You'd have a riot on your hands."

It was true. Her pregnancy hadn't dampened Heather's popularity with the male customers. Her shampoo massages, for lack of a better term, were infamous.

The fact she did most of them standing to the *side* of the men's chairs instead of closer to the sink was none of my business.

I left the two of them to snap at one another as I crossed the salon floor to go set up my station for the day. As I arranged my various brushes and combs and charged my clippers, I couldn't help but keep glancing up at the clock.

9:02 a.m.

The first customers strolled in.

Knowing I didn't have any appointments until later in the afternoon, I approached the walk-ins and gritted my teeth. "So, who wants to go to third base with me?"

I sighed.

It was impossible not to die a little bit inside every time I was forced to say that.

A man in a Big Johnson T-shirt in his thirties smirked as he raised his hand.

I motioned for him to follow me.

As I cut his hair and tried to ignore him staring at my boobs, I continued to glance at the clock.

9:15 a.m.

This was stupid.

Next customer.

A shave and a quick cut.

Another several glances at the clock.

9:35 a.m.

This was absurd.

Anton probably wasn't even going to show up at the Carmichaels.

Someone like him could have any woman he wanted.

He probably screwed a different woman every night. He would have zero interest in a *little thief* in a cheap ill-fitting dress like me.

Another customer. Another cut.

9:50 a.m.

10:00 a.m.

10:05 a.m.

10:15 a.m.

I let out a breath.

There, it was past the appointment time.

Not that it mattered.

It wasn't like he knew to come here or had any way to find me, but at least I could stop staring at the clock as if it were a bomb ticking down.

My misguided misadventure from last night was finally well and truly over.

CHAPTER 8

ANTON

*A*t precisely ten a.m., I knocked on Brynn's door, and was more than a little pissed off when a man in his early thirties answered.

His gaze took in my height, tattoos, and scowl and he immediately took a step back as he swung the door closed until it was only open about a sliver. "Can I help you?"

I could hear the rattle of a chain against the door.

He must be trying to get the door chain ready, as if that would keep me out.

I gave the door a kick.

The man stumbled backward and fell to the floor as I stepped inside.

Taking a deep breath, I folded my hands in front of me and adjusted my shoulders, leveling my cold gaze on the man. "You have two seconds to tell me who you are, and how you are related to Brynn Moore," I said calmly and evenly.

I left out the whole *before I rip your head off* part, but I felt as though that was implied.

Judging by the terrified look on the man's face and the growing wet spot on the denim of his inner thigh, I'd say I was correct.

His mouth moved but no sound came out.

I looked around the apartment.

Something felt off.

Everything was sterile and very beige.

The entire space lacked imagination, as if an IKEA magazine had just vomited page forty-two into an apartment.

My entire career depended on reading people, whether it was a seasoned poker player across a table or a psychotic dictator with an itchy trigger finger and a bad cocaine habit.

I knew people.

I knew Brynn.

This wasn't her place.

The little minx had conned me.

That still didn't mean that this man didn't have a former claim on the woman I now considered my property.

I stepped up to him. Hitching my suit pants, I went down on my haunches and fisted his shirt, lifting his torso. "I'm going to need you to find your words."

"Carmichael."

"Carmichael?" I questioned.

He nodded vigorously as he smiled stupidly as if that would spare him a bullet in the skull.

"Yeah, I'm going to need a few more words."

He swallowed. "My name is Tom Carmichael. Brynn waters my plants."

I raised an eyebrow as I reached into my suit jacket to my side holster and pulled out my OTs-38 Stechkin silent revolver. "For your sake, Tom, I sincerely hope that isn't a euphemism for something."

He raised his hands up. "No. God, no. I have a wife. Brynn just house-sits for us when we travel to New York on business every couple of weeks."

"Do you know where Brynn lives? Where do you send her paychecks?"

"It's all cash."

Remembering I didn't see a cellphone, I asked, "How do you contact her?"

"Through a small jobs app. She never gave us a phone number. She's pretty private about that sort of thing."

I stood up as I holstered my weapon. Looking down at Tom, I said, "We never had this conversation."

He nodded. "Yes, sir."

I reached into my wallet and pulled out a couple hundred-dollar bills and tossed them onto his stomach. "For your trouble … and some new jeans."

I ran into a similar issue, checking the apartment listed on her identification.

Apparently she hadn't lived there in over a year.

As I left that apartment, I pulled out my phone and dialed.

"How'd it go with Mr. Twitchy Fingers?" Mac asked, referring to my meeting with the dictator.

"Fine. I'll fill you in later. Is your piece of shit nephew with you?"

"It's not noon yet, so he's probably still sleeping in the spare room, why?"

"Keep him there. I'm on my way."

I hung up and hopped in my car.

* * *

I ROLLED up to the Four Monks and pulled into the private, secure garage below.

The entire club was actually two nineteenth-century townhouses that were connected through a stunning wrought-iron and authentic Tiffany stained-glass pedestrian bridge, two stories above ground.

I owned the club with my three lifelong friends.

Macarius handled the operations.

Varlaam oversaw all the financial transactions, and Sergius was in charge of security.

I was the general manager and the public face of the club.

Of course, it was all just a front to launder hundreds of millions of dollars of illicit money.

Corporations, puppet governments, Russian, Italian, Polish, Chinese mafia.

It didn't matter.

We washed it all.

And it was stupid easy, given we ran a high-stakes poker game that had hundred-thousand-dollar buy-ins on a weekly basis.

I lived in the penthouse over the main club that housed the poker floor and other gaming rooms as well as the restaurant.

Mac lived in the penthouse located in the second townhouse to the right, over the private suites used by international members who preferred the security of our accommodations to those of hotels, as well as the additional meeting and event space where we hosted the occasional politician or celebrity wedding.

I took the private elevator up to Mac's place.

He opened the door at my first knock. "What's he done now?"

I kicked the door shut behind me. "Same fallout from last night."

I felt for Mac.

Yuri was his sister's kid.

He lost her and her husband to a car accident a few years ago.

Ever since, Mac had tried to steer his nephew in the right direction. He'd brought him here from

Maryland and arranged for him to go to Northwestern University with Mac paying for everything.

The kid had flunked out within the first semester.

After that, every job Mac had pulled strings to get him, Yuri fucked up.

The kid was a lost cause.

For starters, he was acting like a petulant teenager with a chip on his shoulder, which would be understandable given the loss of his mother ... if he was an actual fucking teenager.

But he was twenty-fucking-five, a grown-ass adult, a fucking man.

I had already done two stints in a gulag, been a mercenary in South Africa, and made my first million at the gaming tables in Monte Carlo while this kid was still learning to wipe his ass.

And now he was cheating at cards and had gotten a woman pregnant.

What a fucking mess.

Mac was too good a guy to be dealing with this bullshit.

I followed Mac down the hallway to the spare bedroom. He pounded on the closed door.

There was a muffled, "Go away."

We exchanged a look.

Mac tried the doorknob. Locked.

Mac shouldered it. The door swung open.

Yuri sprang up in bed. "What the fuck, dude?"

Mac planted his hands on his hips. "That's 'Uncle Mac.'

Anton wants a word with you."

Yuri rubbed his head before reaching for his cigarettes. "Can't it wait?"

Mac pointed at him. "You want another black eye, smart ass?"

Yuri was lucky that was all he got for what he tried to pull last night.

We'd killed men for less.

A reputation for card mucking could kill a poker club by chasing away the high-rolling whales and it could bring unwanted attention from the authorities.

We needed the whales to lose big at the tables to cover the massive cash transactions we engaged in as crime bosses.

Yuri had put that all at risk.

Not to mention putting an innocent woman, Brynn, in danger.

Already having had enough of his shit, I stepped forward. "The woman you were with last night, Brynn. What do you know about her?"

He grimaced. "Come on, Uncle Anton. Don't blame Brynny. She was just a last-minute sub and I'll never hear the end of it from Heather."

I clenched my fist when he said the name Brynny.

First, I didn't like the familiarity it implied.

Second, it didn't suit her.

Brynny was something you called a dog, not my girl.

"Don't call her that."

He frowned, flicking his lighter several times as he talked around the cigarette dangling from his mouth. "What? Brynny? That's the bitch's name."

I lunged for him.

Grabbing him by his T-shirt, I lifted him off the bed and slammed him against the wall. His feet dangled a foot off the floor.

He screamed as he strained his neck to look over my shoulder. "Uncle Mac, do something!"

I turned my head to exchange a look with Mac.

Mac leaned against the doorjamb. "Feel free to break his arms. It's not like he has a job to get to."

Yuri's eyes widened. "Look, I'm sorry! I'm sorry! She's not a bitch! Okay? She's actually pretty cool. All right. She didn't want to help last night but she did anyway because she's a nice girl."

I lowered him to the floor. "Where does she live?"

"I don't know. I swear."

"How do you and Heather know her?"

"Heather and her work together."

"Where?"

"The Third Base Salon in Lincoln Square. They are working a shift there now. I'm supposed to pick her up in a few hours."

Mac pushed away from the door. "You let your

pregnant girl work while your lazy fucking ass is in bed sleeping?"

He shrugged.

I laid a hand on Mac's shoulder in sympathy as I left him to deal with his nephew.

I had a lying little thief to go track down.

CHAPTER 9

BRYNN

"So, who wants to go to third base with me?"

The moment the hated salon catchphrase left my lips, all the blood left my body.

Anton slowly stood up.

His stormy gaze slowly moved from my eyes down my body and back up.

Instead of the usual appreciative, slightly leering, occasionally creepy looks I got for my misogynistic uniform, especially the tight, low-cut baseball T-shirt with its even more lurid *slide into third base with me* phrase written across the front, Anton looked absolutely livid.

I didn't have a ton of experience with men, but I knew it wasn't a great sign when their upper lip curled to expose their canine teeth.

His eyes narrowed as he stalked toward me.

Just then, a douchebag in a pair of khakis with a mint green polo shirt with the collar turned up tried to head him off. "Hey, buddy, I was next."

Anton didn't even say a word.

He just turned and looked at the guy.

Just. Looked. At. Him.

And the guy immediately threw up his hands and backed up several steps. "You know what, my bad. You were *definitely* next." The guy stumbled backward into a seat and hid behind an upside-down *Sports Illustrated*.

Anton turned that same piercing glare back on me.

I backed up a step, then another.

I stretched out my hand, blindly searching for the clipboard on the counter. When my hand touched it, I snatched it to my chest, as if it were both a life preserver and shield all in one.

Without looking at it, I said, "You know what—on second thought, I think I may have an appointment coming in."

Anton pulled the clipboard out of my grasp and set it back on the counter. "You don't."

There really was something disturbingly sexy about a man with super scary ink, who had an aura of criminal brute strength, wearing an expensive suit. Like with most men, a suit made sense. It was what society or their job expected them to wear.

But with someone like Anton, there was this

overwhelming impression that he was only wearing a suit to humor society.

To give those around him a false sense that he was suitably civilized enough not to suddenly kill those around him just because he got bored.

He shrugged out of his suit jacket and put it over my shoulders before lifting my wrist and pushing my arm through one, then the other sleeve.

His warmth and the lingering spicy scent of his cologne still clung to the soft wool fabric, which was so big it fell practically to my knees and well past my fingertips.

I looked around for Nigel, who fortunately wasn't on the salon floor at that moment. "I'm really not allowed to cover up my uniform."

Without looking at me, he raised my arm and cuffed the sleeve. "Babygirl, I don't think you understand, so let me explain something to you."

The fact that he was ruining the perfect crease on what was clearly a custom-made thousand-dollar suit didn't seem to bother him in the slightest.

As he worked on the sleeve, he said in a casual tone, as if he were chatting about the weather and not describing committing a graphic violent felony, "I am doing my best not to punch every man in this place who is daring to stare at your tits so hard on the back of the head that their eyes pop out of their sockets."

I gasped.

He picked up my other arm and slowly cuffed that sleeve. "And if you are wondering if such a thing is possible? The answer is yes—and no, you don't want to know how I know."

Finished with his task, he stood less than a foot away from me. He placed a hand under my chin and raised my head to look at him.

He continued through a clenched jaw. "Now, what I would like to do right now is toss you over my shoulder and carry you out of here back to my place, so that I can show you—*in excruciatingly explicit detail*—how displeased I am at having to track you down today."

I licked my lips. "Please, don't do that. I really need this job."

He closed his eyes for a second and breathed in through his nose, almost as if he were praying for patience.

He then opened his eyes and ran his thumb over my lower lip. "You don't, but we will discuss that later. What I am going to do is sit and allow you to give me a hot shave while you explain why you misbehaved… again."

I winced. "Do I have to?"

I hated how I sounded like a little girl, but he already made me super nervous just by standing here, and a hot shave was way more intimate than a haircut. "Couldn't you just leave and I'll stop by the Four Monks after my shift and explain?"

He smiled. "You're adorable." He then tapped me on the tip of my nose. "No."

My shoulders slumped. "Fine. Follow me."

I led him back to my salon chair. Since the place was covered in mirrors, I was able to catch every single appreciative look all my female co-workers sent Anton as he strolled across the salon floor toward my chair.

Not that I blamed them.

Taking off his suit jacket actually made him look even sexier.

He had on one of those vests only sophisticated and cultured men wore with their suits.

There was even a silver chain hooked to a button that ended at a small pocket, which could only mean a pocket watch. *A freaking pocket watch.*

He looked like a tattooed Russian czar. All that was missing was the fur coat and a tamed black bear as a pet.

I gestured nervously toward my salon chair.

Before he sat down, he looked at my mirror. Taking out his phone, he leaned in and snapped a photo before taking his seat.

At first I wasn't sure what he had done, since I didn't keep any personal photos or anything taped to my mirror, only my cosmetologist license as required by law.

Then I realized my license had my current address on it.

I flashed him a disgruntled look as I snapped the towel I had been unfolding more aggressively than necessary.

He winked back.

I placed it around his neck. I then went over to retrieve a steam towel from the steam machine.

As I held it gingerly before his jaw, I warned, "This is going to be hot."

"Don't mind me. I like things hot and wet."

I blushed furiously as I wrapped the warm steam towel over his jaw.

I then went to fetch some warm water for the lather.

As I was at the tap, Heather approached me. "Holy crap. That isn't who I think it is?"

Keeping my head down as I made sure to adjust the right amount of water or it would kill the foam, I said in a hushed whisper, "Yes, so you better keep out of sight if you know what's good for you."

"Fuck! Is he here for me?"

I bit my lower lip. I hadn't thought about that. I shook my head. "I don't think so. Stay in the back as much as you can, just in case."

I swirled the boar brush around the shaving soap at the bottom of the handled porcelain dish, working it into a rich, foamy lather, then I returned to my chair with that and my bowl of extra hot water.

After setting them on the counter, I stepped behind him to remove his towel.

The moment I got close, I was hit with more of the masculine scent of his cologne.

I inhaled more deeply, loving the rich fragrance of cedarwood, bergamot, and spice. The steam of his towel had warmed and enhanced the essence on his skin.

A delicious shudder coursed down my spine as all those sensual pheromones wove their dark magic through me.

Anton's deep voice startled me. "It's called *Oud & Bergamot.*"

My eyes flew open. "What?"

His stormy gray eyes held a hint of amusement as he met my reflection in the mirror. "My cologne. It is Jo Malone's *Oud & Bergamot*. The personal shopper who selected it for me said it had an *animalistic* appeal. I'll be sure to let her know you agree."

My cheeks flamed bright red at being caught sniffing him like a bitch in heat. I snatched the now cool steam towel from his hand.

I scrunched his suit sleeves up my elbows, picked up my porcelain shaving mug, and turned to him.

And promptly froze.

Fuck, he was good looking.

I mean, the salt and pepper hair, the sharp angles to his cheekbones, the smoky gray eyes, the sensual lips, and the way they always seemed to be lifted in a darkly sarcastic smirk.

Even the small lines around his eyes when he sort of smiled were sexy as fuck.

Anton reached out his hand and grasped my wrist, gently pulling me closer to stand between his spread knees. "I think you are supposed to put that lather on my face, *moya malen'kaya vorovka.*"

I blinked, looking around as if coming to from a trance.

Realizing how inappropriate it was to be standing between his thighs, I shifted my hips to move, but he closed his legs, trapping me.

"I have to stand to the side to lather your jaw."

He slipped his hands inside his jacket and placed them on my hips as he drew me flush against the hard ridge of his cock pressing against his inner thigh.

My mouth fell open.

"I think you should stand right here … *and lather me.*"

Oh, God.

My mouth went completely dry.

I forced myself to swallow.

He was so tall that even with him sitting down, he was still at my eye level.

I thought about hitting the pedal on the salon chair to lower it, but then that would put him at eye level with my boobs, which would be even worse.

I schooled my features, knowing I needed to get it together. I was a professional, dammit.

After pulling my gaze away from his eyes, I focused on his jaw.

His chiseled-from-granite jaw.

Clearing my throat, I asked, "Did you want a clean shave or did you want me to just tighten up the beard?"

It wasn't a full beard, more like a sexy, George Clooney five o'clock shadow with killer sideburns to go with his perfectly tousled, slightly wavy, salt and pepper hair.

He wrapped his firm hand around my left wrist and captured my gaze. Without taking his eyes off me, he lifted my arm to his face and tilted his head to rub his jaw along the sensitive skin of my inner wrist. "You tell me. Would this feel too rough on your inner thigh?"

Smashing my knees together, I bit my lip to stifle a moan.

I swore I could actually feel the gentle scrape of his beard on the skin of my inner thigh.

I snatched my hand back. "I'll just tighten up the beard."

He chuckled. "Good choice."

The heat from my burning cheeks practically singed the hairs on the back of my neck when I realized what I had said meant. "I'm only saying that because it will take less time than shaving it off," I said in a rush. "And the sooner I'm done, the sooner you'll leave so I can get back to work."

Which was completely not true and any man who had any experience with facial hair would know that.

Before he could call me out on my lie, I lifted the lathered shave brush to his cheek.

Using slow circular motions, I swirled the soft, white foam onto his cheek and jaw above the beard line and below along the thick muscled cords of his neck, being careful to keep the towel tucked into his dress shirt collar.

As I shifted and leaned close to get the other side, his hand slipped between my thighs.

My eyes widened. I knew the sides and length of his jacket, plus my position between his legs, hid his hands from view … but still.

"Don't stop," he commanded.

I moved the shave brush over his jaw, watching as the swirls of shaving foam clinging to the boar's head bristles smoothed over the hard angles of his face.

He matched the circular motion of my brush with his thumb, caressing my inner thigh, creeping higher and higher with each successive circle.

He tilted his head back and to the side, exposing his neck. "Ask me why I tracked you down today."

I shifted my hips as the thin fabric of the denim shorts pushed against my sensitive pussy lips. "You changed your mind and want to have me locked up."

"Close."

My heart skipped a beat.

He hooked two fingers into the crotch of my shorts and panties.

Using his raised knuckle, he teased my clit, rolling his curled finger in a slow, swirling motion. "After the stunt you pulled with that wrong address, you'll be lucky if I let you leave my bed for a week."

He used his free hand to tighten his grip on my hip as he twisted his wrist downward.

The motion pulled on my shorts until they slipped lower on my hips.

He then pushed two fingers up inside of me. "I'll probably have to get creative with some handcuffs to keep you there."

I dug my fingers into his upper arm as I pushed my lips between my teeth to stop myself from crying out.

His mint-scented breath rasped. "I think you missed a spot on my neck, baby."

I nodded mindlessly as I tried to focus on acting normal. I swept the brush down the column of his neck as he pushed his fingers in deep and used the pad of his thumb to rub my clit at the same time.

My free hand gripped his forearm as I rose up on my toes as my gaze flashed about the salon, surprised to see no one seemed to notice me getting finger fucked.

He continued to torment with his fingers and words. "But that's not why I tracked you down."

He pulsed his fingers inside of mc.

I pushed the shaving brush through the last of the foam and swept it over the final small spot just below his left cheekbone.

His intense gaze was trained on me as his fingers vibrated back and forth faster, teasing every nerve inside of me.

I swallowed a gasp. "Oh, God!"

"That's it, baby. Come for Daddy," he growled.

Fuuuuuccck ... did he have to do the kinky daddy thing? Here?

I twisted my legs, smashing my thighs together as I trapped his hand.

My body twitched as I stiffened my limbs, trying to contain my insanely inappropriate public orgasm.

He pulled his fingers free and put them both in his mouth as he gave me another slow wink.

How was it possible that, even with his face covered with shaving cream, that was still sexy as hell?

He squeezed my hip. "Ask me why I tracked you down."

I was afraid to move on to the next step of the hot shave, afraid to move, period.

Knowing I needed to break the spell but not able to.

I knew he wasn't going to just tell me why he tracked me ... no ... hunted me down.

He wanted me to be curious as to why the wolf preyed on the rabbit. I knew why.

I wasn't going to do it.

I didn't want to do it.

I wasn't going to fall for his trap.

I wasn't going to be lured in.

I needed to put an end to this now before it went any further.

Only a fool would ask him.

To ask would only encourage this madness.

Yes, exactly!

It would be complete and utter madness … *dangerous madness* … to ask him.

"Why did you track me down?" I whispered.

CHAPTER 10

ANTON

hank God I was a possessive man, or I'd be tempted to rip her clothes off, bend her over that counter, and fuck her sideways in this moment.

Christ, I needed to get this woman in my bed ... and soon.

Now.

Before I could answer, she shook her head. "No. Don't answer that."

She turned her back on me and placed the shaving mug on the counter.

I could see her flushed cheeks and bright eyes in the reflection of the mirror.

She really was the most beautifully innocent creature.

It was such a turn-on to see how aroused she became from just the slightest brush of my fingers.

I shifted in my seat as I adjusted my cock along my suit trousers.

A guy two chairs down was staring at us. I raised an eyebrow and he quickly looked away.

I didn't give a fuck if he saw my hard-on, but I'd tear his fucking head off if he was looking at Brynn.

I'd known her less than twenty-four hours, and it was already like that.

And I wasn't bothered one fucking bit by it.

For starters, I wasn't a young man stupid enough to let a beautiful, intriguing woman slip through my fingers because of some misguided notion that my life would somehow be better sinking my cock in as much strange pussy as I could find.

Only immature idiots thought like that.

A real man knew nothing improved the quality of their life like having a good woman by their side. Strange pussy didn't compare.

I also knew better than to just go for looks, although make no mistake, Brynn was beautiful.

With her honey-brown curls, big doe eyes, and heart-shaped face with the small dusting of freckles across the bridge of her nose, she was that sweet kind of beautiful.

Not an ice queen femme fatale who had a cold, untouchable kind of glamorous beauty, but more the warm kind of beauty you wanted to cuddle with on a cold night and spoil with silly stuff like stuffed animals and surprise trips for goofy things like to see the Eurovision Song Contest.

The kind of beauty you could see mothering your children.

I lived a dangerous life constantly in the cold.

I now craved warmth.

She picked up her straight razor and the leather strop bolted to the exposed brick wall to our left. Ignoring me, she raised the strop and pulled it tightly. She then gently ran the razor flat along the leather suede side several times before flipping it over to finish it on the smooth side.

Fuck, it was sexy as hell watching her handle that razor.

When it was sharp, she set the razor aside and moved to take off my suit jacket.

I lifted my chin. "What the hell do you think you're doing?"

"I'm going to start shaving you."

I lifted an eyebrow. "And?"

"I need to put a towel on my shoulder to wipe the blade and I don't want to risk getting shaving cream on your expensive jacket."

"Babygirl, that jacket is the only reason why we're still here. I don't give a fuck about the jacket. Leave it on," I growled.

Apparently she didn't think I was serious when I told her my first instinct was to kill every man in this place for ogling the way her tits and ass were displayed in that fucking uniform.

She is putting a remarkable amount of faith in my level of civility.

She placed the towel on her shoulder and picked up the razor.

Approaching my right side, her cool fingertips touched my scalp as she adjusted the angle of my head.

I closed my eyes and imagined what those fingers would feel like on the heated skin of my shaft.

The sharp blade pressed against the vulnerable flesh of my neck.

It wasn't until that very moment that I realized what I was doing.

I had never in my life allowed someone to shave me, and certainly never would have considered doing so with a straight razor.

It would have been tantamount to suicide in my line of work.

And here I was letting this little slip of a girl, who I had only just caught trying to steal from me, place a sharpened blade to my jugular.

I opened my eyes to slits and observed her.

Her full pink lower lip was pushed between her pearl-white teeth. She frowned in concentration as she deftly handled the blade, applying only enough pressure to slice my coarse beard hair. She swept the razor down my neck several times, swiping the shaving foam off the razor onto the towel on her shoulder.

She moved to the other side of the chair and did the same, before she grabbed another steam towel and gently wiped any excess shaving foam from my face, checking for any place she might have missed.

She picked up the blade and swiped at a place just below my chin before nodding in satisfaction.

When she was finished, I snatched her around the waist and pulled her between my legs before she had a chance to move away. "I love a woman who knows how to handle a piece of thick leather and steel."

She stared up at the ceiling, avoiding eye contact. "You do know I'm still holding a sharp object, right?"

I cupped her ass cheek with my right hand. "I was going to punish this cute ass with my bare hand, but after seeing that leather strop, I can't help but remember the pretty blush my leather belt brought to your ass last night."

Her head pivoted from side to side, making sure we weren't being observed. "Keep your voice down, and what do you mean punish me? You already punished me!"

"That was for last night. I'm talking about this morning's misbehavior, which, by the way, I don't think the Carmichaels will be needing your services again."

Her mouth dropped open, forming an adorable O.

I smirked as I tapped the tip of her nose. "And those lips remind me of your other punishment."

She snapped her mouth shut. Her eyes narrowed as she tried to speak through clenched teeth without opening her lips. "Please tell me you didn't meet the Carmichaels?"

I tilted my head. "I don't think *meet* is the correct word. It implies a level of sociability that was lacking in the interaction."

"Oh my God! Oh my God! Oh my God! They weren't supposed to be back for another three days! They are going to be so pissed! They'll never pay me now. I needed that money."

"You don't, but we will discuss that later."

She tried to pull free, but I tightened my grasp. "Why do you keep saying that? There is no later! Your shave is over. It's on me. I have other customers waiting."

"Are you under the impression I'm letting you stay here?"

Both her eyebrows rose as she blinked several times. "Letting me? Letting me?" She crossed her arms over her chest. "Um, I was under the impression that it was none of your business."

The corner of my mouth lifted. "Interesting. Did you know you have a tell when you lie?"

"I do not!"

"You do."

"What is it?"

"I'm not going to tell you. That would give away my edge."

She threw her hands up in frustration.

The effect was slightly ruined when my suit cuffs came undone and the sleeves tumbled down past her fingertips, making her look like a disgruntled child playing dress-up. "You're impossible."

I nodded. "That's fair. Now get your things. Let's go."

"I'm not leaving with you. I have to work."

I stood up, towering over her, and stroked her cheek. "Babygirl, there are a hundred different ways we can have this argument. At least seventy of those you're naked, but I absolutely guarantee, in not one of those scenarios do you win the argument and stay at this job."

She looked beyond me and gasped.

I pivoted.

Seeing nothing of alarm, I turned back.

Brynn already had my suit jacket off.

Raising her voice, she said, "Thank you so much, Mr. Ivenchenko. I hope you enjoyed your shave. Please tell your friends."

Cheeky little minx.

Before I could respond, a slender man wearing a Third Base T-shirt and a baggy pair of jeans walked past her. "About time, there are customers waiting. And don't break the rules and cover up again. Men want to see that ass."

And then he signed his death warrant.

He swatted my girl's ass.

Brynn's eyes widened.

In one fluid motion, I grabbed the man by the jaw and twisted until his body followed, throwing him to the floor. I stepped on his face and leaned over, pulling the gun from my side holster.

I pressed the barrel to his temple. "Say your name. I like to know who I kill."

Brynn rushed up. "Anton, don't! This is my boss, Nigel. He didn't mean it. He's just a douchebag!"

Nigel pressed his elbows against the dirty linoleum floor as he spit out the cut clumps of hair that clung to his lips as he whimpered, "Yeah! Yeah! Like she said, I'm a douchebag, dude!"

Several of the patrons stood, some with their phones out, others just staring, unsure what to do.

I allowed my Russian accent to come across heavier than usual. "Men, if you don't want trouble, leave now. Ladies, you tell me, should I let your boss live?"

Every customer ran for the door.

The female staff clustered in a group as they stared at Nigel's squirming form.

Nigel called out, "Come on! Tell him yes?"

One of the women put her hands on her hips. "We're tired of you always hitting on us!"

Another one piped up. "And these disgusting uniforms. We want to wear yoga pants."

And another. "And stop stealing our tips!"

I pressed my boot harder into Nigel's face. "That doesn't sound like a yes to me, Nigel."

Nigel blubbered. "Okay! Okay! Just don't kill me."

Brynn looked up at me with tears in her eyes. "Please, don't do this."

God dammit.

Just then a yellow puddle formed under Nigel's prone form.

I took my foot off his face and tucked my weapon into my waistband behind my back. "I'll be sending my men here periodically to check up on you. If these ladies aren't happy, I'll be back and trust me, Nigel, I won't be so nice."

I turned to Brynn.

Wrapping my hand around her upper arm, I marched her into the back where I figured the break room would be. Seeing it to the left, I pulled her over the threshold and pointed to the row of beat-up metal lockers. "Which one of these is yours?"

"Anton, I—"

I sighed. "Brynn, I just watched a man touch you and stopped myself from shooting him. I am in no mood. Which one?"

She pointed to her locker.

I stormed over to it and opened it up.

Snatching an empty plastic grocery bag from a nearby table, I shoved the entire contents into the bag and handed her purse to her. I then walked over to the coat rack. "Which one?"

She pointed to a thin, inexpensive coat.

"This one?" I held it up. "This is not warm enough."

She shrugged. "It's fine."

I held it up for her to put her arms in.

I then picked up the plastic bag and grabbed her hand.

Walking through the salon, I picked up my suit jacket and only paused to collect my wool coat from the customer rack, which I slung over her shoulders before I hustled her out the door to my Range Rover.

Brynn fidgeted with the crystal bead bracelets on her wrist as she sat in the passenger seat. "Where are you taking me?"

I gripped the steering wheel as I stared ahead, trying to ease the homicidal rage in my chest. "Somewhere we won't be disturbed."

CHAPTER 11

ANTON

I could feel her unease mount as I pulled into the underground parking garage of Four Monks.

I circled past the usual parking spots and activated an automated solid steel gate that led to the secure private section for only myself and the other owners.

Catching sight of her twisting in her seat to glance over her shoulder as the security gate slammed shut with a thundering clap the moment my Range Rover cleared it.

It would only increase her agitation if I let her know that gate was two feet of reinforced steel commissioned specifically to withstand a bomb blast.

I rolled the steering wheel to the left as I swung into my assigned parking spot. It was positioned right in front of a private elevator that led directly to my penthouse. It also was specifically commissioned with bulletproof doors.

An uncommon life meant nothing was commonplace.

As I turned off the ignition, Brynn pivoted in her seat to face me. "Is there any version of this where you start the car back up and take me home?"

I tapped her on the nose. "I just can't get over how fucking adorable you can be."

She let out a long sigh before gazing out the car windshield. "So this is what a lair looks like?"

"No, this is what a lair's parking garage looks like." I motioned with my head toward the elevator. "My lair is upstairs."

She twisted the handle of the plastic bag around the tip of her finger, turning it purple. "So we're just going up there to talk, right?"

I pushed her hand away and unwound the plastic handle before she hurt herself. "No, babygirl. We're not going up there to *talk*. In fact, that's the last thing we'll be doing."

I wasn't going to lie to her.

I was an imposing man and sex with me would be aggressive and intense, there was no sugarcoating it. The last thing I wanted was any misconceptions about my intentions.

Once she entered that elevator, there would be no turning back … she would be mine.

The fact I wasn't giving her much choice about

whether or not she entered the elevator was semantics.

I exited the vehicle and crossed to the passenger side, opening the door. Bracing my right forearm along the top of the door, I leaned down and looked into the interior. "Brynn, baby? I need you to get out of the car."

She turned to me. "What about lunch? We could go to a restaurant!"

I raised an eyebrow. "Are you hungry?"

She scrunched her nose. "Not really."

"I'll make you something later if you get hungry."

She gathered her plastic bag and purse. "What about a movie? I haven't been to a movie in ages."

I nodded. "Dimitri, a friend of mine, has a great hookup at the Gene Siskel Film Center. I can arrange for a private showing of any film you want ... at another time."

I stretched my arm into the interior, holding my hand out, palm up. "Enough stalling."

I was trying hard not to fall on her like a Neanderthal on a bone, but if she made me wait much longer I wasn't going to be responsible for my actions.

She placed her small hand in mine. Her skin was soft and cool as her fingers slid along my palm.

I enclosed my hand around hers, trying not to squeeze it too tight. Taking her purse and bag, I lifted her hand high as I helped her step out of the vehicle.

She adjusted my overly large wool overcoat on her shoulders and gathered the extra length in her free hand as I closed the car door and placed an arm around her lower back to guide her to my private elevator.

I entered the nine-digit code and pressed my thumb to the electronic keypad.

Brynn stared at the glowing screen. "So if I memorized the code from last night I'd know how to get into your office and home?"

I glanced down at her. "They are two different codes and they change every forty-eight hours."

Both her eyebrows rose. "You memorize two different crazy-long entry codes every two days?"

"Five nine-digit codes. There are several secure entries around the property."

"That's impossible."

"Not when you are used to memorizing up to six card decks in play at once."

The elevator doors slid open, showing a dim interior with mahogany and black leather paneling with polished stainless-steel railings.

I stepped inside and held the door open for Brynn.

She hesitated.

I looked down for a moment and shook my head.

I'd tried.

I really had.

I wanted to be the good guy.

At least for once.

I'd sat for a hot shave while she tortured my cock with that tight fucking T-shirt and those denim shorts so tiny I could reach her pussy with a flick of my finger.

I'd even denied myself the satisfaction of shooting her piece of shit boss in the head.

There was only so much a man could be expected to take before he … snapped.

I twisted my hands in the lapels of my coat, which hung loose over her shoulders, and yanked her over the threshold of the elevator.

Slamming my elbow into the close button, I used my body to trap her against the wall.

I had wanted to do this right….

I had wanted to do this in a bed….

Now I just wanted her.

I clasped my hands around her jaw and tilted her head back. My mouth captured her gasp of surprise, fed on it.

Fuck, she tasted sweet.

My fingers pushed into her soft hair to hold her tighter as I stepped closer, pushing my hips against her stomach.

Brynn whimpered and grabbed at my sleeves as the tip of her small tongue swirled around mine. The poor thing was trying to keep up with the ferocity of my embrace.

The problem was she was kissing.

I was feasting.

I wanted to devour her.

I pressed my mouth harder against her lips as I pushed my tongue deeper into her mouth.

This was no shy press of the lips, or swish of the tongue.

No coy advance and retreat.

This was a full-on assault.

I shifted the angle of my head as I bit her bottom lip before claiming her mouth again.

Even when the elevator doors opened, I refused to relent.

Shoving my overcoat and her own coat off her shoulders, I bent low and placed my hands just below her ass, around each thigh and lifted her. "Wrap your legs around me," I rasped against her lips, before kissing her again.

The moment she obeyed, I carried her out of the elevator, through the entryway, and down the hall to my bedroom. After crossing the threshold, I kicked the arched oak door with wrought-iron accents closed and carried her to the massive king-size four-poster bed.

I followed her down as I laid her on the edge of the bed on the cream satin tufted quilt. Clasping her right bent knee, I lifted it high as I pressed my aching cock against the juncture of her thighs.

Bracing my left forearm by her shoulder, I leaned back a moment to stare down at her as I brushed her hair back from her forehead. Her high cheekbones had a bright flush of color and her kiss-swollen lips were stained a dark cherry red.

I traced my fingertip around the edge of her mouth, soothing the slight pink marks from where my beard had scraped her sensitive skin. "God, you're beautiful."

She opened her mouth. "No, I…."

I placed my fingertips over her lips. "Haven't you learned yet? I don't like to be argued with."

I captured her mouth again.

I ground my cock against her pelvic bone in an attempt to ease the rising ache as I delayed my own satisfaction. I wanted nothing else in this world than to fuck this woman until she screamed my name, but I also wanted to savor kissing her.

Pleasure like this was not to be rushed, for there was even more pleasure to be had in the anticipation, in the pain of self-denial. A person didn't guzzle a fine wine or wolf down an elegant meal.

Running my right hand down the top of her thigh, I caressed her belly before flicking the button on her denim shorts.

I then slowly lowered the zipper.

Rising to my full height, I grasped the waistband of her shorts and panties and started to pull them over her hips.

Brynn tugged them back up. "What are you doing?"

The corner of my mouth lifted at her sweet nervousness. "You know precisely what I'm doing. Now move your hands before I tie you to the bed."

She shimmied backward, sliding along the slippery satin comforter. "But wait. I thought we were having fun just kissing?"

Narrowing my gaze, I stepped back from the bed.

Reaching in my vest pocket, I withdrew my Jean Pierre sterling silver pocket watch and set it on the nightstand. It was an affectation I had picked up at the European poker tables, where cellphones were frowned upon, since I never liked wearing a watch.

I hated when blood got beneath the wristband.

Watching Brynn closely, I unbuttoned my suit vest as I kicked off my shoes. "No, little one. While I am definitely enjoying kissing you, I'm afraid I'm not some randy teenage boy who'd be happy with a few open-mouthed kisses and a dry hump."

I shrugged out of my vest and tossed it over a nearby oxblood tufted leather chair. I then untucked my dress shirt and slowly unbuttoned it, knowing with each button more of my tattoos would be revealed to her.

Brightly colored, violent imagery telling her precisely who I was and what I had done to achieve the power and wealth I currently enjoyed. Russian criminals didn't wear our hearts on our sleeves; we inked our vicious, cold-blooded resumes on our chests.

After several buttons, I pulled the shirt over my head.

Brynn's eyes widened as she took in the shocking imagery.

From the bejeweled dagger stabbing a barbed wire-wrapped rose in the center of my chest, symbolic of my incarceration before I was barely out of my teens, to the warped military iconography depicting my rise as an elite crime boss in the Russian criminal underground, it was all on full display.

As I reached for my belt buckle, I nodded toward her. "Take off your shorts. I want to see that pretty pussy again. This time I'm not just going to pet it."

I whipped my belt through the loops and threaded the leather tongue back through the buckle just in time as Brynn flipped onto her knees and made a dash for the other side of the bed.

I looped the belt around her left ankle and pulled it tight.

She cried out as she was flattened onto her stomach.

I pulled on the belt, sliding her body toward me.

I then flipped her onto her back.

She raised her palms up as she shook her head. "I can't! I can't do this. You don't understand."

Once again, I grasped the waistband to her shorts. This time, before she had a chance to object, I pulled them over her hips and down her legs.

She tried to kick out, but it was no use.

I easily grasped my belt, which was still around her slim ankle, and stretched her left leg high.

Her cute ass cheeks were just barely over the edge of the bed.

I wrapped my hand around her other ankle and stretched her right leg up high and then spread both legs before stepping close.

Her mouth opened on a gasp as my barely restrained cock pressed against her naked pussy.

"Now take off that fucking T-shirt."

"Please."

"Brynn, you're lucky I didn't rip that thing off your body the moment I saw it. Now take it off," I ground out through my teeth.

Seeing her in the tight, low-cut shirt that was practically molded to her breasts, with its gratuitous third base slogan across the back, had made me see red.

My little girl really didn't appreciate the restraint I had shown in not tearing it to shreds right then and there.

Later, she and I would have to have a long talk about trying the limits of my civility or it would be an unavoidable conclusion that she was going to see me hurt, or possibly kill, someone right before her pretty eyes. Something I was hoping to shelter her from.

She gripped the bottom hem of her T-shirt,

pulling it even tighter over her chest. The thin white material became almost translucent. "This is just moving really fast."

I could see the smooth outline of her bra and just a hint of her dark, dusty pink nipples.

I ran the tip of my tongue along the back of my lower teeth as my mouth salivated at the sight.

There were so many things I had denied myself that first night with her stretched out over my desk as I punished the full curves of her ass. Sucking on those tight buds was one of them.

Releasing her ankles, I pushed her hands away as I reached for the hem of her shirt.

"Time's up," I growled, before tearing it in half.

CHAPTER 12

BRYNN

The pitiful sound of my T-shirt tearing ripped through my body like a gunshot.

His powerful hands then made short work of my bra. Reaching for the center strip of silk and elastic between my cleavage, he actually snapped it in two as if it were nothing more than tissue paper.

My breasts spilled out as the silk cups fell to the sides. I placed my hands over them to shield myself as I tried to twist my hips and curl up on my side. "Anton, wait!"

The mattress dipped as he placed a knee between my thighs and climbed onto the bed with me, resting part of his weight on top of me.

Pinning me down.

It was hard not to panic.

Everything about this man was large and intimidating.

From his height to his muscled chest to the terrifying tattoos of weapons, blood, and military iconography.

He braced one forearm next to my head while he pushed my hand away and cupped my left breast. "I'm done waiting, babygirl."

His mouth seized mine. His tongue swept inside, stealing my breath as he squeezed my breast and pinched my nipple between his finger and thumb.

I screamed against his lips as I tried to buck my hips, but couldn't.

He kissed me with such intensity, my head spun. The moment he released my lips, I sucked in a great gasp of air. It almost felt as if I were drowning.

His lips trailed along my jaw, then down my throat. His tongue laved at the rapid pulse at the base of my throat as he continued to roll my nipple between his fingers, causing ripples of pleasurable pain to dance up my spine.

He shifted his body down along my side to place an open-mouthed kiss on my right breast.

My shoulders came off the bed. "Oh! Oh!"

He used the flat of his tongue to place delicious pressure against my nipple, before teasing it with the tip. Flicking the sensitive nub several times then pulling it deeply into his mouth. Before releasing it, he used the edge of his teeth to gently bite down.

"Oh, my God," I called out as I dug my nails into his upper arms.

I bent my left knee and curled it up over his hip as I unconsciously ground my hips against his hard cock.

He continued to lave, lick, tease, and bite my nipples. First one, then the other.

Holy shit. It was like he was mouth-fucking my breasts.

I didn't even know such a thing was possible. In my limited experience with boys they had usually just painfully squeezed them and maybe quickly sucked on my nipples as they fumbled with trying to get my jeans zipper down, but nothing like this.

He moved to kiss my stomach, then lower.

Again, I got nervous.

I tried to grasp his shoulders and pull him up. "Maybe we should .... "

He slid off the bed to kneel between my legs. "Babygirl, if you think anything is going to stop me from tasting this pussy, you're out of your fucking mind."

He wrapped his arms around my thighs and pulled until my ass was practically hanging off the edge of the bed and the arches of my feet were curled over the tops of his shoulders.

It placed my naked pussy an embarrassing few inches from his mouth.

I knew what his fingers could do. I had just experienced what his mouth could do on only my nipples. And I could only imagine what that would feel like *down there*, but still, this was too much, because afterwards he was going to want sex, and that definitely could *not* happen.

I leaned up on my elbows and stared down my body between my thighs. "You have to stop. We can't do this because you're going to want—"

"Baby, I already want."

"No, I mean—"

He used his thumbs to gently pull open my pussy lips and dipped his head between my thighs.

Just like he had teased in the salon, I could feel the slightly rough brush of his bearded jaw against my inner thigh as he did so.

Keeping his fierce gaze locked on me, he stretched out his tongue and flicked my clit.

My head fell back as my upper body jerked.

He swirled the tip of his tongue around the nub counterclockwise several times, then reversed several times, with each pass gently increasing, then easing the pressure, like the crest and fall of a wave on a beach.

My fingers clawed at the satin comforter until it was bunched in my hands. My head felt too heavy for my neck to support as I remained up on my elbows but with my head draped back.

I shook it from side to side. "Please, we can't. You don't understand."

I tried in vain to pull away from him, from the pleasure he was giving me.

He shifted his head to rub his jaw along my thigh, kissing it. "Tell me, *moya malen'kaya vorovka*, what don't I understand?"

I breathed heavily as I tried to force my mind to focus and form the words.

He returned to teasing my clit, as this time, he pushed one finger, then two inside of me.

My mouth dropped open as my body clenched around his thick digits.

His warm breath caressed me. "I'm listening, baby. Tell me why you think I should ignore what your body is telling me."

He pumped his fingers in and out of me. "Tell me now." He swirled his tongue, gently laving at me. "Because I need you warm, wet, and ready for when I thrust my cock into this tight pussy of yours or I'm going to tear you."

He pushed a third finger into me.

My back arched as I twisted the bedcover in my fists. "Oh! Oh, my … I'm…."

Alarms bells were clanging in my rational brain but I was past reason.

He thrust his fingers in and out faster as he timed the movement with his tongue. "That's it, babygirl," he murmured. The vibrations of his deep, gravelly voice adding to my pleasure. "Come for me. Come for…"

I bit my lower lip, wanting him to say it, but not wanting him to say it.

I could hear the sensual chuckle in his voice when he growled, "Daddy."

Damn it.

My thighs squeezed against the side of his head as my hips bucked.

In that moment, he pressed the flat of his tongue against my clit, applying steady pressure as he pushed his three fingers deep inside of me and kept them there.

I ground my hips against his hand and mouth as I rode wave after wave of crushing euphoria. Somehow, someway this man knew that what I needed wasn't frenzied movement in this moment but steady, almost agonizingly amazing pressure as my body took over and did the rest. If he had moved he would have ruined it.

I shifted my forearms, moving off my elbows to fall back onto the bed as a wave of dizziness washed over me.

Through half closed eyes, I watched as Anton rose to tower over me.

With one cocked eyebrow, he stared down at me as he brought his three fingers to his mouth and slowly sucked each one.

Holy shit.

The raw sexuality of the moment was almost too much to bear.

Keeping his stormy gray gaze on me, his hands moved to his suit trouser zipper. He slowly lowered it and let his trousers and Calvin Kleins fall to the floor.

I blinked several times.

Those alarm bells that I had been ignoring were now screeching.

I grabbed one of the bedposts and used it to swing off the bed.

The moment I was on my feet, I realized I was naked … like, really naked.

My T-shirt lay in shreds on the bed next to my equally torn bra, and my shorts were on the other side of the bed next to Jolly Russian Giant over there.

I snatched one of the satin pillows from the top of the bed and held it vertically in front of me, like the world's worst shield. "I need to borrow a shirt or something."

"I will have the best stores on Michigan Avenue deliver an entire new fucking wardrobe for you right after you get back in that bed and spread your legs."

I clenched my stomach, angry at myself that his crude dirty talk sent a spark straight to my pussy.

I skirted around the bed and kept my front to him. "You left my coat in the elevator. I'll just use that."

"I was going to shoot a man in the head for slapping your ass and you think I'm going to allow you to leave here to prance around the city naked with nothing but a thin coat on?"

"Then give me a shirt to put on."

"Absolutely."

"Thank you."

"After we fuck."

"We are not going to have sex."

"You're right."

"Thank you."

"We're going to fuck."

"Oh, my God! You're impossible."

He stalked toward me, his monstrous cock bobbing between his legs. "I think the word you mean is improbable, and yet"—he gestured toward his cock— "it's real. You'll soon find out how real."

I clutched the pillow tighter as I backed away. "Your *impossible* arrogance aside, that's not what I meant. Look, we just can't have sex, all right, because…."

He stalked closer. "If you are worried, I have a clean bill of health and I've been so busy with the club, it has been a very long time since I've even allowed myself to be distracted by a woman. Certainly never one as entertaining as you, *moya malen'kaya vorovka.*"

While it was reassuring, that wasn't what I was worried about.

I definitely should have been, but it was hard to think straight around him.

"Yes, no, maybe—look, I'm sorry if you think I led you on or something—"

He frowned. "Don't worry. You didn't lead me on."

I sighed as my shoulders sagged with relief. "Well, thank you for that."

He maneuvered to block my exit. "I came to the conclusion I was going to fuck you without any encouragement from you, quite the opposite in fact."

My eyes widened as I saw too late what he had done.

He now stood between me and my only way out of the room.

My head pivoted left and right, but only confirmed my worst fears.

Panicking, I tried to make a dash for it anyway.

I bolted past him.

He easily snatched me around the waist and spun me.

Before I knew what happened I was wedged between his body and the wall, with his hard cock pressed against my stomach.

He stretched my arms over my head and anchored them there by holding both my wrists with only one hand.

The tiny sharp crystal edges from my bracelets pressed into my skin.

He wrapped his free hand high around my throat just under my jaw as he tilted my head back. "What is going on with you? Why are you suddenly so cagey? Are you carrying another man's baby? Is that it?"

I rolled my eyes. "Not unless it's the immaculate conception."

He narrowed his gaze on me. "What about me strikes you as a patient man, babygirl? Tell me. Now."

I swallowed, feeling his grip on my throat as I did so. "I'm a virgin."

CHAPTER 13

ANTON

*S*he said virgin, but all I heard was *only mine*.

I swept down and captured her mouth as I lifted her off the floor. Cupping her by the back of the head, I wrapped my arm around her waist and carried her to my bed.

Without breaking the kiss, I pulled the covers back and placed her in the center, before following her down. I wanted her to feel the cool silky satin sheets on her skin as I pushed her thighs open and drove deep inside of her.

Not just mine.

Only mine.

Blood surged to my already painfully erect cock.

Never in my life had I wanted to sink into the tight warmth of a woman more. Never had it *meant* more to me.

I was wrong.

I wasn't going to fuck her.

I was going to claim her.

Mine.

Only mine.

There wasn't a doubt in my mind, there wasn't a chance in hell I was ever letting this beautiful little treasure who stumbled into my life go now.

She'd be lucky if I let her out of this room after this.

She was a virgin.

All I could hear was a primal drumbeat pounding in my ears.

An ancient call to claim, possess, and protect her.

Wedging my hips between her thighs, I shifted to the left and caressed her pussy with my right hand, teasing her back to full arousal.

She tossed her head to the side as her small hands pushed against my chest. "Anton, wait."

I ran my lips along her neck. "Shhh, don't worry, baby. I'll be as gentle as I can. It will hurt, but I'll kiss it and make it better."

She arched her back and stretched her neck, straining against my embrace. "You don't understand."

I thrust two fingers into her wet heat, twisting and turning them. "I know you're scared but trust me, baby, your body was made for my cock."

And *only* my cock.

She reached up and grabbed a fistful of my hair and yanked on it hard to get my attention. "You're not the one!"

The sting of pain brought a pleasurable rush down my spine but her words had me seeing red.

I rose up on my knees and threaded my fingers through hers, pinning her to the mattress. "You want to say that again?" I growled.

If she was about to tell me about another man while lying naked underneath me, I was going to tie her to this fucking bed and go and put a bullet in him.

Her gaze shifted away. "I didn't have a … normal … high school experience. It's why I'm still … you know… and after I turned twenty, I swore that if I waited that long I might as well wait for the right guy."

I stared down at her flushed face as a heated blush crept over her cheeks.

My cock throbbed against her inner thigh. "Are you asking me to marry you before we fuck?"

As soon as I voiced the question, I realized the idea had merit.

Her eyes widened as her blush deepened. "Hell, no."

The moment she objected, I liked the idea even more.

She yanked on her arms, but I held firm. "I'm saying that waiting for the *right guy* doesn't mean hopping into bed with a tattooed Russian mafia crime boss who carries a gun and threatens to shoot people in the head that I've known less than twenty-four hours!"

I sucked in a breath through clenched teeth as my upper lip curled.

The pounding in my ears turned into a raging howl.

I was a feral beast about to have something I considered mine ripped from my jaws.

What she said was rational and reasonable but I wasn't interested in rational and reasonable.

I released her hands.

Before she got the false idea I was letting her go, I pushed one hand between her legs and wrapped the other around her loose locks as I leaned over her. "You forgot dangerous."

I then thrust three fingers into her tight hole.

Her hips bucked. "Oh!"

I swept the pad of my thumb over her clit as I rasped against her lips, "You think I'm letting you leave this bed to give this sweet pussy to another man?"

I thrust my fingers inside of her several more times while keeping the pressure on her clit.

She grasped at my upper arm. "I didn't say that!"

I nipped at the corner of her mouth. "Let's get something straight, little one. There will be no other man."

I twisted my fingers inside of her, opening her.

Preparing her.

Her fingernails dug into my flesh.

I fisted my cock and placed the head at her entrance. "Whether you like it or not, I am *the one* and will be *your only one*."

I braced my forearms on either side of her head. "Say it," I commanded. "Now."

Her big, beautiful brown eyes stared up at me. "You're the one," she whispered.

I thrust in deep, breaking through her maidenhead.

My mouth crashed down on hers, swallowing her momentary cry of pain.

I clasped her to me and rolled until I was on my back, placing her on my chest.

I could feel my heartbeat pulse along my shaft as it was sheathed in her incredibly tight heat.

Still, I willed myself not to move, not to thrust.

Sweat broke out on my brow as I wrapped my arms around her shoulders and lower back and held her close.

I kissed the top of her head. "Fuck, babygirl, if I could have taken that pain, you know I would have."

She didn't answer, only nodded.

I regretted the pain I'd caused her, but not taking her virginity.

I would be goddamned if I was going to just let

her leave my bed without claiming her fully as my own.

After all, I hadn't become a high-ranking mafia boss because I was afraid to take what wasn't mine.

I stroked her hair. "I'm going to start moving, baby."

She shook her head. "No, don't. It will hurt."

I smiled against her hair. "Yes, but you'll like this pain."

There was a difference between the having your delicate flesh torn pain and the sweet soreness from being pleasurably fucked.

I rolled to place her beneath me, wanting to feel her softness under me. I grasped her right knee and gently pulled it up over my hip to open her up more.

I then pulled out a few inches and pushed back inside.

Brynn's back arched as she tossed her head to the side and whimpered.

I kissed her cheek. "Shhh, babygirl. Daddy's going to make it all better."

Although she kept her eyes closed, I watched her sink her teeth into her bottom lip at my kinky promise.

Daddy kink.

If that's what did it for her, I had no fucking problem being her dirty daddy.

I thrust again.

Brynn moaned as she tilted her hips up slightly to meet my next thrust.

I leaned down and swirled my tongue around her nipple before blowing on it slightly.

She let out the cutest gasp.

I really loved how responsive she was when I sucked on her tits. Next time I would have to see if I could make her come just from teasing her nipples with my tongue.

I flicked the sensitive nub with the tip of my tongue as I pulled back and thrust more forcefully this time.

Brynn moaned again as her body rocked with my thrust.

"That's it, baby. You're being such a good girl, taking Daddy's big cock."

Brynn's eyes sprang open at that.

I winked. "Hey, pretty girl."

She blushed.

I ground my hips against the juncture of her thighs. "Tell me you're ready for me to thrust harder."

She buried her face against the crook of my shoulder.

I continued to slowly thrust. "Go on, babygirl. Tell me."

Her voice was muffled as I felt the warmth of her breath against my skin. "Will it hurt?"

"Yes."

I wasn't going to lie to her.

My cock was big and she was still tight and untried.

It would fucking hurt, but I wanted her to want the pain.

I wanted her to want to please me.

I wanted her to trust that I would turn the pain into pleasure.

She twisted her fingers into my chest hair. "Thrust harder … *Daddy.*"

Fuck, yes.

I grabbed her hips and for the first time allowed myself to thrust straight to the balls.

Christ, it felt good.

Brynn cried out from the impact.

I claimed her mouth, sweeping my tongue inside as I shifted my hips and increased the pace of my thrusts, pounding into her with unleashed fervor. As I did so, I once again reached between us and brought her to the crest of release with my fingers.

My balls tightened, but I held back. "Come for me, baby."

"I can't. It's too much," she said, out of breath as she tossed her head from side to side.

"Do as you're told," I scolded, as I pinched her nipple.

Her shoulders shot off the bed as her legs wrapped tightly around my hips. She threw her head back, exposing the delicate skin of her throat as she let out a long, keening moan.

I placed an open-mouthed kiss at the base of her throat, wanting to feel the vibrations of her orgasmic moan the moment my shaft swelled and I came, pouring my hot seed deep inside of her.

I rolled, collapsing on my back with her on my chest.

Her body rose and fell with my labored breathing.

Jesus Christ, that was the greatest fuck of my entire life.

I'd never felt so sexually satiated.

If I didn't have meetings at the Four Monks tonight, I wouldn't leave this bed.

Pushing her tangled honey-brown hair away from her eyes, I looked up at her adorably flushed face, certain she felt the same way.

Brynn blinked down at me. "Can I leave now?"

CHAPTER 14

*A*nton scowled at me.

For a moment I thought he was going to yell.

He then tilted his head back and closed his eyes.

After several seconds where I was pretty sure he was counting to ten, or whatever the equivalent was to counting to ten in Russian, he got out of the bed without saying a word.

He crossed the massive room, giving me a rather impressive view of his tattooed, muscled back and tight ass before he crossed the threshold of the bathroom and slammed the door behind him.

I scooted down in the bed as I pulled the covers up to my chin.

Now what?

I looked around me.

If I ever wondered what it would be like to sleep

in a king's bedroom, this would be it. The entire room looked like it belonged in a Russian palace, from the enormous four-poster bed, draped in a thick ivory satin coverlet, to the gilt-framed art over the headboard.

Across from it was a carved black marble fireplace flanked by two oxblood leather chairs and a small round table with a chessboard set up on it. The walls were a dark hunter green and filled with more really expensive-looking artwork.

I shimmied to the edge of the bed and leaned over the side, to see if I could reach my denim shorts.

Just then, the bathroom door swung open.

I was so shocked, I almost tumbled out of the bed.

He was wearing a pair of soft gray sweatpants that hung low on his hips.

I breathed out slowly.

He really had good reason to be so freaking arrogant. The man was sexy as fuck.

Anton marched over to me carrying a cobalt blue and gold paisley robe lined with terry cloth. He swept the covers back and pulled on my wrist until I was sitting upright. He placed the robe over my shoulders.

Still without saying a word, which was seriously starting to alarm me, he shoved my arms through.

I opened my mouth to say *I'm sorry*, but a dark look from him stopped me.

He placed a hand under my chin and tilted my

head back. "I have started a bath for you and I will lay out something for you to wear. I'm going to make us something to eat."

I sucked my lips between my teeth and just nodded.

He kissed the top of my head and left.

I waited several minutes before sliding off the bed and making my way into the bathroom.

The second I crossed the threshold, I groaned, "Oh, come on!"

Seriously? Who lived like this?

The room was bigger than my bedroom. Everywhere I looked was green marble with threads of gold. There was a huge claw-foot tub off to the side, already mostly full of silky bubbles. There was even one of those cool rain showers. I wiggled my toes and stared at the marbled tile floor.

Bending down, I pressed my palm flat against the floor and sighed.

Heated floors.

Shutting the bathroom door and locking it, I shrugged out of the robe, wrapped my hair in a towel to keep it dry, and climbed into the tub.

It was glorious.

Too bad I was too nervous to enjoy it.

And I wanted so badly to enjoy it.

But I just couldn't relax knowing that Anton was prowling about on the other side of the door.

I had no idea what was supposed to come next.

Should I strip the bed before heading into the kitchen?

Was I supposed to stay and eat?

Would he take me home or just hail me a taxi?

No, he had mentioned several times wanting me to stay. I should probably be more worried about him *not* calling me a taxi.

Unable to take the uncertainty any longer, I climbed out and dried off.

Putting the robe back on, I crept back into the bedroom.

The bed was already stripped and laid out on the bare mattress was a sweatshirt with some Russian writing on it. It was so big, it would reach well past my knees.

Resting on the bureau was my purse and plastic bag, on top of my neatly folded coat.

Casting a quick glance over my shoulder to make sure Anton was not in the hallway, I crept over to my stuff.

Oh, my God! Yes! I had forgotten that I had a change of clothes in my locker. Anton must have shoved my yoga pants in the plastic bag.

I bit my lip.

It was obvious he didn't want me to leave.

If he remembered I had clothes, he might take them away.

Picking up my coat, I partially unfolded it and

placed it over the plastic bag, hiding the contents. I then tossed his sweatshirt over my head.

I couldn't resist wrapping my arms around my middle, just for a second.

It was so cozy and warm and boyfriend-y.

Underneath the sweatshirt was a pair of new white athletic socks. I pulled them on. They were so big they reached to my knees with the heels reaching halfway up my calves.

Pushing my hair forward over my shoulders, I took a deep breath and ventured down the hallway in search of the kitchen. After passing the elegant entranceway with its crystal chandelier and fresh flower arrangement that I'm embarrassed to say I hadn't even noticed because I'd been too busy being kissed senseless by Anton, I found it.

Compared to my cramped kitchen with the tiny, frosted window that looked out over the back-alley dumpsters, it was definitely a step up with its cream cabinets, black polished granite island, and gorgeous high-end stainless-steel appliances.

The insanely hot man making food at the stove certainly helped.

Anton looked up and winked. "Come here."

As I neared where he was standing, he flipped several pieces of golden toast in the pan before turning to me.

Lifting up my left arm first, he rolled the sleeve until my fingers appeared.

"You're making French toast?"

He lifted my other arm and rolled my other sleeve. "No. I'm making *grenki*."

I inhaled the warm buttery sweet scent and looked at the bowl of beaten eggs and the glass canister of sugar. "It looks like French toast."

He wrapped an arm around my lower back as he picked up the spatula again. "You are with a Russian man now, little one. It's *grenki*."

I played with the bracelets on my left wrist. "About that … when you say I'm with you…."

He squeezed my side. "I mean in every sense of the word, including biblical."

"See? I can't tell if you are being sarcastic or serious."

He placed his hands on my hips and lifted me up to sit me on the black granite island. He then placed the *grenki* on a plate, covered it with blueberries and drizzled it with bright swirls of golden honey.

He spread open my thighs and stepped between them as he reached for a fork.

Slicing through the stack of honey custard toast with the side of his fork, he then pierced a piece with the tines and brought it to my mouth. "Open your mouth."

Butterflies fluttered in my stomach at his suggestive turn of phrase.

I opened my lips and took the forkful into my

mouth. I closed my eyes at the sweet buttery flavor hitting my tongue.

They shot open when I felt his tongue flick the corner of my mouth.

He winked. "You had a drip of honey on your lips."

I swiped the area with the tip of my finger as I blushed. "It's very good."

He nodded.

I couldn't resist adding, "But it's totally French toast."

He laughed as he brought a larger bite up to his mouth.

After chewing, he said, "I wish I didn't have meetings this evening in the club, but unfortunately there are several … gentlemen … who are in the country for only a few hours specifically to meet with me. Otherwise, I would be more than happy to stay in bed with you."

He caressed the top of my thigh, slipping his hand under the hem of the sweatshirt. The skin-to-skin contact sent a shiver of awareness up my spine.

This man really was dangerous in more ways than one.

I shook my head no when he offered me a second bite.

I didn't want to, but I had to ask him.

After losing the Carmichael money, I couldn't really afford to be taking a taxi from the Gold Coast all the way to my apartment. "Will you have time to drive me home before you have to work?"

Anton frowned as he cut a large piece of toast with the side of his fork.

He swirled it through the pools of honey on the plate before raising it to his mouth. He paused before taking the bite. "What are you talking about?"

"Home? I'm talking about my needing to get back to my apartment. I forgot my cellphone there when I left for work today so I need to check my messages to see if I still have a job."

Left my cellphone behind because I was out of data and minutes for the month and didn't have enough money to buy a better plan was more accurate but he didn't need to know that.

He slowly chewed as he stared at me. Finally, he said, "Babygirl, you're not going back there."

I shrugged. "I know my boss can be an ass sometimes and so can the customers, but he's not that bad and the tips are really good. I'm saving up for—"

His hand pressed into my thigh, squeezing it. "I know I did not just hear *my woman* talking about shaking her ass for fucking tips from a bunch of dickheads?"

I sat up straighter.

At least sitting on the counter I was at eye level with him for once. "How dare you? Don't make it sound like I'm some stripper on a fucking pole! I'm a cosmetologist and a damn good one! And for your information, I happen to be saving up for a chair at a better salon downtown."

At that, I tried to push on his chest so I could hop off the counter and storm off.

He wouldn't budge.

Because he was wedged between my legs, he had me trapped.

I crossed my arms and turned my head to the right. "Kindly move back so I can leave."

He moved both his hands to my thighs. "You're not going anywhere. You're going to finish your meal like a good girl and then I'm going to go to work."

I flipped my head back to glare at him.

The nerve of this man. "You can't tell me what to do! Just because you had your cock inside of me doesn't mean you own me now! I'm. Going. Home!"

He leaned in close as he wrapped his hand around the back of my neck.

My heart skipped a beat.

"That is *exactly* what having my cock inside of you means, babygirl."

He then kissed me hard on the lips. "Apparently, I made a mistake in not punishing you for that little stunt you pulled this morning. It's time you learned who's in charge here."

CHAPTER 15

ANTON

I pushed my shoulder into her stomach and flipped her squirming form onto my shoulder.

"Put me down!"

I slapped her ass. "No."

I stormed down the hallway back to our bedroom.

Yes … *ours.*

I dropped her in the center of the bed.

The moment she hit the bare mattress, her body bounced up as she rolled onto her stomach and then up onto her knees in an attempt to crawl to the other side of the bed.

I grabbed her ankles and pulled until she slid half off the bed. The movement pushed my sweatshirt up, exposing her thighs and ass as her legs dangled off the side.

Fortunately, my belt was still within reach from earlier.

I grabbed it and pushed the metal buckle into my palm as I wrapped the leather tight around my fist. "I'm doing this for your own good, babygirl."

She clawed at the mattress, once again trying to crawl away. "You're a bully and I hate you!"

I grabbed onto her hair at the back of her neck. "I'll prove you don't later, but for now, you need to be punished."

She pushed her hair away from her face and turned her head to glare at me. "I didn't do anything wrong!"

"Cheating at poker. Stealing. Giving me a false address. Talking back when I give you an order."

She reached behind her and tried to push the sweatshirt back down over her ass. "I wasn't the one cheating, Yuri was. Besides, you caught me before I could actually help steal anything. And giving a boy a fake address is not a crime!"

I smirked. "I'm no boy, little one. And when I tell you to do something I expect to be obeyed."

I wrenched the sweatshirt back up over her ass and raised my arm.

The leather belt struck across her ass with swift precision.

Brynn cried out as she moved her hands behind her to cover her vulnerable flesh.

I clasped her wrists at her lower back, and swiped

her ass with the belt a second and third time.

"Stop! You can't do this! It's not fair."

The curves of her ass cheeks bounced with each lick of my belt as her creamy pale flesh turned a bright cherry pink. Not wanting to punish her too severely in one place, I directed several swipes to her upper thighs as well.

"You will learn to behave. Disobeying me could get you killed in my world."

She sniffed. "I don't want to be in your world."

The simple statement would have cut me to the quick if I hadn't already had a glimpse into *her world* without me.

Her good nature had been taken advantage of by Yuri when he convinced her to try to steal from my club, an extremely dangerous proposition.

A degrading job with a dickhead boss.

Multiple side jobs that took her into strangers' apartments and still barely enough money to live on, judging by her thin winter coat and need to take Chicago's Metra late at night despite the risks.

All this and I still hadn't seen where she lived, but given the address listed on her cosmetologist license, my assessment of her situation was not going to improve.

All this made her vulnerable and culminated in her sweet innocence being taken advantage of and claimed by a violent criminal … me.

My world may be dangerous but at least in my

world, I was there to protect and shelter her from the rest of the world's evils.

In my world, she would want for nothing and never again feel the need to work to scrape by a meager living.

"You should have thought of that before you willingly entered it. Now you're mine and I'm not letting you go. So I suggest you stop fighting this."

I brought the leather strap down on her ass several more times for good measure.

As Brynn sobbed into the mattress, I tossed the belt aside and gently rubbed my hand over her punishment-warm flesh. Gathering her to my side, I sat on the mattress and slid back to lean against the headboard.

At first she resisted, but I subdued her by pushing her head against my chest with her ear over my heartbeat.

Her shoulders still vibrated softly from her tears that wet my skin.

After several minutes, when she still hadn't calmed down, I remembered how upset she had been from her first punishment and what had seemed to soothe her.

I pulled down the waistband of my gray sweatpants and pulled out my already hard cock.

The sight of her bent over the bed with her punished ass in the air had sent the blood rushing to my shaft. Just the thought of her hot skin pressed against the tops of my thighs as I pushed inside of her almost had me coming, but I had known I wouldn't fuck her again tonight.

She would be too sore.

And now was not the time to initiate her into some of my darker bedroom pursuits.

I fisted my shaft and applied gentle pressure to the back of Brynn's head as I guided her to lie down perpendicular to my hip. "Open your mouth, baby-girl. Suck on Daddy's cock. It will make you feel better."

She shifted her head to turn wide, tear-filled eyes up to me. "You won't push it down my throat, will you?"

I stroked her hair. "No, baby. Just put the head in your mouth and suck."

She encircled my shaft with her small, soft hand and pulled the top of my cock into her warm, wet mouth.

I leaned against the headboard and focused on not thrusting deep into her tight throat as I rested my hand on the back of her head.

Soon her body relaxed, her breathing evened and her lips went slack around my cock.

I carefully eased out from under her.

Slipping a clean pillowcase on the pillow, I placed it under her head. I then retrieved a soft quilt from the lower bureau drawer. I hated that she was sleeping on the bare mattress but wasn't going to wake her. I tucked the blanket around her sleeping form.

Standing over her, I ran the backs of my knuckles down her still damp and flushed cheek.

I felt an uncustomary stab of regret.

I had been too hard on her.

I'd never felt so protective or possessive of a woman before.

I knew I was probably holding onto her too tightly.

It was no wonder she was scratching and clawing to escape my grasp.

The problem was, as much as I was drawn to her sweet innocence and cute sass, those same qualities terrified me.

They made her vulnerable.

It was all I could do not to handcuff her slim wrist to the bedpost to reassure myself she'd be safe while I was at work.

I moved my hand to caress the delicate thin skin on her inner left wrist.

I smiled at the cheap elastic bead bracelets I had yet to see her take off. I would have to take her to my jeweler and buy her something more appropriate.

I shifted the thin beads with the tip of my finger and frowned.

What the fuck?

Marring her skin was a thin white line ... an unmistakable scar.

CHAPTER 16

BRYNN

I came awake with a start.

I blinked as my eyes adjusted to the semi-darkness. It was disorienting to feel warm and cozy yet confused at the same time.

The moment my fuzzy brain caught up to the moment, I sat up and looked around.

The bedroom was empty.

It was clear from the view through the curtains that it was now quite late in the evening. There was a soft glow coming from the nightstand. Next to a small globe light there was a plate of fresh fruit, a glass of white wine, and a note.

I picked up the heavy ivory card stock with the masculine scrawl in black ink.

Brynn,

Please eat something. I will be home later.

*If you need anything, pick up the phone and press #
and ask for Polina.*

A-

I SHIFTED on the mattress and hissed.

Rolling onto my left hip, I rubbed my ass, which
was still sore from my punishment. While, like the
last time, he hadn't spanked me very hard, it was still
humiliating to be punished like a child.

I really didn't know what to make of the man
at all.

One moment I was enthralled by how handsome
and charming and sweet he was and the next I was
desperately looking for the exit.

One moment he was turning me on, the next he
was terrifying me.

He was both the most infuriating man I'd ever
known and the most intoxicating.

He was like a drug.

You thought it would be fun.

Just a taste.

What could be the harm?

And at first it was.

It was a rush.

You felt lightheaded and free.

Every nerve was firing.

There were sparks and bursts of light.

But then the room started to spin and spin and spin.

And things moved too fast and you no longer felt in control.

I needed to break free before I got sucked in too deep.

I wasn't stupid.

A girl from a broken home who had a troubled childhood.

I looked down at my wrist and rubbed the scar I hidden under bracelets.

It was easy to see why I would be drawn to an overbearing yet protective man who promised to fix all my problems.

In fact, I was so textbook I was boring.

And it wouldn't take long for Anton to realize it as well ... and get bored with me.

Daddy kink was only fun when it was a *kink* ... not when it became part of your girl's abandonment issues.

Besides, right now this was an infatuation.

Soon I would be dumb enough to believe it was love.

And then it would be heartbreak ... at least for me.

I slipped out of bed and crossed to my purse and plastic bag.

The air in the bathroom still felt heavy with steam and the scent of cologne. Across the edge of the tub were his discarded gray sweatpants and the marble countertop had several drops of water and a toothbrush next to the sink.

Anton must have only just left.

It was odd seeing signs of domestic normalcy from a man so fierce and bigger than life like Anton.

It was like seeing a demi-god eating at McDonald's.

Shaking off the feeling, I quickly slipped my yoga pants on under his sweatshirt. Searching in the bag, I realized he hadn't grabbed my shirt, just the yoga pants and my sneakers. I pulled off his oversized socks and slipped on my pale pink canvas sneakers. Shoving the plastic bag with the remaining items in my purse, I slipped on my coat and made my way down the hallway.

Taking a deep breath, I pressed the button for the elevator.

"Leaving so soon?"

I screamed and turned as I flattened my back against the wall.

Standing before me was the elegant silver-haired woman from last night.

Crap, was it really only last night that I first met Anton?

She held out her hand. She had long pale fingers with black nail polish. Her ring finger had a stunning massive sterling silver and black opal ring. The kind of bohemian ring, popular in the seventies, that went with her chic all-black outfit vibe.

"I'm Polina but you can call me *Tetya* Polina."

"Tet … ya."

"*Tetya* Polina." She twirled her wrist. "It means Aunt Polina in English. All the server girls at the Four Monks call me that."

I placed a hand over my chest. "Oh, I'm not a server girl here."

She placed a hand on my shoulder and gently guided me toward the kitchen. "Of course you're not, kitten." She wagged her index finger. "Antonius never, ever sleeps with the staff. Ever."

I thought about asking her his policy on sleeping with thieves who try to steal from him but thought better of it.

She walked over to the sub-zero and pulled open the freezer door. She selected a frosted bottle of vodka and set it on the island. She then brought down two shot glasses from the cabinet, poured two shots, and slid one in front of me.

My eyes widened. "I'm not much of a vodka drinker."

She raised the shot glass. "You're with a Russian now, kitten. *Za zdorovye!*" She then drank it.

I raised the glass and sipped half of the gasoline before I went to put it down.

Tetya Polina put her fingers under my wrist. "Bad luck not to finish shot."

I coughed as I finished the rest.

Her heavily kohl-lined gaze roamed over me from head to toe. "Antonius said you were staying. By the looks of it, you have other plans?"

I gripped the strap to my purse tighter. "Are you going to stop me from leaving?"

She raised her palms in the air. "No."

I frowned, not quite believing her.

"But—"

I sighed. Okay, here it was.

She patted her perfect French knot. "It will be bad enough when he learns you're gone. Let's not add to the male drama by having him learn you took a taxi or worse, the train. I'll have Boris drive you home."

I must have made a face because she laughed and patted me on the shoulder. "Don't worry, kitten. I know, it's unfortunate. The poor man is as sweet as can be but you Americans have a silly hang-up with the name Boris. You all think he's going to be some assassin or something." She twirled her wrist again. "The man knits, for good- ness' sake."

I raised my eyebrows. "Knits?"

She shrugged as she walked back toward the elevators. "He's the driver for the club so he spends lots of time waiting in the car. He doesn't like to read."

The elevator doors slid open.

I stepped inside.

She held the doors open. "Boris is waiting for you in the garage. He's in a black Escalade."

Again, something must have shown on my face.

She laughed. "Really, kitten. You are so distrustful. If you are worried this is some kind of trap you can always stay here."

Seriously, the woman was some kind of Svengali.

"Will I get you in trouble?"

She twirled her wrist again. "I've known these boys since they were hoodlums on the streets of St. Petersburg. They cannot stay mad at their *Tetya* Polina for long."

She let the elevator doors go, but I stopped them from closing. "Why are you helping me?"

She patted the back of her French knot again. "He's never brought a woman up here before, let alone left someone of such short acquaintance unattended in his"—she looked around her—"sanctuary."

She then gave me a cryptic smile like the proverbial cat that ate the canary as she lifted her hand and wagged her index finger at me and then winked. "But he was a little … how do you say? Too confident … when he talked to me about helping you move in here. Snapping his fingers. Talking about a new wardrobe and books and jewelry as if you are a flower he can just pluck from a garden and put in a vase with no life of your own!"

The more she talked, the more animated she became, as she waved her hands about.

It was clear she loved Anton in a motherly way, but also didn't take any of his crap.

I marveled at her as if she were displaying a superpower.

When she finished she clapped. "Now go, before he returns and catches us both misbehaving."

As the elevator doors closed, I waved. "Thank you, *Tetya* Polina."

Boris was actually very sweet and not an intimidating-looking Russian assassin at all. He even showed me the scarf he was knitting for his niece.

Still, I was glad when I finally got home.

The moment I walked through the door, my cousin Jonathan approached me. "You worked late. I was getting worried. You forgot your phone. It's been ringing."

I tossed my purse and coat onto the small kitchen table, headed to the refrigerator, and grabbed the container of leftover Kung Pao chicken.

Fishing out a pair of chopsticks from the utensil drawer, I leaned against the kitchen counter and dug through the container, selecting a piece of cold chicken. "It's a long story."

I looked up to see him searching through his tool bag.

My aunt Janice, Jonathan's mom, had taken me in after my foster family didn't want me back after *the incident*. Jonathan usually lived out in the suburbs with his girlfriend, but occasionally crashed on my sofa to save money when he could get lucrative construction gigs in the city.

I nodded. "Are you headed out?"

"Only to the hardware store. I need some supplies for tomorrow. I'll be back." He gestured to Anton's sweatshirt. "What are you wearing?"

I looked down and crossed my arms, hiding the Russian writing with the Chinese takeout container. "It's an even longer story. It's been a long day. I'm just going to go to bed."

I would deal with what was certain to be a hundred text messages from Heather and the situation at work tomorrow. Right now I just wanted a shower and to not think about Anton.

He nodded. "I'll keep it down when I get back."

* * *

AFTER TAKING A LONG, hot shower and hiding Anton's sweatshirt in the back of my tiny closet, I crawled into bed and hugged a pillow to my chest.

First, I curled onto my side, then flipped onto my back, then back onto my side.

As hard as I tried to empty my mind and fall asleep, all I could think about was Anton.

The memory of his weight on top of me.

How his hips forced my legs open.

The pleasurable burn as his cock thrust in deep.

My hand moved over my stomach as my finger-tips teased the edge of my panties.

I thought of all the dirty sexy things he growled into my ear as he thrust harder and faster.

With a frustrated growl, I kicked the covers off, stomped over to the closet, pulled Anton's sweatshirt out of its hiding place, and put it on.

I slipped back between the covers, curled up and inhaled the spicy scent of his cologne that clung to the worn cotton.

Imagining the warmth of the fabric was really his touch, after several moments I finally fell asleep.

Until the sound of my apartment door being kicked in woke me up.

CHAPTER 17

ANTON

I checked my watch as the smarmy politician droned on with all his bullshit reasons why he was using our services to launder and hide his country's money.

Mac leaned back in his chair as he rubbed his finger over the top of his right eyebrow.

Our silent signal.

There was no fucking way we were doing business with this asshole. There was something to the old adage, honor among thieves.

We may be criminals but we were honest ones.

There was something to be said about a corrupt bastard who waltzed into our offices with a leather satchel filled with cash and a cocky grin who balls-out admitted to stealing the money and wanting us to clean it.

Varlaam, my other partner, who handled the

financial exchanges for the club as well as our auxiliary activities, leaned forward and interlocked his fingers. Not one to mince words, he said, "The answer is no. Get out."

Mac snorted.

I slapped him on the shoulder as I tried to contain my own laughter.

While we may not want to launder his money, there was still probably other business to do with him.

The politician choked on the sip of Chardonnay he had been taking.

That should have been our first clue. Chardonnay.

"Do you know who I am?"

Before we could respond, the heavy steel security door beeped.

The concealing oak panel slid open and in strolled Dimitri Kosgov and Vaska Rostov.

Vaska stretched out his arm to the politician. "If you have to ask that question halfway through a meeting, you haven't made much of an impression, my friend."

The politician shook his head. "I am not your friend and these men have insulted me."

I winked at Vaska as I reached for my vodka glass and drained it. "To be fair, we meant to."

The politician's extra chin wobbled as he struggled to respond.

Dimitri shot me a dark look as he placed a

placating hand on the man's shoulder. "Ignore them. I understand your country is still using those old black market MIM-14 Nike Hercules surface-to-air missiles. How about we discuss your country purchasing some 2K12 Kubs and perhaps I can arrange for an off-the-books discount?"

Code for overcharging his country, the corrupt politician keeping the cash.

Vaska sat to next me and pulled a flask out of his breast pocket. After twisting off the top and pouring vodka into an empty glass, he raised an eyebrow at me.

I cast a disdainful glance at his flask. "Still drink that rotgut shit?"

"If you mean the people's vodka, Moskovskaya Vodka, yes."

"Pass."

He shrugged, then gestured with his chin. "So why no welcome?"

"Selling him weapons is a better deal. One and done. The way this asshole wants us to do business is too traceable. He'd have us leaving a paper trail a kilometer wide." I checked my watch again.

Vaska caught the gesture. "Are we boring you?"

I thought of Brynn tucked upstairs in my bed. "Yes."

I had never let a woman distract me from business before, but then again, Brynn was no ordinary woman.

Vaska shook his head. "Make sure she's not a bitch or Mary will eat her alive."

I frowned as I pushed an empty glass toward Dimitri as he sat down after showing the politician out.

Mac raised his glass in a toast as Var poured. "Is that the cute little piece you caught cheating at cards?"

"Technically it was your piece of shit nephew who was cheating."

Mac raised his glass to that. "I'm going to have to ship that kid to Russia, I just know it."

"You may want to reconsider that with his girl being pregnant."

Var slapped him on the back. "You're going to be a granduncle."

Mac pulled his gun on him. "Don't anyone ever call me that. Jesus fucking Christ, I'm barely forty-two, how does that math work out?"

Dimitri smirked. "I think it's biology, not math. Don't worry. You're going to *love* the midnight feedings."

Vaska pointed at him. "Don't you say a word about my goddaughter. She is an angel straight from heaven."

Dimitri laughed. "An angel with the lungs of the devil."

As they joked I thought of Brynn pregnant with my child. I ran the tip of my finger over my lower lip.

The idea had merit. I had never thought of myself as a family man, but I could see it with someone as sweet yet sassy as Brynn.

I rose, buttoning my suit jacket. "Gentlemen, I trust you can continue this without me?"

Dimitri stretched out his arm to shake my hand. "I'm glad you've found someone, my friend. Bring her over to meet Emma."

I clasped my hand over his. "That is a great idea. I have a feeling my girl needs a better class of friends. No offense to Yuri's girl, Mac."

Mac reached for the bottle of vodka in the center of the table. "None taken. I've met her. You're not wrong."

Making my way through the labyrinth of corridors, I entered the security code for my private elevator.

As I waited for the doors, Polina approached.

I gave her a kiss on the cheek before turning back to face the elevators. "Thank you for looking in on Brynn for me."

She folded her arms across her middle. "She is not there."

I turned to look at her. "What do you mean? You didn't let her wander onto the poker floor alone?"

My stomach twisted.

I didn't like the idea of my girl on the floor of the Four Monks without me by her side. Our members needed to know who she belonged to, needed to know the consequences if they so much as looked at her.

Even her being flanked by bodyguards would not be good enough.

She needed to be on my arm for that.

Polina twisted her wrist with a dismissive wave. "Of course not."

I relaxed.

The elevator doors opened and I stepped inside, pressing the button for the penthouse.

Just as the doors started to close, she said, "She's not in the building."

I slammed my palm against the left door, stopping it. "What?"

Polina shrugged. "She's gone."

I stormed out of the elevator. "You let her leave?"

"What is this let her leave? What do the Americans like to say? It is free country?"

My gaze narrowed. I spoke through a clenched jaw. "You know goddamn well I wanted her kept in my penthouse, Polina."

She reached up and patted my cheek. "I know, *mishka*, that is why I let her fly away."

"Calling me your little bear will hardly make me less mad at you, *Tetya* Polina."

She shrugged again as she turned her back on me and sashayed away. "Yes, but it will help make you more mad at me."

I called after her, "That doesn't even make sense!"

Tetya Polina was truly like an aunt to us all at the club and I had known her since I was a little boy running wild in the streets of St. Petersburg. But that didn't mean I didn't want to wring her neck right now.

Changing course, I stepped into the elevator and hit the down button for the private parking garage.

* * *

WHEN I PULLED up to Brynn's apartment building, I wasn't any happier.

The only thing that was saving her at this moment was that her apartment was on the second floor and not the first.

The building was at least forty years old with rotting wooden frames around the windows and no visible security.

In short, a burglar's dream.

Except there was probably very little worth stealing in any of the apartments inside.

Climbing the stairs to the second floor, my anger increased as I stalked down the dimly lit narrow corridor, counting off all the ways Brynn could be grabbed and attacked as she made her way from the nearest Metra station to her apartment door.

Tonight would be the very last time she darkened the doorstep of this building, I vowed as I raised my fist to pound on the door.

I didn't care that by now it was after midnight.

At first there was no answer, so I pounded harder, prepared to break the door down if she didn't answer.

Finally, I heard a chain rattle.

I tilted my head back and prayed for patience.

If the chain was rattling, it meant she was putting it in place to answer the door, instead of it already being securely in place.

As the door creaked open a crack, I expected to see her sweet cherubic face; instead I saw a strong jaw and a five o'clock shadow.

"Who the fuck are you and why are you banging on our door?" asked the man.

Asked the man.

The man in my girl's apartment.

At midnight.

Asked the man alone in my girl's apartment at midnight.

Fuck, I was getting fucking tired of men answering doors every time I went in search of this damn woman.

What had he said?

Our door? As in his and my girl's?

Was he the reason why she had been so cagey earlier?

All rational thought left my mind.

Including the fact that I had taken her virginity only hours earlier.

My primal irrational side took over.

Grabbing the doorknob, I pulled the door toward me and then shoved it forward, snapping the metal security chain and slamming it into the man's face, breaking his nose.

The man cried out.

As blood gushed over his mouth and chin, I twisted my fist in his shirt and pulled back my arm, prepared to strike him in the face again, when Brynn came rushing out.

"Anton! Let go of my cousin!"

CHAPTER 18

*A*nton rubbed his hand over his mouth and lower jaw as his stormy gray eyes glowered down at me. "Your cousin?"

I snatched a dish towel off the kitchenette counter. "Yes, my cousin!"

I turned toward Jonathan with concern as I held the towel gingerly up to his gushing nose. "Lean your head back."

Anton pulled the towel from my grasp. "No, lean your head forward." He nodded toward me. "Go get some *margantsovka* crystals and some clean water."

I pulled the towel from his hand. "I've treated plenty of bloody noses and you're supposed to lean back to stop the bleeding and what the fuck are *margarita* crystals?"

He snatched the bloody towel back with a glare.

"Don't curse. *Margantsovka* crystals. You call it potassium permanganate here."

With a huff, I yanked open the kitchen drawer and got a fresh towel. I then turned back toward Anton and Jonathan. "Pomegranates? Now you are not even making sense. And I'll fucking curse if I want to. You are in my fucking apartment in the fucking middle of the night and you just tried to fucking kill my cousin! I think fucking cursing is called for in this fucking situation."

Before I could replace the bloody towel with my fresh one, Anton snatched it from my hand.

Through clenched teeth, he said, "Not pomegranate, *potassium permanganate*, it is like your hydrogen peroxide. And don't think that comment about dealing with a lot of bloody noses escaped my attention. We will talk about that later."

He placed his large hand behind Jonathan's head and pushed it forward as he held the towel to his face.

He glowered at me over Jonathan's bent form. "If you hadn't disobeyed me and stayed in my bed where you belong, then none of this would have happened. I'm losing patience with tracking you down only to have a strange man open the door, babygirl," he ground out.

I pulled on the sleeves of his hoodie, which hung well past my fingertips, in my agitation. "I told you I wanted to go home! And he's not a strange man, he's my cousin and you just tried to kill him."

"If I wanted to kill him he'd be dead."

Jonathan's wide eyes shifted between me and Anton. "Whud the fucd? Brynd whod id thid guy?"

Anton and I answered at the same time.

"Her man."

"Nobody."

Anton released his grip on Jonathan and stalked toward me.

I retreated until my butt hit the sofa.

He kept coming.

I arched my back, bending over the sofa.

He placed both of his hands on either side of my hips and leaned over me. His mouth only a few inches from mine.

I tried to look around him to see if Jonathan was witnessing this and going to come to my aid but it was like trying to look around a freaking wall.

And it was pointless to do so.

Jonathan was clearly distracted with his bloody nose.

Anton's gaze slowly moved from my eyes to my mouth and back up. "What did you just say?"

I swallowed. "Nothing," I squeaked.

His right eyebrow rose as he pressed his hips into mine.

My mouth opened on a gasp as I could feel the hard press of his cock.

He bared the sharp points of his canine teeth, like a feral beast. "I ever hear you deny you're mine again, especially in front of another man, I will bend you over the nearest surface and fuck you senseless to prove to you, and everyone watching, who you belong to, do you understand me?"

"But he's not another man, he's family."

"I don't give damn if he was your father. The shared blood in your veins is nothing compared to the blood on my cock from today. I'm your first and will be your only. I'm your *daddy* now."

The possessive bloodthirsty threat should have had me screaming for the police in the hopes my neighbors would care enough to call.

Instead it gave me a sick and twisted thrill.

He couldn't possibly know that my own father never gave a damn about me. That in fact he was the reason why I had witnessed so many bloody noses. It did something to a daughter's head when her own father didn't care enough about her to stick around, let alone want to protect her from the big, bad world.

And yet here was this incredibly intoxicatingly dangerously sexy man who, despite only just meeting me, not only cared enough to want to protect me, but was actually *laying claim* to me.

My body reacted to the emotion.

It was as if I had just submerged myself into a bath after spending hours in a cold, freezing rain.

A girl could get lost in the soothing warm comfort and gentle silence underwater.

Until she needed to breathe….

I thought of my mother and what my father's betrayal and abandonment did to her.

I thought of finding her….

I thought of my own reaction….

The scar on my wrist itched.

Before I could respond, Jonathan called out. "I thinkd id stopped bleedingid, but it might be brokend."

Anton stepped toward Jonathan.

It was alarming seeing them side by side.

I had always thought of my cousin as a relatively big guy. He was over six feet tall and worked in construction.

Anton dwarfed him.

It didn't help that poor Jonathan was in boxer shorts and a T-shirt, and Anton was wearing a cashmere overcoat and what looked to be a very expensive three-piece suit underneath.

Anton reached into his inner pocket and pulled out a thick wad of cash, secured with a brightly polished silver money clip.

He flicked open the money clip and siphoned off a literal chunk of crisp hundred-dollar bills. Folding them in half, he pressed them in Jonathan's palm.

He then pulled out his phone and sent a text as he continued to talk. "It is not broken. I can tell. Head to the Four Monks on Astor Street. Ask for Sergius Tabakov, he is the head of Security. I am letting him know you are coming. He will take care of you."

I straightened as Jonathan and I exchanged a look.

Jonathan stepped back from Anton. "Take care of me—as in—?"

Anton clapped him on the shoulder as he chuckled. "We find it—useful—to have several doctors of varying specialties on call. There is even a clinic with a fully equipped operating room for just that purpose on the premise. Why pay an outrageous American hospital bill, right?"

I suppressed a shudder. It was hard to ignore the macabre, yet strangely practical, reasons as to why a dangerous mafia organization would want its own private mini hospital. Everyone knew doctors in America were required to report signs of violence, like bullet wounds, to the police.

Jonathan curled his fist around the money and walked around the sofa to his overnight bag. He grabbed the pair of jeans on top and pulled them on. He swiped the bloodied towel under his nose as he looked at me. "Are you going to be all right?"

I looked at Anton.

What could I say? It was my fault my cousin was injured so I couldn't very well tell him not to take advantage of Anton's offer of help.

I nodded.

Jonathan tossed the dirty towel onto the kitchen

counter, grabbed his Carhartt jacket, and left through the open doorway.

Anton shook his head as he shrugged out of his own coat and suit jacket, leaving him in only his suit vest and dress shirt. He then walked over to the door and lifted it off its broken hinge and slammed it into place within the doorframe. "That was disappointing. He should have stayed."

I frowned as I stretched out my arm, gesturing toward the now closed door. "You gave him money and told him to go get medical help."

Anton picked up both bloodied towels and tossed them in the garbage. He then crossed his arms over his chest as he leaned against the kitchen counter.

Leveling a hard stare at me for several moments before speaking, he said, "The more I see of the men in your life, babygirl, the more I know why fate crossed our paths."

I pushed a paint chip dislodged from the door with the toe of my sock as I stared at the floor. "There are no men in my life and fate didn't bring us together, that asshole Yuri and his stupid card scheme did."

For such a large man, he moved with surprising speed and virtually no noise.

Before I knew it, he was across the room, standing in front of me.

He cupped my chin and raised my head to meet his gaze. "Your boss was a pig. Your cousin should never have left you alone with a violent man like me. He should have thrown my money back in my face and stayed to protect you. And I have no intention of telling our children that piece of shit Yuri is how we met. *It was fate.*"

Our children?

Our children!

I lifted my head up and to the right, breaking his hold.

I then backed around the sofa and casually slid my foot to the side, positioning myself closer to the hallway that led to my bedroom. "We had sex once and you already have me knocked up and chained to you."

The corner of his mouth lifted as his gaze moved over my body. "Chained to my bed at least."

I slid my foot back, hoping he wouldn't notice my slow retreat. "If I asked you to leave, would you?"

He tilted his head to the side as he observed me for a moment.

I could feel the elevated vibrations of my heartbeat pounding in my chest as the seconds ticked by.

His gaze narrowed. "What do you think?"

I slid my other foot back as I shifted closer to the wall, bracing my palm against it. "Why me? I'm not sophisticated. I didn't go to college. The furthest I've been from Illinois was a camping trip to Michigan with my foste—with my family. I don't even have a passport. I mean ... we literally don't even speak the same language and we're born decades apart."

He grinned. "Ouch."

I frowned. "You know what I mean. There is absolutely nothing we have in common, so why me? Why are you chasing me around the city? Why are you here in the middle of the night breaking down my door? Why won't you just let me go?"

My voice raised an octave on that last question as I started to shake. I wasn't used to all this attention, let alone from a man, especially one like Anton.

Abandoned by my father.

Tossed into the foster system after my mother's suicide.

Then worse, until my aunt took me in.

I got used to making myself nondescript, unnoticeable.

The places I'd been, getting noticed only brought trouble.

He stepped closer and leaned his shoulder against the same wall. His large form filled the narrow hallway space. "Because you need me."

I drew back. "I don't need you. I don't need anyone."

Before I knew what he was doing, he reached down and wrapped his powerful hand around my left forearm.

He then wrenched the sleeve of his hoodie down. Since it was the middle of the night, I had taken off the crystal stretchy bracelets I always wore to cover the long thin scar on my inner wrist. It helped avoid awkward questions about my past.

He moved closer, pinning me against the wall. "Tell me."

CHAPTER 19

ANTON

*S*he yanked on her arm, but I only tightened my grasp.

"It's none of your business."

"Wrong, babygirl. Now tell me."

She turned her head. "It was years ago. Just a stupid teenage prank for attention."

I ran the pad of my thumb over the delicate line. "No."

"No?"

"No, that is not the truth."

She turned to look back at me.

Her cute stubborn chin rose. "Really? Because I don't recall you being there."

I pressed my lips to her inner wrist. Speaking against her warm skin, I said, "This was pain, not a prank."

I pulled my shirt out of my waistband and placed

her hand against my side over my own scar. "Do you feel that? Knife wound. My first stint in a Russian prison when I was sixteen."

I then unbuttoned the first two buttons of my shirt and slipped her hand inside, sliding her fingers just under my collarbone by my right shoulder. "That is a bullet wound. It was when I decided to get out of arms dealings and turn to other pursuits."

She pulled her hand free and locked her fingers together. "Your scars are different."

I shrugged. "Scars are scars. They are proof you survived a painful experience. Nothing more. Nothing less."

She swiped at a tear on her cheek as she kept her gaze averted. "So is this the real reason why you've been chasing after me? Why, you think I need you? Because you saw my scar and took pity on me?"

"I don't *think* you need me. I *know* it. And no."

She shook her head. "You Russians sure don't waste a lot of time with elaborate explanations or long sentences, do you."

I picked up a lock of her hair and ran the silky length between my fingers. "We prefer action to words."

She pulled her hair from my grasp. "It doesn't really matter. Now that you've seen it, whatever this was between us is definitely over."

She slipped between my body and the wall and ducked into the nearest doorway.

Before she had a chance to close the door, I followed.

The bedroom was small and neat.

A double bed dominated the space, its wooden frame mismatched with the bureau that was jammed at an awkward angle into a corner between a window and panel door closet. Its surface was bare except for a pink hairbrush. The walls were adorned with art posters and one of the Chicago skyline over the bed. Like the rest of the apartment, there were no family photos and few personal items.

She whipped off my hoodie and tossed it to me.

Although I appreciated the view of her cute sleeping shorts and tank top, I preferred the idea of her cute body being kept warm by something I owned.

She crossed her arms defensively over her middle. "You wanted to know how I could still be a virgin at my age? Easy. There are only three types of boys."

She counted off on her fingers. "Those who are freaked out by the idea that I might be"—she then raised her arms to do air quotes—"*damaged* when they find out I didn't have the perfect little cookie-cutter suburban childhood. Or they take pity on me and start treating me differently with kid gloves. Or they like to play hero and think I'll be so grateful for their affection because of it, I'll put up with their bullshit."

She crossed to the far side of the room, which was

barely two strides away from me, placing the bed between us. "Clearly you are the latter and I just don't have time for that in my life right now."

I nodded. "I understand."

I turned my back on her and crossed to the bedroom door, not missing the soft catch of her breath as I did so.

I knew what my babygirl was thinking … *she was wrong*.

After closing the bedroom door and locking it, I turned to face her as I slowly unbuttoned my suit vest. "I've told you before … I'm no boy. It's one of those … how did you put it? Decade differences in age?"

I raised an eyebrow as I shrugged out of my vest and crossed to a beat-up nightstand next to her bed.

Her eyes widened as she stretched out her arm, but then pulled it back. "What are you doing?"

I smirked. Judging by her reaction, I knew exactly what I was going to find in it. I pulled on the loose brass drawer knob.

Inside was a collection of vibrators and a small bottle of lube.

"Close that drawer. You have no right to poke around my belongings."

Selecting a twenty-centimeter-long silver metal bullet-shaped vibrator, I placed it and the bottle of lube on top of the nightstand. "First, I'm going to prove to you that I have no intention of treating you any differently now that I know. Then later, you can tell me who caused you this pain, so I can deal with them."

"He's not an issue. I mean, there is nothing to deal with it. Now I want you to leave."

He. Another asshole man in her life that had obviously let her down. Jesus Christ.

Was there no man who had stood by this beautiful creature to protect her?

I should be grateful.

If there had been, she wouldn't have fallen prey to someone like me.

"No."

"You can't say no. This is my apartment."

"Fine, then get your things and we will continue this at my place."

She huffed. "I'm not leaving with you."

"We either settle this here and now, or at my place. Those are your only options, babygirl."

"I could call the police and have you arrested for breaking and entering."

"You could try, but I think you are smart enough to know that a powerful man like me has friends within the police department."

Pulling my shirt over my head, I tossed it over the footboard on top of my vest as I kicked off my shoes.

I observed her gaze flashing over my tattoos. I flattened my palm over my abs, drawing her eye, as I moved my hand to my belt buckle.

She gasped and stepped backward, colliding with the wall. "What are you doing?"

The cool leather strap slipped over my palm as I pulled it through the buckle. I then drew the belt from around my waist and folded it in half, snapping it. "I should punish you for sneaking out like that."

Brynn's body jerked at the harsh sound as it reverberated off the walls in the small confines of her room. "You wouldn't dare."

"Haven't you learned better than to challenge me like that?"

Her gaze remained riveted on the belt stretched between my hands. "Tell you what, I'm a gambling man. I'll make you a bet."

Her lips thinned. "What kind of bet?"

"If you win, I will walk out that door and you can return to your old life before you met me, even your old job."

She shifted her gaze downward for a moment. She then nervously tugged on a lock of her hair, twisting it. "And if you win?"

I rubbed my finger over my lower lip as I studied her. "If I win … you have to play a game with me."

"A game?"

I nodded.

"What kind of game?"

"You'll find out when I win."

She bit her lower lip. "So how do we bet?"

"It's simple. I ask a question and you answer it. If you tell the truth, you win. If you lie … I win."

She shifted her weight from one hip to the other. "Just one question?"

The corner of my mouth lifted. "Just one question."

"And if I win, you'll leave?"

"You have my word."

She hesitated for several more moments, then said, "Fine, what's your question?"

I tossed the belt on the bed and approached her.

She slid along the wall. "What are you doing?"

I continued to stalk her. "Asking my question."

I placed my forearm over her head as I leaned in.

She was so tiny.

I had to constantly remind myself to be gentle.

Although this would not be one of those times.

Quite the opposite in fact.

I needed to prove to her that the stupid scar on her wrist didn't define her.

I wouldn't call it a moment of weakness.

I hated when people called it that. It was a moment of strength. It wasn't weak to contemplate ending your life; that was human.

It showed strength to overcome that impulse and carry on against whatever odds were overwhelming you.

That thin line was proof my girl was a survivor. The fact she didn't see it that way, that she hid it behind stupid bracelets and let it impact her life, ended here and now.

The bastard in me wanted to be grateful that the boys who came before me were too immature to realize all this and left this sweet, amazing creature alone and untouched for fate to send her to me to protect and treasure.

But even I wasn't that selfish.

If it would have spared her this pain and saved her from being so vulnerable now, I would have gladly preferred it if someone worthy had come along sooner.

No one deserved to think they were in any way *less than* or deserved less for something they did when they were young. I should know that better than anyone.

But now it was time to prove to her that I was nothing like any of those boys that came before me.

I cupped her jaw with my left hand as I leaned down to whisper in her ear, "I want you to tell me the truth, *moya malen'kaya vorovka.* Earlier tonight, when you were curled up, all alone in that tiny, cold bed. Were you thinking of how it felt to have my hands on your body, to have my weight pressing between your thighs, to have my cock fill that pretty little pussy of yours, when you put my hoodie on to comfort you?"

Her body trembled.

I leaned back to observe her.

Her desire was obvious, from the way her pert

nipples pressed against the thin ribbed cotton of her tank top, to the rapid beat of her pulse at the base of her throat.

But I was watching for her tell. The one she didn't know she had.

Brynn swallowed as a soft pink flush crept over her cheeks. The tip of her tongue swept over her lower lip.

My mouth watered, remembering the sweet taste of her as my cock swelled.

The tension in the room stretched.

Soon.

I watched … and waited.

And then there it was … her eyelids flickered.

The dark fan of her eyelashes fluttering like the wings of a butterfly.

Her tell.

My adorable little thief was about to lie to me.

Brynn inhaled a shaking breath. "No, of course not. I accidentally had it on when I left your place is all, and didn't bother taking it off when I got home."

The side of my thumb stroked the edge of her jaw as I tilted her head back. I placed a soft kiss on her lips. Then rasped against her mouth, "Liar."

She gasped. "I'm not!"

I sank my teeth into her plump lower lip, nipping her, before responding. "I can prove it."

She tried to escape.

I placed a hand on her waist, restraining her. "Tsk, tsk, tsk."

She huffed. "Fine. Prove I'm lying."

I skimmed my lips along the edge of her cheek before kissing the corner of her eye. "Your hair smells of jasmine and is still slightly damp, which means you showered here. So you had to have deliberately put my hoodie back on to feel it close to your skin."

I slipped my hand under the hem of her tank top to touch her soft skin.

She inhaled sharply as her abdominal muscles tightened.

"The sheets and blanket on your bed are all twisted. Meaning you were restlessly tossing and turning."

I skimmed my fingertips along the waistband of her sleep shorts as I moved my mouth down the column of her throat, tasting her rising pulse. "There's that cute little tell you have when you're lying."

Her back arched away from the wall. "I don't have a tell."

I bit her earlobe. "You do and it's adorable and before you ask, no, I won't tell you what it is."

I pushed my hand inside her panties.

Her eyes widened as she wrapped her small fingers around my thick wrist.

Our gazes clashed.

I raised one eyebrow. "You know what I'm going to find the moment my fingers touch your pussy."

She pouted. "Fine. You win. It doesn't mean anything."

"It means everything," I growled before claiming her mouth.

I pinned her against the wall, pushing my hips into hers as I thrust my tongue into her warm, wet mouth.

I kissed her so feverishly, our teeth scraped. I didn't care. I tilted my head in the other direction, grasping her jaw as I pushed my tongue in deeper, devouring her.

When I finally broke free, her poor lips were stained a deep pink. "You lost our bet. Time to pay up, babygirl."

Her soft brown eyes darkened. "What do you want as payment?"

I stroked her cheek. "I told you. You have to play my game."

"What's it called?"

I ran my thumb over her swollen lower lip. *"Punish me, Daddy."*

CHAPTER 20

BRYNN

"*I*'ve changed my mind!" I blurted out.

"Too late."

"No fair!"

"First rule of gambling. Don't gamble if you're not prepared to lose."

"Like you would have just walked out of my life if you had lost?"

"I never said I would."

"Yes, you did!"

"No, I said that you could return to your old life."

"Exactly!"

I smiled. "I never said I wouldn't be there."

Her mouth dropped open. "Cheater!"

"Says the poker cheat. And I disagree; you should have paid closer attention to the phrasing. Now stop stalling."

"I really hate you."

He chuckled. "I think I've proven the opposite, babygirl." He then leaned down and whispered, "And I'm going to prove it again right now."

I bit my lower lip. "Please, I'm still sore from earlier."

"Don't worry. I'll kiss it and make it better. Now kneel on the bed."

There had to be something seriously twisted and wrong with me that despite my objections, I found all this fucking arousing.

All. Of. It.

His entire overbearing, domineering, arrogant, push me up against the wall demeanor was doing it for me.

And that was what was so terrifying about him.

On shaking legs, I walked over to the bed and gingerly sat on the edge facing him.

He wrapped his fist into my hair and wrenched my head back. "Did I say sit on the bed or kneel?" he growled.

I clenched my thighs. "Kneel," I whispered.

"One… two…"

It took me half a second to realize he was counting and I really didn't want to see what happened if he got to three.

I scrambled to the middle of the bed and knelt on all fours.

"Good girl. Now pull down your shorts and panties. Let me see that cute ass of yours."

I clenched my butt cheeks, still remembering the sting of his belt from earlier. "You're not going to punish me with your belt again, are you?"

"No. Now do as you're told."

Feeling self-conscious and a little like a petulant child, I leaned up and hooked my thumbs in my shorts and panties and slipped them over my hips until they fell down over my thighs before returning to all fours.

I inhaled a sharp breath when his warm palm slid over my exposed left cheek. Because my double bed was so small, his long arms and tall frame easily reached me in the middle of the bed.

"What's the name of this game?"

My cheeks flamed. "Please don't make me say it."

He spanked my ass with his open palm.

I cried out and fell to the side on my right hip.

He grabbed my hair and lifted me back up onto my knees. "What's the name of this game?"

"Punish me, Daddy," I whimpered.

His palm rubbed circles around the stinging flesh where he had struck me, sending a strange thrilling buzz through my limbs. "How do you want me to punish you, little one?"

I squeezed my eyes shut.

Oh, God. He was going to make me say it.

His large hand slipped over my ass to cup my pussy from behind.

My back curled as he pushed two fingers past my pussy lips to tease my clit.

I was already embarrassingly slick.

He pushed in one finger.

I moaned as I pushed back against his hand, already wanting to feel the fullness of another finger.

"Say it, babygirl. Tell me what I want to hear."

It was so *fucking dirty wrong*.

He pushed a second finger into me.

My fingers crushed the blanket beneath me as I threw my head back.

Fuck. The man was the devil.

He knew I wanted to know what it felt like to be spanked and dominated by him. He knew I wanted the sting and the pain and the degradation. The release that came from giving myself over completely.

I gritted my teeth and then finally caved. I cried out, "Spank me, Daddy!"

Before I had even gotten the full plea out, he had raised his arm and landed his heavy palm down on my right cheek. The white-hot pain shot up my spine like lightning.

A volley of stinging swipes from his hand followed, each more painful than the last.

My flesh burned as I fell partially forward, burying my head in the covers.

"Ow! Ow! Ow!"

My feet kicked up as my body absorbed the punishment.

He moved his hand from my butt cheeks to my upper thighs.

I knew I wouldn't be able to sit for a week after this.

"Please! Please!"

I didn't even know what I was asking….

"Please what?"

"Please stop, Daddy! I've been punished enough!"

"We're only just getting started."

I bit the blanket as tears blurred my vision. I barely noticed when the spanks stopped.

My ass throbbed. It was as if every drop of blood in my body was pulsing just below the surface of every piece of skin he'd touched.

I could hear him move around the bed, but was too caught up in processing my own emotions to even lift my head to see why.

His powerful hands wrapped around my hips and shifted my body until I was kneeling perpendicular on the bed. He caressed my inner thigh, moving his fingers in soft circles as he inched higher. "Open your legs wider, baby."

I sniffed. "Is my punishment over?"

"Have I punished your pretty button before?"

I frowned, not sure if this was a trick question and not wanting to get in trouble for lying again. "Yes … with your belt."

He teased my clit with his fingertip.

I arched my back. Unlike before, his touch felt even more electrifying. It was like the punishment and pain had heightened my senses and nerve endings, making everything more intense.

"And what did you say about those stupid boys?"

I couldn't focus. Not when he was rubbing my clit. "I don't know—" I breathed.

"You told me they treated you differently."

I pushed my hips against his hand. "Yes … um … okay."

"So, babygirl, this punishment game isn't over until we've done something … *different.*"

I stilled.

I didn't like the sound of that.

I looked over my shoulder.

He was looming over me from behind—all six feet three inches of hard tattooed muscle of him.

He raised his hand and spanked my ass. "Eyes forward."

I turned my head. "What are you going to do?"

"I told you … something different."

He pushed two fingers inside of me and pumped them several times. I was still sore from earlier but it was a pleasant kind of pain. Like that twisted kind of satisfaction you got from pressing on a bruise.

I was so aroused with conflicted emotions of pain and pleasure, I was sure that a few more thrusts and I would orgasm just from the touch of his hand.

Then I felt it.

His other hand, pressed against my lower back as his thumb moved between my cheeks to tease my dark hole.

I squeezed it hard as I tried to shift my hips forward.

He shifted his hand to grab my hand. "Don't move."

My breathing came in short bursts. "No. Not there."

"This is my game. You don't make the rules."

He moved his hand back to my lower back and placed the pad of his thumb against my asshole and pressed.

I dug my fingers into the bed blanket.

As much as I tried to resist, his thumb pushed inside to the first knuckle.

It felt strange and violating.

He swirled his thumb around as he pushed it in further.

I whimpered.

"Shhh, baby. Just relax. You're going to take far worse than my thumb before this game is over."

I tried to turn my head to look over my shoulder again. "What?"

"Eyes forward," he barked. "Or I'll really teach you a lesson and shove my cock up there without preparing you first."

Fresh tears poured down my cheeks. I knew how

much his cock had punished my tight pussy. He was so fucking big. There was no way I could take his hard length up my ass. No freaking way. "Please, Anton. You can't."

"You didn't think you were going to be with me and not give me this virgin ass, did you, baby?"

"Yes! I didn't think I was giving you my *real* virginity! Of course I didn't think about my anal virginity!"

His deep chuckle rolled over me. "You really are adorably innocent."

He pumped his thumb in and out of my asshole several more times, each time applying pressure in steady circles, opening me. At the same time, he continued to tease my clit.

"This might feel a little cold."

"What?"

I gasped as a cool dollop of gel slid down between my cheeks. His fingertip swirled over my puckered hole.

"Oh, God, please, you're not going to put your … your … cock in there … are you?"

He leaned over and placed a kiss between my shoulder blades. "Push your hips up."

"You didn't answer my question."

"I know. Do as you're told."

He shifted his hand from between my legs to put pressure on my lower back, forcing my hips up. At the same time, something hard pressed against my hole.

"What is that?"

"It's your vibrator. Now be a good girl, and open your ass up for Daddy."

"I don't know how to do that."

"Stop fighting me and relax your bottom hole, or I'll be forced to spank you to distract you."

I held my breath and tried to force myself to stop clenching.

The cool metal of the vibrator quickly warmed as it slipped deeper inside of me.

"Ow! Ow! Ow!"

It wasn't a sharp pain as I had been expecting as much as it was a strange, full pressure.

He pushed on my back as he thrust the vibrator in and out of my ass. "Good girl."

With each thrust, he pushed it in a little deeper.

After several minutes, he pulled it free.

I felt oddly empty, but that was short-lived.

"Let's try a bigger one."

My eyes widened as I heard him open my night-stand drawer. Over my shoulder, I saw him lift up a silicone, penis-shaped dildo that was still in the package. It was nine inches long and at least two and half inches thick. I'd received it a few years ago as a gag gift for my birthday from a long-forgotten friend.

"No! That was just a stupid joke gift."

He winked at me as he tore open the package with his canine teeth.

"Please, Anton! It won't fit."

"You don't have a choice, baby. This is smaller than my cock. Eventually you *will* be taking my cock up that sweet tight ass of yours so you might as well start with this."

He shifted me to the center of the bed and placed one knee on the bed as he grabbed my hair. "Open your mouth."

I licked my lips. "Why?"

"The only thing hotter than watching your tight ass swallow this fake dick will be knowing you felt it fill your mouth and pushed down your throat first. So when it pushes against your little hole, you will know exactly what's coming next as I shove it in deep."

I gasped, which was a mistake.

He pushed the purple silicone head past my lips and along my tongue until it pushed against the back of my throat.

My shoulders lurched as I gagged.

"That's it, baby. Try to swallow it."

My tongue swept over the rubber dick as I made obnoxious gurgling noises.

He placed his hand around my throat, tilting my head back as he pulled the dildo out and pushed it back in. "Feel your lips stretching around the thick base. Imagine what it's going to do to your tiny untried hole."

My eyes teared as his vivid dirty talk sent a dark, twisted, humiliating thrill through me.

He pulled the dildo free and shifted to move behind me. "Now ask Daddy to shove this in your ass."

I choked as I rubbed the back of my hand over my mouth.

He pressed his left hand against my left ass cheek, opening me. "Say it, Brynn," he warned, his sexy voice dark and low with command.

I swallowed. "Shove it in me ... Daddy."

He spanked my ass.

"Ow!"

"I can make this pleasurable ... or painful, baby. Your choice."

I sniffed. "Please shove the dildo in my ass, Daddy."

"Good girl."

I closed my eyes with relief when another cool glob of lube hit my already sore and stretched hole. Then the thick purple rubber head pressed against my ass.

Anton was right.

If he had just pushed the dildo inside of me, it would have been bad ... but this was so much worse. After sucking on it, it was a much more visceral experience. It was as if I could still feel it in my mouth as he slowly pushed it into my ass.

I could feel the lines of cach fake vein and the thick ridge of the head as it popped past my tight ring.

I fisted the blanket and desperately tried not to clench as the pressure increased as he slowly pushed it deeper and deeper inside of me.

It felt so full.

I was breathing in such quick gasps I made myself dizzy.

Anton rubbed my back and encouraged me. "You're being such a good girl for Daddy. You should see how your tiny ass is swallowing this dildo like a greedy little mouth. Too bad this isn't flavored lube, or I'd shove it back down your throat."

Fuck, that was so wrong. So why did my thighs just clench?

"Two more inches, baby. You got this."

I lowered my head, letting my hair cascade to hide my shame. "Please, no. It hurts. It's full. It's already full."

"No, baby. Trust me. Your ass can take a few more inches. I'll prove it to you. After tonight, I'll get you an even bigger toy for your ass."

Oh, God.

He pushed it the final inch.

My body jerked forward.

I expected him to move it or thrust, but he didn't. He just left it there, deep inside of me.

My body clenched and throbbed around the intrusion.

The mattress dipped as he shifted again. He stood next to it and shed the rest of his clothes before joining me back on the bed.

My eyes widened as he deftly lifted me as if I weighed nothing, then had me kneel over him with my knees on either side of his hips and my palms near his head.

I shook my head. "No! You promised we weren't going to fuck! I'm sore and you can't put your cock inside of me with this thing in my ass! It's too much!"

He reached for the hem of my tank top and whipped it over my head.

I pushed my hair out of my face. "I mean it, Anton. Game or no game. No way."

"Babygirl, I am always a man of my word."

Before I could object, he grabbed my hips and lifted me until I was straddling his face.

"Oh, my God!" I exclaimed.

I tried to climb off him, embarrassed by the position.

Anton reached between our bodies and twisted the dildo inside my ass.

I rose up on my knees, inadvertently shoving my pussy in his mouth. "Ow!"

He laughed, his warm breath teasing my oversensitized flesh. "That's more like it. Now hold onto the headboard."

Seeing no other option, I gripped the headboard for dear life.

As Anton gripped my thighs and pressed them open wider, his tongue licked and laved at my pussy, tormenting my clit with delicious pleasure.

"Oh! Oh!"

I rose up on my knees again, wanting more but also shying away from the vulnerable position.

He moved his hands around my thighs to grip me just below my ass and then reached for the end of the dildo lodged in my ass. He pulled it out a few inches and pounded it back inside me.

I cried out as I thrust my hips forward against his mouth.

Anytime I tried to move away from him, he would pull on the dildo and push it ruthlessly deeper into my ass.

After several minutes, I was only holding onto the headboard with my left hand. My right was gripping Anton's hair as I shamelessly rode his face, grinding my pussy against his mouth.

I came so hard I thought I would pass out. Bright flashes of light burst behind my eyelids as my lungs burned from lack of oxygen. I fell backward, until my head was between his open legs, by his knees, my ass propped up on his chest.

Anton leaned up as he wrapped my legs around his middle.

His mouth twisted in an arrogant grin as he twisted the dildo inside of my ass. "So did you like my game?"

I flung the crook of my right arm over my eyes to hide my humiliation as my cheeks burned. "I still hate you," I groaned.

"Brave words for someone who still has a dildo deep in their ass."

CHAPTER 21

ANTON

*M*y adorable little 'damaged' thief.

It would take time, but eventually I would prove to her that I was nothing like the parade of idiots in her past who had let her down, starting with, it sounded like, her father.

Brynn snatched at a rumpled corner of the blanket and tried to drag it over her naked form.

I placed my arms around her back and pulled her up into my arms with her legs still wrapped around my middle. With her cute ass nestled against my cock and her breasts pushed against my chest, I could definitely get used to the position.

The only way it would be better was if I were balls deep inside of her.

I nuzzled her neck just under her ear. "What do you think you're doing?"

"I was going to cover up before I rolled off you and got this *thing* out of my butt."

"Who said you were allowed to pull it out?"

She lurched backward and stared at me. "You're not going to make me keep it in there, are you?"

I touched the tip of her nose with the tip of mine. "The thought had occurred to me, at least until we got back to our place."

She frowned. "*Our* place?"

"Yes, the Four Monks."

She wedged her arms between us as she covered her face and rubbed her eyes. "Anton, I've already told you, I'm staying here."

"And I've already made it clear that was unacceptable."

She squirmed in my embrace. "I'm not having this conversation with a dildo in my ass!"

I ran my hand along her thigh and over her hip. Cupping the curve of her ass cheek, my fingertips teased the smooth edge of the dildo.

Just to punish her a little further, I twisted it inside of her.

She lurched upward, pushing her beautiful tits against my mouth. I turned my head and captured a nipple between my lips as I palmed the back of her skull, holding her in place.

She dug her nails into my shoulders. "Oh! Oh! Wait … no. You're not going to distract me again."

Giving her nipple a final, teasing bite, I carefully pulled the dildo out of her bottom.

Her lips formed the cutest O as I did so, as if she were begging for me to slide my cock between them.

Brynn blinked several times as her chest rose and fell with her heavy breathing. "It's strange how it felt so intrusive going in and now it feels empty without it."

My mouth quirked at the corner as I raised an eyebrow. "I can always put it back in."

She shifted her hips as she covered her ass with her hand. "No!"

I tossed the dildo on the floor and wrapped my arms around her waist. "Is there anything in here you want? I can send my men to pack it up for you. Otherwise, I do plan on buying you a new wardrobe and anything else you may want. I can take you shopping this weekend or if you need something sooner I'm sure Polina can go with you tomorrow."

"You're doing it again."

"Doing what?"

"Railroading me."

"You said you weren't going to discuss it with a dildo in your ass. The dildo is gone."

"You know that is not what I meant. I'm not moving in with you, Anton. We only just met."

"So?"

"So what happens when it's over?"

I flipped her onto her back, pinning her beneath me. "And people say Russians are pessimistic."

"It's not pessimistic. It's realistic. You expect me to throw my entire life into chaos for a man I barely know, so what happens when you tire of me and toss me on the street?"

"I will never tire of you, babygirl."

Her eyes darkened with a sad, haunted look as her gaze shifted to the side. "That's what all men say, until they do."

Fuck. I would really have to watch every word and deed around her.

"I will pay you."

Her gaze narrowed. "I'm not a whore."

"I never said you were. I am a man of business. This is a business venture."

Her lips thinned as she studied my face. "I'm listening."

"You mentioned you were saving for a salon chair at some fancy place downtown."

"You remember that?"

I tapped the tip of her nose with my finger. "I remember everything you've said."

She rolled her eyes. "Don't act so smug. You've known me for what? Two days? And I've spent half that time running from you. It's hardly that impressive."

"Damn. You are a little ballbuster, aren't you."

She smirked. "See? Something you didn't know before you rushed to move me into your penthouse. Change your mind yet?"

I leaned down and nipped at her bottom lip. "Nice try. No."

She huffed. "You were saying about the salon?"

"Have your chair at the Four Monks."

"What?"

"We have the space. It would be a nice service for the women. I've talked with the partners before about adding a spa space. This would be a small step to see if there is interest."

Her beautiful soft brown eyes lit up with excitement. I knew she remembered the clientele from her adventure in crime. It would give her a chance to do the hair and makeup of some of the most influential and rich women in the city.

"It would be a chance to develop a client base before I went out on my own," she said, thinking out loud.

There wasn't a chance I was letting her take that step, but I knew when I had won the battle, there was no reason to start another skirmish.

She eyed me skeptically. "Of course, if I did this, you'd be my boss, so…."

I ground my hips against hers. "Don't even finish that thought, babygirl. Offering you a chance to start your business at the Four Monks is all the compromise I'm willing to offer. It is that, or I keep you naked and handcuffed to my bed."

Her mouth fell open. "You know, technically, this *is* still America, not Russia. Option three is, I go back to saying *no thank you, sir, I don't wish to date you.*"

I kissed her on the forehead before rolling off her and swiping my shirt from the footboard. "It's adorable you think what we're doing is dating." I pulled the shirt over my head and buttoned the last few buttons, then reached for my suit vest. "Get dressed."

She sat up in bed as she grabbed the blanket and covered her breasts. "What are we doing if not dating?"

I shrugged into my vest and headed toward the door as I repeated, "Get dressed. I'm going to make some calls to get my men here to repair your door. Grab what you need for tonight and make a list of what you want them to pack up. We leave in five."

She was still calling out to me as I headed down the hallway. "Anton? Are we not dating?"

Brynn was correct.

We barely knew one another so of course she wouldn't know that I had never brought a woman up to my penthouse. She would have no way of knowing how unusual it was for me to shirk off work to chase a mere slip of a girl around Chicago for two days straight.

She would be completely ignorant of the impact she'd had on my psyche since meeting her.

From the moment I laid eyes on her sweet innocent face and saw the fear and anxiety etched there, I knew … I just knew my purpose in life from that moment forward was to protect her.

I wouldn't call it an epiphany, but it was as close as a hardened criminal with a usually jaded perspective on life could get.

As I reached the main living room, I took a good look around and shook my head. She was out of her fucking mind if she thought I was going to allow her to stay in this tiny, unsecured apartment for one goddamn minute more.

Brynn followed me down the hall, the blanket from the bed wrapped around her middle.

I turned to stare at her as I finished sending a text to Sergei telling him to send men to my location. Nodding in the direction she came, I said, "Get back in the bedroom and put some clothes on. My men will be here soon."

She stared up at me. "What is this, if it's not dating?"

If she was hesitant to move in with me, it was probably best not to inform her that I had no intention of ever letting her leave my side, and planned to see her bear my children.

I cupped her face. "Dating implies something informal and casual. So let me be very clear, little one. You are mine and mine alone. I do not share and my interest in you is not in the least bit casual, do you understand me?"

She slowly nodded.

"Good."

I placed my hands on her shoulders and turned her around to face the bedroom door. "Now do as you are told and put some clothes on." I then swatted her ass.

She yelped as she scurried down the hall.

I sent a few more texts and made my way back to her bedroom. Leaning a shoulder against the door-frame, I watched as she carefully packed a few spare items in a small backpack.

Crossing my arms over my chest, I asked, "Are you only taking a few items because you've finally decided to take advantage of me and my money or are you secretly assuming you will be returning here in a day or two?"

She puckered her lips as she shifted her gaze to the floor. "Totally not the second thing."

I stormed into the room and grabbed the back-pack. "Liar."

I placed a hand on her lower back and ushered her toward the door, swiping the hoodie from the end of the bed as I went. When we reached the main room, I turned her toward me. "Arms up."

"I put a sweater on."

"Arms up," I repeated.

"Is this how it's going to be? You just ordering me about all the time?"

"Yes. Now do I have to take off my belt?"

Her arms shot up.

I pulled the sweater over her head and replaced it with my hoodie. I then wrapped her in my overcoat.

She pushed out her lower lip. "This coat is like a thousand times too big on me."

I rolled up the left sleeve until I saw the pink tips of her fingernails. Then I picked up her right arm to do the same to the other sleeve. "It's also *like a thousand times* warmer. First order of business is to get you a proper fucking coat."

She smirked. "You sound like a *daddy*."

I yanked up the collar as I pulled her against my chest and kissed her roughly on the lips. "And you're a brat."

Before I could do more there was a discreet knock on the door.

Several of my men nodded in greeting after I swung open the broken door, keeping their gaze respectfully averted from Brynn.

I fired off instructions and then bundled Brynn to my side and out into the dark night.

A frosty cloud left her lips as she sighed. "So you're really taking me back to the Four Monks?"

I looked down at her as I quipped, "You could act like it was a multimillion-dollar, luxury penthouse ... *like it is* ... where I plan to pamper and spoil you...

instead of like I'm dragging you off to some remote fortress to hold you prisoner."

Her beautiful eyes darkened.

Her whisper was almost lost on the winter wind. "Are you sure about that?"

I tightened my grasp around her waist.

No. I wasn't.

CHAPTER 22

BRYNN

*S*houlders tense, I woke up, but kept my eyes closed.

My lungs contracted as I tried to keep my breathing unnaturally shallow and even. I resisted the urge to tighten my stomach muscles where Anton's arm rested.

I tried to take in as much information as possible without the benefit of sight.

The room was quiet, strangely so.

I was used to waking to irritating noise.

The bang, clatter, and squish of residents tossing garbage bags out of their windows in doomed-to-fail attempts to hit the open dumpster in the alley outside my bedroom window. The usual tire screeches and errant horns of traffic congestion. The clang of old plumbing pipes strained beyond their limit as people showered for work. My occasional roommate cousin hocking a loogie he coughs up right before I hear him flush the toilet, combining into a fairly disgusting image in my head.

But this morning there was ... nothing ... just peace.

It was as if Anton's home were in a freaking meadow and not in the center of Chicago.

I wiggled my butt slightly. Then there was, of course, the impossibly comfortable pillow top mattress. If I were that type of girl, I might stay with this man just for this mattress.

It truly was like sleeping on a cloud, just like the commercials said.

It beat the hell out of my secondhand double bed. And it was so freaking big! I could stretch out my arms and legs and flop around all I wanted as I slept and I hardly even knew there was another human being in the bed with me.

That was another annoyingly thoughtful thing about Anton.

Despite his arm cuddling my waist now, he hadn't pinned me down with his body all night long. Despite being a virgin, I had spent a few disastrous nights with a couple of failure-to-launch boyfriends and it was always awful.

I liked to toss and turn and I hated how they clung to me like a thousand-degree weighted wet blanket.

What was it with guys and their furnace-like body temperatures at night?

It was like they were burning through their unused testosterone through their skin.

Not Anton, probably because he didn't have any unused testosterone at the end of the day.

He'd obviously used *all* his up throughout the day … and then some.

He had settled us in the bed, gave me a soul-searing kiss, and then placed a possessive hand on my hip as I turned on my side, but didn't try to pull me against him or smother me.

This morning, his arm was around my waist but there was still a bit of distance between us.

I was both grateful for it … and bothered by it.

I wanted the space because all this was a bit over-whelming, but at the same time, I kind of wanted the warm and fuzzy feeling that came from snuggling against his chest.

I inhaled softly, careful not to expand my lungs too deeply, not wanting to alert him to the fact I was awake. There were hints of leather, tobacco, and musk from his cologne that still clung to his skin and the cozy blankets that surrounded us.

I sucked my lips between my teeth to stop myself from smiling.

Okay, I'll admit it.

It was kind of nice waking up in a peaceful, warm, and cozy bedroom that smelled faintly like sexy cologne, next to the even sexier man wearing it.

There was a soft caress on my cheek. "You know I know you're awake, right?"

My eyes flew open to see Anton with his head resting on his right hand as he leaned over me.

His left hand cupped my jaw as his thumb caressed my lower lip.

I frowned. "How long have you been staring at me?"

He gave me a crooked smile. "Since the first moment I saw you walk through the doors of the Four Monks in that terrible black cocktail dress."

I rolled my eyes. "I meant this morning."

He shrugged one shoulder. "No idea. You're even cuter when you sleep. Well, except for the snoring."

My mouth dropped open. "I do not snore!"

He laughed. "You most certainly do, but I thought it was adorable, my little deviated septum baby."

I snatched the pillow out from beneath my head and whacked him with it. "Take that back!"

"It had the faintest little rattle, like the purr of a kitten."

I straddled him as he flopped onto his back. I stretched my arms to the right and whacked him with the pillow. I then raised it again to the left and swung it in an arc, but before it could land, Anton flipped me onto my back.

I pushed out my lower lip. "You are the worst! You're supposed to tell a girl she slept like a princess and she's the most beautiful woman you've ever seen, even in the morning without makeup. You're not supposed to tell her she snored like a truck driver!"

He leaned down and kissed my left cheek. "You slept like a princess." He then kissed the tip of my nose. "You are the most beautiful woman I've ever seen, even without makeup." He then kissed my right cheek. "And I said you sounded like an adorable purring kitten as you snored."

I twirled the tip of my finger in his chest hair as I continued to pout. "You were the one who insisted I stay here."

He nuzzled my neck just under my jaw, sending shivers up my spine.

I gripped his strong upper arms as I stifled a moan.

He rubbed his hard cock against my upper thigh. "I was the one who insisted that you *move in* here … not stay," he corrected.

With a growl, he leapt out of the bed and scooped me up into his arms.

"Where are you taking me?"

He continued to kiss my neck as he carried me across the bedroom. "To the shower. I want to be careful and give you until tonight before I fuck that gorgeously tight pussy of yours again."

He set me down in front of the glass door as he leaned in and flipped the brass lever that started the rain shower. Focusing his heated gaze back on me, he tore off the T-shirt of his he had given me to wear last night.

Since he was already naked, he pulled us under the steaming spray of water.

He cupped my face as he stared intently down at me. "So I'm going push you to your knees and jerk off on these amazing breasts of yours and then I'm going to personally suds up all the naughty places I made dirty." He winked.

I gasped from the overtly dirty sensuality of his words, and he swooped down to claim my mouth with a searing kiss.

As he did so, he walked me back until I collided with the glass shower wall.

I could feel him reach between our slick bodies to grasp his cock.

When I was breathless, he broke our kiss and rasped, "Get on your knees, babygirl," as he pushed down on my hip.

And completely without shame or hesitation, I obeyed.

* * *

TWO HOURS LATER, he escorted me downstairs to a posh employee lounge.

Anton placed a hand on my lower back and guided me to the side of the woman standing there.

With a sardonic twist to his mouth, he said, "I'd introduce you two, but I believe you've already met."

She was, of course, looking impossibly elegant with her silver hair pulled back in a flawless, tight bun at the top of her head and her signature all-black attire and bold jewelry.

She tilted her head to the left, exposing her cheek. "Don't be surly, *mishka.* It is morning and I haven't had my tea yet."

Anton leaned down and kissed her cheek. "Pour me a cup. Brynn?"

Tetya Polina was standing in front of a stunning cobalt blue enameled samovar. She lifted the elaborately decorated porcelain teapot from the top and poured a heavily concentrated black tea into a clear glass with an etched silver *podstakannik* holder. She then flipped the lever on the samovar to fill the rest of the glass with hot water.

She handed the cup to Anton and turned to me. "Tea?"

I inhaled deeply. It smelled divine, like a smoky campfire. "What kind is it?"

"It is called Russian Caravan. It is a very popular black tea in Russia, a blend of lapsang souchong, oolong, assam, and pu-erh. It's smoky yet sweet. I think you will like it."

"It smells just like a campfire. I'd love to try it."

237

She nodded and turned to make me a cup.

As she did, I asked, "So what does *mishka* mean?"

Anton looked up as he paused in stirring a spoonful of orange marmalade in his tea. "Don't you dare—"

"Little bear," she responded with a Cheshire cat grin as she handed me my tea.

I turned to Anton with delight. "Little bear?"

Anton scowled at *Tetya* Polina. "Really?"

She placed a sugar cube between her teeth and took a sip of tea before shrugging. She then reached up and patted his cheek. "She asked. Besides, it's a cute nickname."

I hid my smile behind the rim of my glass. "Yes, *mishka*, be a good sport!" I scolded, before I erupted in giggles.

He swatted me on the butt. "No. Don't even think about it." He then shook his head as he turned to Polina. "Am I going to regret leaving her with you today?"

She twisted her wrist as she waved her hand. "Probably."

One of the staff approached her with a question, so she turned and left us alone.

I looked up at Anton. "I thought you were showing me the salon space today?"

"I'm having some of the men clean it up." He nodded toward Polina. "In the meantime, *Tetya* Polina is going to take you shopping."

I bit my lower lip. "I don't need to go—"

He leaned down and kissed me on the forehead. "Babygirl, I'm planning on using this sweet body of yours for dirty, gratuitous, borderline illegal sex. Use me for my dirty, gratuitous, borderline illegal money. I'll see you later tonight." He gave me a wink and left.

The rest of the afternoon was a surreal mashup of *Pretty Woman, What Not to Wear* and *The Godfather*.

First there were the three black Cadillac Escalades that rolled up to the curb of the Four Monks as we exited.

I didn't realize *all three* were for us until *all three* pulled away from the curb at the same time after we got into the center one.

When I asked *Tetya* Polina about it, she just gave me a twist of her wrist and said that Anton was particular about security.

As we emerged from the vehicle, four men in suits would follow us, two staying outside by the entrance and two following us into the store.

At first, *Tetya* Polina said she would let me just wander around the store and pick out the items I would like to try on.

That lasted for approximately twelve minutes.

When she saw the graphic T-shirt and simple scarf, the two cheapest items I could find in the high-end Michigan Avenue store, in my hands, she threw up her arms, uttered something in Russian that I'm pretty sure was not complimentary, and took over.

Next thing I knew, she was pressing our bodyguards into service as valets. She became a whirling dervish as she circled around the store tossing expensive dresses, lingerie, skirts, and blouses into their outstretched arms while anxious sales associates followed her around offering champagne and fashion suggestions.

The final surreal thing was after trying on one outfit after another and either receiving a twist of her wrist, which I took as approval, or a dismissive shake of her head, which I took as a no, we never actually *purchased* any of the clothes.

The sales associates carefully wrapped everything in tissue paper and handed the boxes and bags to the bodyguards as *Tetya* Polina just tossed over her shoulder as we waltzed out the door, "Send a bill to Antonius Ivenchenko at the Four Monks."

That was it.

No credit card.

No ID.

Nothing.

Just tossing out Anton's name.

And it wasn't just that store. The same thing happened store after store along The Magnificent Mile; *Chanel, Gucci, Louis Vuitton, Prada, Giorgio Armani, Escada*.

Even at Harry Winston, where she selected several outrageously expensive diamond and pearl jewels to match some of the cocktail dresses she had chosen.

I tried objecting, but she wouldn't hear it. "If you have a problem, take it up with Anton. He is the one who gave me my marching orders."

She then turned to the sales associate and said, "These will be on trial of course until Mr. Ivenchenko approves."

The man bowed. "Of course, madam. We will send a representative to the Four Monks in a week to see if everything is satisfactory. Should we take the liberty of bringing a few additional pieces at that time?"

She laughed. "Of course!"

After an exhausting afternoon, I slumped down on the soft leather seat in the back of the Escalade. I rolled my head to the side. "*Tetya* Polina, tell me the truth. How much money did we just spend?"

I had absolutely no idea since I never saw a single price tag and we never even approached a cash register all afternoon.

She sighed. "Darling girl, do you not understand that your man is worth a stupid amount of money? Billions upon billions and worse, he can easily make more whenever he wants it. Money, it is like nothing to him. A game. What we spent today is … how do you American's say? A drop in bucket."

I covered my face. "That much, huh?"

She patted my knee. "Yes, darling girl. That much."

I turned my head in the other direction and stared out the window as I watched a line of people waiting for a bus, knowing how easily that could have been me right now.

There was no point in kicking up a fuss about all the extravagance. I might as well enjoy it while it lasted. It was not like I was going to take all the clothes and jewels with me when we broke up.

My heart twisted at the thought. When, *not if*, we broke up.

Despite Anton's objections to the contrary, I knew it was *when*.

It was a hard lesson I learned early from my father.

I could not depend on a man to be there for me.

Always and forever did not mean the same thing to them as it did to women.

I learned that soul-crushing lesson from my mother.

I pushed aside my crystal bead bracelets and touched my scar.

In the end, I was the only one I could depend on to save myself.

I learned that lesson from my own survival.

Still, as I stared at the city's skyline out the window, I couldn't help *wanting* to believe in the sincerity of Anton's words when he said always and forever.

It's what made being with him so dangerous.

For the first time in a very long time, he was making me have hope in love again.

And I really needed to stop it.

CHAPTER 23

ANTON

When I awoke, Brynn was not in bed with me.

It had only been one day and already I had looked forward to waking up by her side.

I threw on a pair of jeans and a gray knit sweater and went in search of her.

It was still early so most of the staff were not on property yet.

Below stairs, The Four Monks felt like a strangely empty luxury hotel when there was not the frenetic energy of staff and members.

After looking through the lounge, I finally found a steward who pointed me in the right direction.

Last night, I showed her the beginnings of what would be her salon space.

A perk of having money and being in the mafia was fantastic construction contacts. I was able to get a crew of men on property at a moment's notice to turn a thousand-square-foot empty space into a charming salon complete with mirrors, sinks, a private bathroom, and salon chairs. I had an interior designer drop off paint swatch books so Brynn could choose what colors she wanted them to paint it today.

It was a bit bare bones and I definitely planned to do something better for her in the future, but I was pleasantly surprised at how overwhelmed and pleased she was at the simple gesture.

Although my plans for her to show me how grateful she was fizzled when my poor babygirl practically fell asleep in her plate of pasta later that night over dinner. It seemed she wasn't accustomed to marathon shopping trips.

After tucking her into bed, I had stayed up for a few more hours with my laptop, doing work next to her, enjoying the quiet domesticity of the moment. Well, almost quiet, except for her cute kitten purr snoring.

But then I woke with her gone.

I stormed down the hallway in the direction the steward pointed. I should have known to check her new salon space first. Of course my babygirl would be excited about her new venture.

As I neared her partially closed door, I heard her animated chatter ... and a deep male voice. "I don't think the sides are even, can you take a closer look?"

Brynn replied, "I think they are but let me check."

God. Fucking. Dammit.

Would there ever come a time where I could approach a fucking door and *not* find my woman with another man behind it?

I didn't even bother with the doorknob.

I just kicked it open with my bare foot.

The door swung open so forcefully, the knob broke through the wall plaster behind it.

She was standing between his spread-open knees, bent over, giving him a terrific view straight down her fucking V-neck sweater as she held his face in her hands.

He had his hand barely an inch from grabbing her ass as she was distracted checking his haircut.

They both turned as the door crashed open.

I'm sure I meant to say, "What the fuck is going on here?"

But all that came out of my mouth was a primal roar.

Brynn stumbled out of the way as I grabbed the salon chair by the arm and swung it around to face me.

I grabbed the man who I recognized as one of my poker dealers by the front of his partially unbuttoned tuxedo shirt and lifted him bodily out of the chair and off his feet. A violent pitch to the right sent him sailing across the room to slam against the wall.

He lifted his hands. "I didn't know she was yours!"

I snatched his shirt again and pulled back my arm, making a fist. "You dare insult me by sitting there with my woman standing between your fucking legs?"

His cheekbone crunched beneath my knuckles.

Brynn wrapped her arms around my outstretched arm and clung to it like a monkey hanging off a vine. "Stop! I was just giving him a haircut!"

"He was staring at your tits and about to grab your ass!"

Brynn's outraged shriek rang over my poker dealer's protests. "He what?"

"I'm sorry, Boss! I thought she was fair game!"

My red-hazed gaze barely focused on her as I lifted the man's crumpled form off the floor by his neck. "Get out of my sight," I ordered through clenched teeth before shoving him toward the open doorway.

Before he crossed it, I called out, "Wait."

The man's shoulders hunched as he turned, braced for another strike from my fist, which he knew he more than deserved and worse. He was lucky I wasn't armed.

My hands gripped the edge of the heavy oak door and ripped it right off its hinges. I then shoved it toward my employee. "Take this with you."

The man staggered back from the weight of the door. In his haste he tried to leave through the doorway with it still upright. It crashed against the frame, sending small splinters of wood and dust raining down onto his back. He then tilted the door forward and awkwardly ran down the hallway.

Deliberately unclenching my fingers one by one, I slowly pivoted to face off with Brynn. "What did I tell you about touching other men?"

"Anton, you're being—"

I stalked toward her. "And what have I *repeatedly* told you about being alone behind closed doors with other men?"

"Seriously, Anton. The door was barely closed and besides—"

I pinned her against the wall. "How am I supposed to protect you when you insist on putting yourself in these bullshit, dangerous situations?"

Her cheeks blossomed into a furious flush as her beautiful eyes hardened into chips of ice. "I never asked for your protection! I was just doing my job! I wasn't doing anything wrong. You're acting like you caught me fucking him against the mirrors!"

I snatched her around the waist and yanked her to me as I placed a hand around her throat.

Glaring down at her, I seethed, "I thought I had made myself clear that you were to take *female clients* only. Obviously this was a mistake. I'm forbidding you from working from now on."

Her mouth opened and closed several times as she made a choking, gurgling sound.

Finally she spit out, "Forbidding me? Forbidding me! What is this, the 1950s? You can't forbid me."

I tightened my hold. "You're forgetting where you are and who you're talking to, babygirl. My word is law, and no woman of mine is going to work for a living, understood?"

To punctuate my command, I seized her mouth, pushing my tongue past her lips to prove to her who had the dominating hand in this relationship.

Brynn fought my embrace, scratching my bare arms with her fingernails.

It did nothing to deter my wrath or my desire.

The harder she fought, the harder it made my cock.

I lifted her up by her ass and swung left, placing her on the mirror-backed countertop as I pushed between her knees. I fisted her hair and wrenched her head back as I pushed my tongue deeper into her mouth.

Only the taste of her submission would ebb the fury still pounding through my blood.

She wrenched her head to the side. "No! We're not doing this!"

She shoved against my shoulders. "You're not going to go all Neanderthal on me and then try to distract me with a kiss."

I yanked her hair. "I wasn't stopping at a kiss," I growled as I pushed my hand inside her sweater to grasp her breast.

She pulled on my wrist as she began to tremble and all the color drained from her face.

Fuck.

I eased back and cupped her cheeks. "Baby?"

Anger had gotten the better of me, and now I had truly scared her.

She was such a sassy little fighter, always giving as good as she got, I lost sight of just how intimidating my temper could be.

Hell, larger, prison-hardened men had pissed themselves at just the sight of my approach when I was enraged and out for blood.

Brynn shook her head as she pushed against my bare chest. "I … I need some air."

Without thinking further, I swooped her up into my arms. Down the hallway, I pushed my back against the metal stairwell door. I then launched myself up eight flights of stairs until I reached the private rooftop deck. Storming through the glass-enclosed lounge, I kicked open the French glass doors and carried her to the wrought-iron gazebo in the corner.

Sitting down on one of the padded benches that encircled the enclosure, I cradled her on my lap.

As I smoothed her hair away from her ashen cheeks, I kissed her forehead and held her close. "Baby, talk to me."

"I can't do this," she whispered. "I thought I could, but I can't."

I tilted my head back and closed my eyes for a moment as the beast inside of me raged. I resisted the urge to tighten my hold on her slim and trembling frame. Taking a deep breath, I looked down at her as I cupped the back of her head in the palm of my hand.

I let out a frustrated sigh. "Look—I'm not sorry about why I lost my temper but I'm sorry about how I lost it in front of you."

She frowned. "Is that supposed to be an apology?"

My lips thinned. "I'm not accustomed to apologizing."

Both her eyebrows rose. "Yeah … it shows."

"I'm trying to say I'm sorry for scaring you."

"And I'm saying that you're *really* bad at apologies."

I leaned my forehead against hers. "Somehow I feel like I'm going to get a lot more practice with you around."

She twisted her fingers in her lap. "No, you're not … because I'm not going to be around."

My stomach muscles tightened. Again, the beast inside my chest howled with rage, clawing, and scratching to be released.

My hand shook as I moved it down to caress her lower back. "We've been through this. I'm not letting you go."

Call me a selfish, overbearing, misogynistic bastard.

I'm. Not. Letting. Her. Go.

This tiny slip of a girl was my salvation and my redemption.

Fate brought her to me, to protect and love.

No matter how hard she tried to resist and fight our attraction, I wasn't going to back down.

She was mine.

Now and forever.

And yes … I fucking said love.

One of the benefits of age was knowing when you had the real thing in your arms. And not being dumb enough to let it slip away.

She let out a faint sigh. "It takes two to be in a relationship, Anton."

"You've obviously never dated a Russian man before."

My attempt at levity fell flat.

"I like you, Anton. I mean I really like you, probably too much."

"What is too much?"

"Too much is a trap. I can't do it. I can't become dependent on you. If something should happen…"

"Why are you assuming something will happen?"

She tucked a lock of hair behind her ear. "It must be nice to be so confident. I can't take that chance. We've only just met. We barely know one another. You are this rich, powerful … male. Of course you're not worried if this whole thing blows up in our faces because your life won't be ruined by it, but mine will."

I stroked her cheek. "I don't give a damn if I've known you for one hour or a hundred. A man knows when he has found the right woman for him. This is real. Nothing is going to separate us."

"You can't know that—"

"Yes, I can, because I won't let anything separate us—and I am a very stubborn man."

She shook her head as she swiped at a tear. "I'm sorry. It's too big of a risk. I'm already half in love with you. If I stay I'll fall completely in love with you."

"And what would be so bad about that?"

She finally turned and looked at me. Her pretty brown eyes filled with tears. "I know it sounds stupid. You're offering me the fairy tale. The hand-some, rich Prince Charming come to save Cinderella. The problem is my life experience has been more the Grimm version than Disney when it comes to fairy tales."

I ran my palm in comforting circles on her back, trying to keep from snatching her to me and screaming *mine* like a child about to be deprived of his favorite toy. "Trust me, babygirl. I am far from Prince Charming."

That at least earned me a slight half smile.

She lowered her head, as her hair slipped from behind her ear and fell in a soft wave to cover her face. "It's been a really long time since someone's given a damn about me and I'm scared. You have these big strong shoulders and you want me to lean on them. You want me to depend on you and turn to you for help."

I pushed her hair back to try to catch her gaze again, but she shifted her head to the side, avoiding me. "You want to explain to me why that's a bad thing?"

"It's bad because *wanting* to be with someone and *needing* to be with them are two very different things. The more I learn to depend on you, the more vulnerable I will become."

I reached over and placed my palm on her cheek to force her to face me. "Babygirl, accepting help, especially from someone who can easily afford to give it, is not a sign of weakness."

She climbed off my lap. "I'm not saying this right."

Against my better judgment, I let her.

She shook her hands out in front of her as she paced around the gazebo like a cute, agitated little brown squirrel. "I know this sounds insane. There are thousands of girls who would line up for the chance to lie around all day in the lap of luxury and do nothing but spend your money."

I threw an arm over the back of the bench as I watched her. "I'm glad you think so."

She ran a hand through her hair.

I adjusted my seat as I ran a hand down my thigh,

pulling on my jeans. Now was not the time to think about pulling on those long silky locks as I drove my cock into her from behind … and yet, that was exactly what I was thinking about.

Fuck, even when this woman was doing her best to try to break it off with me, all I could think about was bending her over this bench, ripping down her pants, and hammering into her with my cock, like I was driving nails.

There was absolutely no fucking way I was letting her go.

She was lucky I was even letting her *talk* about leaving me.

If I could, I'd find a way to stop her from even thinking about it.

Hell, I had tried earlier with that kiss, but it backfired.

She paused in front of me. "I'm not like other girls."

Running my gaze appreciatively over her, I said, "I'm very well aware of that, little one."

God, did she really not know how amazingly intriguing and beguiling she was?

How utterly fucking adorable?

How she made a man just want to pick her up and put her in his pocket like a sweet little sparrow with a broken wing that only he could save?

She continued as if I hadn't spoken. "I actually like working. It gives me a sense of security and purpose.

It calms the bad thoughts in my head. And no matter what, I know that I always have a plan B. *I need a plan B.* My mother didn't have a plan B."

I clenched my jaw.

A plan B.

In other words, an escape plan—from me.

I rubbed my jaw and remained silent, not trusting myself to speak.

Unfortunately, she filled the silence and only made things worse.

Brynn paced again, avoiding eye contact. "That's why it won't work between us. You should look for one of those other girls who would want what you're offering and would better appreciate"—she swung her arms out—"all this. Not that I didn't. It's great. The shopping trip was lovely. It just comes with too many strings."

She stopped and crouched down before me, placing her hands on my knees, her eyes finally meeting mine in entreaty. "Please tell me you under-stand? I know you're just trying to protect me and give me everything I don't have… but I can't be with someone who takes away my plan B. I can't be trapped like that."

Fresh tears fell down her cheeks. "I stopped believing in Prince Charming and fairy tales a long time ago and I can't allow myself to start believing in them again now. It's too risky."

She bowed her head, breaking eye contact.

I stared down at her for several minutes.

Finally, I leaned down and placed a soft kiss on the top of her head.

Without saying a word, I stood up and walked away, leaving her alone in the gazebo.

The last thing I heard was the sound of her sobs.

CHAPTER 24

ANTON

*A*s I crossed through the enclosed glass lounge, I moved to the wall-mounted phone.

Picking up the receiver, I dialed Polina's extension, knowing she would be in her office at this hour.

She picked up immediately.

Without preamble, I said, "Whatever you are doing, drop it. I need you to take care of Brynn until I return. She's in the gazebo. She is your top priority. I don't want her left alone for a minute. Anyone has a problem with that, tell them to fuck off and see me."

For once, she did not have a sassy retort. She had known me for too long to know that now was not the time. "Absolutely, I will be right up."

"Good."

Resisting the urge to turn and look at Brynn,

knowing my resolve would falter, I slammed the receiver down and headed toward the stairs.

Minutes later I was in my car, speeding through the city streets as I punched in the address to an office complex construction site near O'Hare Airport.

I drove my Range Rover into the center of the dirt-packed site.

As I emerged from the driver's side, a man in khakis and wearing a white hardhat approached, waving a clipboard in the air. "You can't park here. This is a restricted construction site."

I pierced him with a glare. "I'm Antonius Ivenchenko. I need to speak to a Jonathan Moore. Now."

The man's eyes widened as he bowed. "Yes, Mr. Ivenchenko, I'm sorry. I meant no disrespect. I will have him sent for immediately." He bowed twice more.

I grimaced as I lowered my aviator sunglasses. "There is no reason to bow. Just go get him. I'll wait in your office."

The man bowed again. Then snapped upright, catching himself. "Of course, sir. The door to the trailer is open. Make yourself at home."

After climbing the rickety wooden set of stairs, I swung open the dented metal door to the white office trailer.

A blast of musty smelling heat hit me as I entered

the narrow, cramped space. There were two desks crammed at opposite ends with a man sitting at one of them and another leaning over him as they studied a set of blueprints.

I barely glanced at them. "Out."

Without a word, they scrambled to roll up the blueprints and stumbled over their boots to hustle out of the door.

One of the perks of being in the Russian mafia and money laundering was our tight ties with the construction business. There wasn't a man in the industry from the owners to the hourly grunts who didn't know who I was.

I walked over to the coffee machine. The acrid, smoky scent of burnt grounds assailed me as I lifted the stained-glass pot with its thick mixture that only slightly resembled coffee sloshing around the bottom. I replaced it on the hot plate, no longer interested.

Just then, the door swung open, bringing with it a much-needed fresh burst of winter air.

Jonathan stepped inside, squinting as his eyes adjusted from the bright sunshine to the flickering artificial fluorescent lights.

The moment he saw me, his eyes widened. "Is it Brynn?"

I raised up a palm. "She's fine."

He visibly relaxed as he reached into his shirt pocket for a pack of cigarettes. He pulled one out and offered me one. They were a cheap American tobacco but since he was soon to be family, I obliged, making a mental note to send him a case of superior *Sobranie Black Russian* cigarettes.

After I accepted a light and blew a cloud of smoke into the already thick air of the trailer, I said, "You shouldn't have left me alone with her."

I was being a bastard.

There was no way I would have allowed him to stay and interfere between me and Brynn, and yet it still bothered me that he left so easily.

It bothered me that before me, she had no one in her life willing to stand their ground and protect her.

It just wasn't fucking right.

Dark shadows of my childhood and my mother threatened to bring the past to the present.

I ruthlessly suppressed them.

He set his hardhat and jacket aside and leaned against the other desk as he looked at his cigarette and then scratched his head.

He looked up at me, both of his eyes bruised from the knock I'd given his nose. "I knew she'd be safe with you."

I shook my head. "I inspire many things, son, but a warm and fuzzy feeling of safety is typically not one of them. I'm generally considered a violent man."

He took a long drag, then blew a smoke ring before responding. "There's a difference between using violence and a violent man. A violent man would have kept hitting me even after learning I was Brynn's cousin."

I smirked. "You're perceptive."

He lowered his head. "Nah, just guilty."

My shoulders tensed as I controlled my temper, waiting for him to explain what he meant by *guilty*.

He took another long drag. "When Brynn came to live with us, after what happened, I was a douchebag teenager caught up in my own bullshit, more concerned with getting my dick wet than getting to know a female cousin I barely knew."

He sighed. "I wasn't … there for her. I should have been, I don't know … a big brother or something to her. By the time I was older and realized it, it was too late. She had shut down. You know what I mean?"

I nodded. I knew exactly what he meant.

He stubbed out his cigarette. "I know you're here for answers and I don't have any for you. You should talk to my mom, her Aunt Janice."

I looked down at the burning ember of my cigarette. "You've been to the Four Monks?"

He looked away as he uttered a nervous laugh. "Yeah, that was an interesting experience."

"So you know who I am—what I am."

There was no point in denying it. I had a dangerous reputation with even more dangerous affiliations.

He stared at me.

"Why are you helping me?" I asked.

He shrugged into his jacket and picked up his hardhat, holding it before him. "As bad as you are—Brynn's piece of shit father is worse. I think it's time she had someone strong enough in her life to protect her from him."

The tension in my shoulders increased as I crushed the cigarette I was holding in my hand, caring little for the sting from the ember against my palm.

He headed for the door. "I have your number. I'll text you my mom's address and let her know you're coming."

As he swung open the door, he turned and looked at me. "Brynn is a good girl. She's deserved better than what life's given her so far."

"And I plan to give it to her."

He nodded and left without another word.

* * *

BRYNN'S AUNT Janice lived out in Joliet in a tidy two-bedroom suburban home.

If she was alarmed at a large, tattooed gangster showing up on her doorstep, she didn't show it.

As the floral-wreathed front door swung open, she greeted me with a warm smile. "You must be Anton. Come in! I just made a pitcher of iced tea."

The kitchen chair creaked as I settled my weight into it at the head of the table.

She placed a tall glass of iced tea and a small plate of sugar cookies in front of me and sat on the chair opposite. She folded her hands in front of her on the braided placemat and met me square in the eye. "So, are you going to kill that bastard who killed my sister and almost killed my precious niece?"

I choked on my sip of iced tea, not expecting such a bloodthirsty request from such a sweet, matronly looking woman. Carefully setting the glass aside, I raised an eyebrow as I took a closer look at her.

Tilting my head to the side, I answered truthfully. "Probably."

She beamed as she reached out and patted my forearm. "Good."

I leaned back in my chair as I rubbed my finger over my lower lip. "Now that we have that settled, would you mind telling me why I'm killing him?"

"That depends; would it be enough that he hurt our Brynn?"

I nodded. "Yes."

She winked as she picked up a sugar cookie and took a bite. "Right again. You should try one, I baked them myself. I add extra cinnamon."

I obliged by selecting a cookie and taking a bite, nodding my appreciation.

She took a sip of her own iced tea. "My son said you want answers. I'm not sure I can give you any about Brynn. She's a sweet girl, but learned the hard way to close herself off from people. I've tried over the years but…."

"Just tell me what happened. I'll work out the rest between Brynn and me."

She patted my forearm again. "I like you. You're stubborn. That will be good for her."

I reached for another cookie, which seemed to please her.

She sighed before she began. "Unfortunately, it's a tragically common story. My sister fell for the wrong man. He was a mean bastard who abused her, probably Brynn as well. He was a drug dealer who got my sister addicted to his dreadful product. We didn't know until it was too late. He had cut her off from her family so we barely saw or heard from her and rarely even saw little Brynn. Then he abandoned them both. Her mother committed suicide over it."

She lowered her head. "I just wish my sister had reached out to me. He left her without a penny and a kid to support. She had no job and no real skills, plus she just couldn't kick the drugs. I guess she just lost hope."

I rubbed my hand over my face as I absorbed all the horror of my girl's childhood. I had already suspected as much, but it didn't make it any easier.

I remained silent, giving her time.

Her mouth curled in a sneer. "He never even married her. He was supposed to after she got pregnant but when she had a little girl, he refused. He berated my sister. Telling her he wanted a son and she couldn't get anything right. Saying he wasn't going to give his name to a pathetic girl."

She took a deep breath. "There was an administrative clerical error for a year after she died, and the courts placed Brynn with a foster family instead of searching for us. Then her father reclaimed her for a month or so. Something happened. I don't know what. Brynn would never say, but that is when she tried to commit suicide."

I clenched my fist as my thoughts went to a *very dark* place.

Her gaze fell on it. She covered my fist with her hand as her gentle eyes consoled me. "Not that, dear. I do know that much. I think he tried the same manipulative, abusive bullshit on her that he did on my sister. I wouldn't be surprised if he even tried to get her addicted to drugs so he could control her like her mother, but our Brynn was too smart for that. I've always gotten the impression he convinced Brynn it was her fault her mother killed herself. That she was too much of a burden, that sort of nasty shit."

She brushed cookie crumbs off the table into her palm and got up to toss them in the sink. "It was actually a twisted blessing in disguise. The hospital she was rushed to had my contact information because of her mother's frequent visits and after a brief time in an institution, the courts allowed Brynn to come live with us."

She turned and leaned against the sink. "We've tried to make her feel like our daughter, but I'm not sure she feels the same. Don't get me wrong. She loves us and she knows we love her, but she's very guarded. And who can blame the poor thing?"

I stood, feeling like a dark primitive force in her cozy kitchen that was filled with cow art and flower wallpaper. "Where is he now?"

She shrugged. "Who knows? That's the terrible thing. He'll disappear, sometimes for years, and then like a nasty penny he'll turn up." She sighed. "He always seems to find Brynn. The last time he threatened to break her arm if she didn't empty out her bank account and give it to him. She was in cosmetology school at the time. She would have had to drop out if he'd made good on his threat."

She crossed to the table and cleared our glasses. "The worst part of that was I didn't even find out about it until she casually mentioned it a year later. She never even told me at the time. Poor little thing just took it on the chin and struggled to find rent and make tuition on her own." She shook her head. "So stubborn. Never asking for help."

"What's the bastard's name?"

"Mark Davies."

I picked up the plate of cookies and carried it over to the sink. "Thank you for taking the time to speak with me."

She placed her hands on my chest as she gazed up

at me. "You're going to protect her from him, aren't you? You're going *to take care of him*. That's why you're here, right? Because you love her."

I stared down into her worried eyes, years of anxious fear etched into their depths. Laying a hand on her shoulder, I reassured her. "Yes, Janice. That's exactly why I'm here."

"Good. I could tell you were the right man for her."

I smirked. "You and your son are strange judges of characters."

She gave me a dismissive wave. "The criminal thing? What do I care? What did the police do to protect my sister? What has the law done to protect my niece? They had their chance. You fight fire with fire. Only a man not afraid of the devil would know how to kill him. The man ruined my sister's life and he is ruining Brynn's life too."

My gaze narrowed. "Not anymore, he isn't. You have my word."

She fisted my sweater in her hands. "Don't make our same mistake. Don't let her close you out. Don't let her push you away. Hold on to her. She's worth it."

"Trust me, nothing on this earth, *including her*, will convince me to let her go."

Especially now that I had the ammunition I needed to go into battle against her demons.

CHAPTER 25

BRYNN

I lifted my tearstained face as a warm hand rested on my shoulder, unwilling to accept the dizzying rush of relief that washed over me, knowing Anton hadn't left.

That I hadn't managed to fuck up and chase off the first man who truly seemed to care about me.

Rubbing my eyes, I pushed my hair away from my face as I blinked my eyes into focus.

The crushing disappointment was like a physical blow.

It wasn't Anton's stubborn, handsome face staring down at me, but *Tetya* Polina's kindly, concerned one.

Unable to stop myself, my face crumbled on a sob as I buried it in my forearms where they rested on the bench seat of the gazebo. I hadn't moved from my kneeling position after feeling Anton's goodbye kiss on my forehead.

She patted my back. "I don't mean to sound critical, kitten, but this ... is not a good look for you."

"Heeees guuoon. Iees mif feelt. So stupid," I sobbed against the seat cushion.

She sat next to me. "Get off the floor. It is not ladylike," she scolded.

I climbed onto the bench and slouched down as I leaned my head back. "I'm so confused. I know I've made the smart decision. The safe decision, but—" I gave myself a mental shake. "No, this is silly. I made the right decision. I'm just having a momentary ... *moment*. I'm fine."

Tetya Polina cast me a side-eyed glance then laughed so hard her usually tight bun loosened. A cascade of thick black hair tumbled down over her shoulders.

I frowned. "What's so funny?"

Reaching her elegant arms high over her head, she twisted her thick ponytail and wrapped it back into a bun, securing it with a sterling silver sword-shaped hairpin.

She rolled her eyes at me as she pierced her hair with the razor-sharp point. "You."

I sat up straighter as I swiped at the remnants on my cheeks and smoothed the wrinkles from my sweater. "What about me?"

She leaned back as she cast her dark cat eyeliner gaze over me. "You don't seriously think Antonius just meekly took you at your word and walked away, do you?"

I smoothed my tangled hair over one shoulder to hide my sudden uncertainty. "I think ... he ... respected my decision ... yes."

She patted my knee and laughed again. "He is right, you really are adorable."

I huffed as I slammed my palms down on either side of my hips. "I'm sorry but I don't understand the humor in this."

She stood and ran her hands over her hips. "You will. Now, come."

I slumped back. "I'm not in a mood to be cheered up or go shopping right now."

She placed her hands on her waist. "Good, because I wasn't offering either of those things. I'm going to put you to work." She raised an eyebrow. "That is what you keep saying you want, isn't it? To work? To be useful?"

I stood. "Yes. What do you need?"

"You'll see. Come."

As I fell into step next to her, I continued to insist, "I really am making the right decision, you know. Anton and I won't work. He wants a completely different kind of woman. I'm never going *to be* that type of woman."

The silk lining of her tight figure-hugging skirt swished as she elegantly led the way down the stairs and through a series of hallways and doors. All while remaining silent.

A silence I continued to try to fill. "He knows it too. That's why he walked away. We are both being responsible adults in this. We are cutting it off before either of us gets in too deep and gets hurt."

She cast me a dark look as her red lips thinned but still said nothing.

I sighed. "I really wish you would *say* something."

She held open a door for me as she waved an arm for me to proceed first. "You seem to have it all figured out with all the answers. What could I possibly add?"

I gave her a curt nod as we entered a back corner of what seemed to be Four Monks' commercial kitchen space that served its upstairs restaurant. "Good. I'm glad we are agreed."

She chuckled. "Oh, kitten. I didn't say we were agreed."

A beautiful woman in a chef's coat came bouncing up to us. "Is this her?"

Tetya Polina nodded. "This is her, although she is currently denying it."

Another gorgeous woman dressed casually but expensively, with an adorable baby boy on her hip playing with the eye-popping diamond choker around her neck, approached. "Didn't we all?"

A third woman dressed like a sexy gothic librarian, pushing a baby carriage with a bundle of pink and lace inside, closed the distance. "I didn't. Technically, I don't think I was given a choice!"

They all laughed.

Before I could ask what was happening, another woman with arresting crystal blue eyes carrying an SLR camera appeared, as if out of nowhere, over my shoulder. "Hold on! I want to capture this!"

All the women smiled, and she fired off a few snaps, then she turned to me. "You too, jump in there. You're one of us now."

One of us now?

Why are they making it sound like a cult?

Confused, I looked to *Tetya* Polina.

She wrapped her arm around my waist and pulled me to the edge of the friendly group of women.

The woman with the camera called out, "Say *syer*!"

They all called out, "*Syer!*" Which I could only assume was Russian for cheese.

The woman in the chef's coat burst out, "Crap! My dough water is boiling over!"

She circled around the large stainless-steel table to the stove top where a large pot was hissing as water hit the open gas flame.

The gothic librarian approached me as she unwound her scarf from her neck. "Hi, I'm Emma. I'm married to Dimitri. He's one of Anton's oldest friends." She pointed to the woman in the chef's coat.

"Over there fussing with the pot is Carinna, an amazing pastry chef. She is dating Maxim who works for…." She turned in a circle and found the elegantly dressed woman who was handing her baby boy to *Tetya* Polina. "Dylan's husband, Ivan."

The woman with the camera waved her hand to indicate that we should stand together.

Emma pressed her cheek to mine and smiled as she took a picture, then held out her hand. "And I'm Katie. I'm married to Luka."

I shook her hand and smiled weakly. "It's very nice to meet you all. I'm sorry, I didn't mean to intrude on your family thing. I'll just go."

Dylan pushed her arm through my elbow. "You're family now, too. We're being pressed into service by Carinna and *Tetya* Polina to make homemade *pelmeni*."

"What is *pelmeni?*"

Tetya Polina looked up from the baby she was cradling in her arms. "It is traditional Russian dumpling. Very good."

Katie chimed in. "They are cooked in huge batches in winter because they freeze well. It will be fun. Is Mary coming?" she asked Emma.

Emma looked up from tucking the blanket more firmly around her babygirl. She raised an eyebrow. "For a cooking activity? You're not serious? No. She's torturing Vaska at a tequila tasting event at some funky new restaurant on Morgan Street."

Carinna leaned over the stainless-steel table and tossed white aprons to everyone. "Put these on. *Tetya* Polina, if you want to start with the filling?"

Tetya Polina nodded as she placed the baby in a small pen Dylan had set up in the corner.

I watched as Carinna added salt and several cups of flour to the boiling water and butter mixture and stirred it with a large wooden spoon. She then slid it off the heat. After transferring it to a standing mixer, she cracked several eggs into it and added more flour. She then wrapped a damp towel over the top and started the process over again with another pot of water and butter.

Emma nudged me with her elbow as she twisted the ties of her apron over her waist. "Put on your apron. Trust me. The flour is going to get everywhere."

I turned so I wasn't facing the group. My cheeks burned as I whispered, "There's been a mistake."

Her sweet brown eyes so close in color to my own looked at me in understanding. With a decisive nod, she whispered back, "Come with me."

She then said louder, "Brynn and I are going to go sneak some wine from the front bar before the bartenders arrive for their shift."

I was a little surprised she already knew my name since in the flurry of introductions, I couldn't recall it being mentioned.

Had Anton talked about me to them and their husbands and boyfriends?

Dylan smiled. "Good idea."

Tetya Polina winked. "The good stuff is in the wine cooler on the right. We already have glasses back here."

"We're almost ready to start the first batch of dough," called out Carinna. "Don't be long!"

I followed Emma out of the kitchen. Like errant teenagers, we scurried down the hallway, trying to avoid the security guards and staff and snuck into the main poker room.

It was odd to be in the majestic ballroom with its massive crystal chandeliers and elegant green velvet and mahogany gambling tables when it was silent and empty.

My gaze was drawn to the table where Yuri had been sitting that fateful night.

Barely a week ago.

The night my entire life was sent into a topsy-turvy tailspin.

I wrapped an arm around my waist, pressing my palm against the spot on my hip where Anton's hand first touched me.

You're in big trouble, little one.

He had growled it into my ear.

I bit my lip. I had thought he meant with the police.

I wished I had known he had meant my heart.

My attention was drawn back to Emma as she wandered behind the bar. She grabbed a few bottles of wine but then placed two shot glasses on the bar top. She then unscrewed the cap off a bottle of Jose Cuervo Tequila and poured two shots.

I grimaced. "It's a little early."

She waved me off. "It's eight hours later in Russia right now and we're practically standing on their sovereign territory. The Four Monks might as well be a Russian embassy."

She raised the shot glass and laughed. "To being the heroine of your own story!"

I smiled. "That's a great toast."

We both took our shots.

I choked as the cheap tequila burned my throat. "God, that's awful. I'm surprised a place like the Four Monks even carries it."

She screwed the cap back on. "Vaska makes them for Mary."

She leaned her elbows on the bar and pointed in two different directions behind me. "There is an exit to the right and left, but I have to warn you ... you won't get far."

I stilled. Was she threatening me?

She tossed the dirty shot glasses in the sink. "You're in love with him."

I frowned. "No offense. You seem really nice, but you don't know me."

She leaned back on the bar. "That's fair. Let me

put it a different way. I *have* gotten to know Anton, through my husband. And he's a pretty amazing guy, so I find it hard to believe that a woman *wouldn't* be in love with him."

I lowered my head as I tucked a lock of hair behind my ear, not really wanting to answer.

She continued, "Especially if it was stupidly obvious that he was in love with her."

My gaze shot up to lock with hers. "What makes you say that?"

She rolled her eyes. "You're lucky we're in here and not in front of the others for this conversation or they would have bombarded you with stories. Let's just say … for as scary and dangerous as our Russian men can be … they have some *predictable* patterns when it comes to the women they fall in love with."

I helped her gather the wine bottles as we started back to the kitchen. "Like what?"

"Stubborn. Possessive. Jealous. Pretend not to understand the English word no. Arrogant. Demanding. Bossy as hell."

My mouth fell open. "Oh. My. God. Yes! Yes to *all* of that!"

"The good news is, with all that bluster and testosterone also comes fierce loyalty. Undying love. Devotion. Strength. Unwavering support. Protection. And mind-blowing sex," she winked.

My cheeks flamed. "Yeah, I'm not sure I signed up

for all that. We really only just met and I've spent half the time fighting with or running from him."

She turned and pressed her back against one of the doors to open it. "Well, I hope I didn't make you feel less special, but trust me, it's kind of *a truth universally acknowledged that a single Russian man in possession of a good fortune who finds the woman he wants will pursue her with a singular obsessive purpose,*" she quipped, paraphrasing Jane Austen.

We were nearing the kitchen so I needed to talk fast. "That's what I wanted to tell you. You are all being so nice and welcoming, but I'm afraid I broke it off with him this morning. Things were just getting too intense, too quickly. I just don't want you and the others to have the wrong idea about Anton and me."

She stopped just outside the kitchen door and stared at me.

I frowned since this was the second silent reaction to my declaration of independence from the great Antonius Ivenchenko.

Finally, Emma burst out laughing. "Anton was right. You *are* adorable!"

For the love of....

ALL OF US women had settled into a finely tuned dumpling assembly line, as Dylan used a biscuit cutter to cut out the three-inch-wide circles, then Emma placed careful scoops of golden-brown ground pork and onion filling.

Tetya Polina and I would then carefully fold the circles in half and crimp the edges.

Carinna then scooped them up and tossed them straight into a pot of boiling water with some bay leaf and peppercorns. Others she flash fried until they were a crisp golden brown on both sides for us to enjoy right then and there.

Into this cozy atmosphere stormed Anton.

My heart seized the moment I saw his handsome face.

All baking activity stopped as his intense, masculine energy immediately changed the casual mood.

Ignoring everyone, his dark gaze zeroed in on me and me alone.

Without preamble, he declared, "I've been to see your aunt. I know all about your father and I'm going to handle it for you. So there should be no more issues with you doing as I say, and staying right here, and no longer working."

I blinked, too stunned to speak.

There was a scuffling of feet as my new girlfriends shifted to circle protectively around me.

I could hear Emma say under her breath, "Oh, Anton, you didn't."

Katie murmured, "Holy shit, she's going to murder him."

At the same time, Carinna whispered, "Does anyone know if she owns a gun?"

Dylan groaned, "This feels like Ivan's bad advice."

Tetya Polina sighed. "Oh, dear, *mishka,* I certainly hope you have a plan B."

CHAPTER 26

ANTON

"*P*ut me down," cried Brynn.

Plan B.

I kicked the doors leading out of the kitchen to the labyrinth of staff hallways, secretly designed to also confuse any attacker should anyone be stupid enough to try.

I thought about taking her to my private office but decided this was a conversation for the penthouse.

As I rounded a corner, I encountered Dimitri, Maxim, and Ivan.

They didn't so much as raise an eyebrow at seeing me with a screaming woman slung over my shoulder.

Maxim pointed beyond me. "Are we in time for some warm *pelmeni?*"

I motioned with my chin. "Your girl is taking them out of the pan now."

Maxim rubbed his hands together. "Good, I'm starving."

Ivan said, "I see you took my advice. Good man! We already saw Mac. He's waiting for us downstairs." His lips twisted in a sardonic grin. "Should I tell him you're occupied?"

Brynn took that opportunity to try to bite my back.

I spanked her ass for her troubles. "Give me thirty."

"Ow! You beast! I hate you!"

I spanked her ass again. "Better make it an hour."

He nodded as he followed Maxim toward the kitchen.

Dimitri circled around and bent in half to look up at Brynn's flushed face. "You must be Brynn. Welcome to the family."

He then slapped me on the shoulder and followed the others down the hall.

Brynn called out, "For the last time! I'm not family!"

"You are if I have anything to say about it," I growled as I headed toward my private elevator.

The moment the door opened, I swung her forward, wrapping her legs around my waist and pinning her to the elevator wall as I slammed my fist against the button for the penthouse.

Twisting my hand into the fabric of her sweater, I

lowered my head until my lips were skimming hers. "Tell me again that you hate me," I dared.

She whimpered.

My mouth claimed hers.

My tongue swept inside, tasting the sweetness of the wine she had been sipping all afternoon. The moment I heard the ping, I grasped her around the waist and backed out, just as the doors slid silently open on my floor, still keeping my mouth on hers.

I crashed into the entry table, sending the center floral vase tumbling to the floor. Rose-scented water flowed over the black marble as I kicked the glass shards aside, uncaring, as I carried her to the bedroom.

The moment I set her down on the bed, she broke free.

Pushing her mass of curls back from her face, she then held both arms out to ward me off. "Wait. We're not doing this!"

Without acknowledging her threat, I pulled my sweater over my head and tossed it aside as I kicked off my boots. "Take off your clothes."

"You're not listening. We. Broke. Up."

"No, you tried to leave me, a status to our relationship I reject."

She raced across the bedroom to the lounge area in front of the fireplace, stepping behind one of the tufted chairs as she continued to defy me. "I reject your rejection!"

My fingers flipped open the top button to my jeans. They slipped low on my hips. "Noted and denied. I'm losing patience, Brynn. Take off your clothes, before I tear them off."

She threw her arms up into the air. "This is not how a couple settles an argument!"

I smirked as I tilted my head, gazing at her through a lowered brow. "This is how Russians do."

Her hand rubbed her forehead. "I can't believe you went to see my aunt behind my back."

Two steps to the right had me circling around her position, caging her in. "You left me no choice."

She raised a pointed finger at me. "No. I left you with a choice you didn't like."

I shrugged. "Same difference."

She huffed as she pounded the back of the chair. "It *so* is not!"

"In case you are wondering, I have your aunt's blessing."

She frowned. "Her blessing? For what?"

My gaze rested on her, studying her reaction. "What do you think?"

She blinked several times as she broke my gaze. Then her eyes widened. "Oh, my God. You didn't tell her we were *getting married*, did you?"

"No."

Her shoulders sagged as she visibly relaxed.

I continued casually, "Although we are, and soon."

She leaned over the chair. "What? What part of *broken up* don't you understand?"

I smirked. "All of it."

Her hand rubbed over her forehead again, then her eyes as she shook her head. "So if you didn't mention marriage, then what do you have her blessing for?"

As she was distracted, I stalked two more steps closer, almost within arm's reach. "To kill your father."

She staggered back, hitting the back of her head on the edge of the fireplace mantel.

The moment she raised her hand to check for an injury and turned to see what she had collided with, I pounced.

Snatching her around the waist, I dragged her out from behind the chair and secured her arms behind her back as she struggled. "My father is my problem."

I pulled her flush against my chest. "Wrong, baby-girl. Your father *was* your problem. *Now I'm his.*"

Her eyes filled with tears as she lowered her head. "Anton, look, I don't want you involved. It's messy and ugly and it's a part of my life I'm not proud of, my father…"

With both of her wrists anchored at her lower back in one of mine, I used my right hand to tilt her chin back to force her to look at me. "No longer exists to you. I'm your *daddy* now," I growled.

It was twisted to mix a fun sex game with family, but in this instance, it applied.

I wasn't just the man who pulled her hair, spanked her ass, and made her call him Daddy for kinks.

I was also the man who would fiercely protect his babygirl from anything ... and anyone ... who threatened her happiness.

I captured her mouth, swallowing any protest, my gut knotting as I tasted the salt of her tears.

My thumb stroked her swollen lower lip after pulling back. "Claw. Scratch. Fight. Run. Scream. Do whatever you need to do, babygirl. Push me away a thousand times." I released her wrists and cupped her cheeks, brushing away the tears. "Just try not to be surprised when I kick down that door a thousand and one times to get you back."

Her head shook. "If I learned anything from my childhood, promises like that from a man don't mean anything."

I winked. "How many times do I have to tell you? I'm no ordinary man. I am a Russian man and yes, it is an iron-clad promise."

Intent on kissing her again, I leaned down, but she turned her head at the last minute.

Her head bowed under my arm as she scampered across the room out of my reach. "You're doing it again. Trying to charm and distract me with promises and words."

She raised up her palms as she reached the other

side of the room. "I've already told you. This isn't about you. It's me. It's a self-preservation thing. Trust me. You're better off."

I crossed to the arched wrought-iron and oak bedroom doors and slammed them closed.

Her eyes widened. "What are you doing?"

With my gaze trained on her, I reached behind me and locked them.

The heavy metallic thunk of the bolt sliding in place had her stepping back. "Anton?"

I reached for the zipper of my jeans. "Since I haven't been truly counting up until this point—*one*."

CHAPTER 27

BRYNN

*T*he backs of my thighs hit the footboard. "One?"

One as in the first out of a thousand times.

As in this stubborn, domineering, arrogant, controlling… amazing, caring, wonderful, sexy AF Russian man was not going to give up on me, no matter how hard, or how many times, I tried to push him away.

"Take off your clothes."

I shook my hands in front of me. "Stop saying that."

"Take off your clothes and I'll stop saying it."

I shoved my hands into my hair as I paced in front of the bed. "Wait. Just wait. I need to think."

Could this be real?

Was it possible?

There were literally thousands of books and

movies dedicated to the outlandish possibility of finding love like a bolt of lightning on a clear spring day. So it wasn't that insane to think that maybe our feelings for each other were genuine.

And no man I'd ever been with had ever—*ever*—put in nearly this much effort to stay with me.

A man would almost *have* to be in love to go to all the trouble Anton had.

My brow furrowed as I looked up at him.

He tapped the side of his head with his finger. "That is the problem. You think too much."

My gaze traveled over his powerful frame, covered in colorful violent imagery.

He was literally a walking billboard for action over words.

I waved my hand in his direction. "You couldn't possibly understand what I'm feeling. To you danger and risk are a rush … a high … *a freaking resume builder*. It's not the same for me. The consequences are *way* different."

He lowered his head as his gaze slowly wandered over me. Rubbing two fingers along his jaw, he seemed to consider my argument. "I will give you one month to get used to the idea you are to be my wife. You live here and I am a silent investor in your new salon with five percent of the profits. No men."

Was this?

Could this be?

No….

Maybe?

Was it possible?

Was Anton … *compromising*?

For me?

My heart leapt.

In that moment … that precise moment …

I knew I wasn't half in love this man.

I was fully head over heels.

Stupidly.

At risk.

Danger ahead.

Wave the white flag.

I submit.

Take me, I'm yours.

In love with him.

I slipped my lips between my teeth to try to hide my smile. Reaching for the hem of my sweater, I pulled it over my head. "Six months. I live at my own place paying my own rent, but I'll promise no more roommate. Standard for an angel investor is twenty-two percent. I don't want special treatment and it is literally against American law to turn away men."

His voice lowered to a growl as he stalked toward me. "Two months. Ten percent and you live in a place I choose. I pay. No men. I don't give a damn what the law is in America. That is what I have expensive lawyers for, to twist the law."

I slipped my yoga pants and panties off my hips and kicked them aside. "Three months. Eighteen percent. I live where you choose but I pay half the bills. Men, but my staff caters to them."

He shirked off his jeans. "Ten weeks. Fifteen percent. I'll let you buy the groceries. You don't even look at the men that enter that salon," he growled as he stalked within arm's reach of me.

I unhooked my bra, excited but a little nervous at his hungry look as his gaze focused on my curves. "So do you need me to sign something?"

His warm hands snatched me around the waist. The hot, hard press of his cock against my naked stomach sent a shiver of fearful anticipation up my spine as he wrapped his hand around the side of my throat and leaned in close. "I just need that mouth to say yes."

It was now or never.

Adrenaline coursed through my blood, making me lightheaded.

It was as if I were standing on the prow of a ship staring at a bright horizon full of beguiling and tempting promise ahead while also painfully aware that the tiniest slip could mean a tumble into a black stormy abyss of nothingness, of pain and betrayal.

A rushing noise filled my ears as I stared into his dark gray eyes, lost in their stormy ocean depths.

I took a deep breath and held it for second and then said, "Yes."

His response was immediate, overwhelming, and fierce.

After claiming my mouth in a searing kiss that made me feel as if I had truly just signed away my soul to the devil himself, he lifted me off the floor and flipped me onto my back on the bed until my head was hanging just off the side.

"Open your throat for Daddy."

I had flashbacks to the first night we met. Me draped over his desk like a pagan sacrifice and him commanding just this submission.

I licked my lips before lowering my jaw and tilting my head back as I stared up at him.

He laid his palms on either side of my head as he stepped closer. The rough hair on his thighs brushed my cheeks as the head of his cock pushed against my lips.

I sucked a deep breath in through my nose as I closed my eyes, tasting the salty tang of his skin on my tongue.

He slid in several inches.

My hips bucked.

HIs hands moved to grasp my breasts, teasing my nipples.

I whimpered as I sucked his cock harder.

"Good girl."

His praise sent a delicious spike of twisted pleasure straight between my thighs.

My hand moved to tease my own clit, but before my fingertips could find the nub, Anton's large grip enclosed around my hips and lifted me off the mattress.

With his cock still deep in my mouth, he curled my body upward toward him, placing the tops of my thighs on his shoulders.

We were a standing sixty-nine.

With my shoulders resting on the mattress, his cock slipped a little deeper, into my throat, as he wrapped his arms around my thighs and nestled his face between them.

He then flicked his tongue over my already sensitive clit, applying just the right amount of pressure.

He swirled his tongue around the nub several times before growling, "You better suck my cock hard and fast, babygirl, because I'm not pulling back until you come."

Oh, God.

With that warning, he thrust deep down my throat, choking me.

Tears streamed down my cheeks as I struggled to swallow his thick girth, all the while wave after wave of tremors ran up my spine as he tortured my clit with soft and hard, fast and slow, perfectly timed swirls and flicks.

At first it was hard to concentrate on giving him pleasure while also receiving it, but after a few moments I learned to time the movement of my tongue with the pulses of sensation.

After that I finally did what Anton asked ... I stopped thinking and just felt.

I felt his touch. His skin. His heartbeat.

I felt us.

Together.

It was as if time stood still.

My throat relaxed even further and he slid in deeper still. There was a strange sense of pride, taking his shaft so deep inside my throat. My jaw ached and my cheeks burned from the salt of my tears but it was worth it.

In that moment, I let go.

My thighs clenched around the corded muscles of his neck.

He held me tighter as his fingers dug into my soft skin.

The tip of his tongue pressed and held against my clit as he pushed three fingers deep inside of me.

As my hips bucked, he pulled me closer against the warmth of his chest.

Bright bursts of light and color exploded behind my eyelids, probably from both my intense orgasm and lack of oxygen as I'd become so lost in my own pleasure I'd choked myself deep on his cock as he hugged me close. The little death as they used to call it.

Anton released my legs and they fell back to the bed.

He pulled free from my mouth as he reached for my waist.

Lifting me as he lay on his back on the bed, he had me straddle his hips.

"Sit on my cock," he ordered roughly.

I reached between us and grasped his shaft. Placing the head at my entrance, I gingerly lowered myself onto him, my mouth opening as he stretched me with each painful inch.

"That's it, baby. That's it. Keep going."

I bit my lip as I pushed my hips down. Despite having just come and being incredibly slick, I was still really tight and he was still really big. Slowly my body adjusted to his thick cock and opened for him as, inch by inch, he pushed deeper into me.

I pressed my palms onto his flat stomach as I clenched my jaw and rocked my hips back and forth.

He reached up and wrapped his hand around my throat. "Eyes on me."

His other hand pressed into my hip. "Your choice, baby. Do you want to be in control? Or do you want me to take over?"

I stared down at him.

It was strange.

I was on top, and yet he was still the one with all the power.

But he was offering it to me.

Did I want it?

I kept saying I wanted it.

I thought I wanted it.

Yet at the same time, I couldn't deny it was really nice having someone else in control every once in a while, to have someone else watching over me, taking care of me, *giving a damn about me.*

I pressed my fingertips into his abdomen as I ground my hips down on his shaft. "Maybe, just this once—"

His weight was pressing me into the mattress before I finished the sentence.

"—am I going to regret this?"

"Never," he vowed, and he wasn't just talking about tonight as he thrust hard and fast into me.

CHAPTER 28

ANTON

*M*ac looked up from lighting his cigar as I entered the private poker room. "Did you get enough beauty sleep?"

"Shut the fuck up."

He winked and finished lighting his cigar.

In the center of the poker table, neatly arranged on the lush green velvet, were eight gleaming gold bars. I quickly calculated the math in my head; at four hundred troy ounces a bar, it was roughly five million United States dollars' worth.

Dimitri looked up at me while he effortlessly broke the card deck into four sections and shuffled it in a flourishing Z formation, executing a perfect Sybil cut, a leftover from our professional gambling days. It was all flash and showmanship … and a complete con. When you were done shuffling, despite it looking like the deck had been completely tossed, all the cards were in the exact same order they were from the start.

He raised an eyebrow. "A gift from our friendly dictator."

Varlaam leaned back in his chair as he blew a perfect smoke ring. "*Durakam zakon ne pisan.*"

No law is written for fools, an old Russian proverb.

I took a seat. "If we keep it, there could be problems."

Maxim rolled a custom Four Monks poker chip over his knuckles. "If we don't, then how will he learn his lesson?"

No one in the room wanted to make an enemy of a peevish, immature dictator. They were a pain in the ass when they got their feelings hurt.

Mac rolled his cigar along the edge of the heavy crystal ashtray, careful to not disturb the burning ash. "Dimitri, he was happy with the weapons exchange?"

Dimitri shuffled the card deck with one hand as he nodded. "Very. Vaska is arranging for a shipment of 2K12 Kubs and a sizable *donation* to his favorite charity next week. The problem is he wants your services."

I exchanged a look with Mac and Varlaam before shaking my head. "I don't like it. I agree with Maxim. We keep the money because of the audacity of it and fuck him."

Ivan poured himself a drink. "It's been awhile

since I sent my boys out into the field. We could cross the border and poke around in his country, see if he's a threat? Use it as a training exercise."

We all nodded in agreement.

Mac leaned forward. "Now that's settled, I have a personal matter that needs to be addressed."

I closed my right hand into a fist.

I knew why I was here, why we were all here, why I was being dragged away from my girl's side. Yuri, that ungrateful piece of shit.

Mac rubbed his eyes. "Serg has confirmed it. He's not just on drugs. He's fucking selling them."

We all leaned back in our chairs.

Fuck.

We didn't get involved in drugs or human trafficking. Period.

No exceptions.

And just because Yuri was technically not part of our business did not mean there wouldn't be blowback on us. There was very little chance he wasn't trading on our reputations out on the street to build up his little drug hustle.

Mac continued, "Look, gentlemen, I know the rules."

Ivan placed his hand on Mac's shoulder. "Fuck the rules, Mac. He's still your nephew. We're not going to kill him."

Mac visibly relaxed.

He would have accepted the group's decision if

Yuri had to be dealt with in that manner. It wasn't just that he had broken the rules and risked our organization.

There was a reason why we didn't deal in drugs. Drugs made people unstable, untrustworthy, and unpredictable, several things that were not good for business.

And while killing them may seem unsympathetic, usually it was more a matter of being pragmatic, since second chances usually turned into third, fourth, and fifth chances with a drug addict and we had neither the time nor the patience for that kind of bullshit.

Especially since the drug trade came with violence.

As backward as it may sound, arms dealing, gambling, and money laundering were all still gentlemen crimes. There were rules, an etiquette to how things were done.

Drugs were messy.

As I said, unstable, unpredictable, and untrustworthy.

The kind we wanted no part of.

Ivan shrugged. "We're still going to send the little *mudak* to a military camp in Siberia where he can learn some manners, though. I haven't forgotten the bullshit he pulled with my girl."

Another failed attempt on Mac's part to put his nephew on a better path. He set him up as an intern at Dylan's real estate firm. That lasted for about two weeks, until Ivan learned Yuri had made copies of the keys of vacant penthouses and was using them for parties. If it had been found out by her select clientele, it would have ruined her reputation.

Yuri was lucky Ivan didn't kill him then.

Keeping a watchful eye on Mac, I said, "There is a complication. He got a girl pregnant. She's pretty far along. I'd say at least eight months."

Mac raised his cigar to his mouth. "No freaking way she goes to Russia with him. I'd bet on it. My plan is to pay her off after my grandniece or nephew is born."

I nodded. "Good plan. So Yuri?"

Maxim leaned forward. "We know he's dealing, which means we need to send a clear message on the street that it was without our permission."

Dimitri set the card deck aside. "So a decisive strike. Something with lots of flash so it gets noticed. Kill his main supplier. Send a message."

Maxim pointed at him. "Exactly. We're thinking tomorrow. No point in waiting."

I looked around the table. "Do we know the supplier's name?"

Mac shook his head. "Serg couldn't find out, which means it must be some low-level player. We caught this early, which is the only bright spot. We do know the exchange is happening in the back of a bar in Streeterville. He's supposed to pick up two kilos of product, twice his usual, so he's ramping up."

We all stood.

Dimitri slapped Mac on the back. "Until tomorrow, my friend. I will make the arrangements."

Ivan cupped him around the neck and pressed his forehead to his. "Don't worry. My men will whip him into shape in Siberia. He will come back a better man, a good man, and a proper father to your new grandnephew!"

I smirked. "Or niece."

Maxim rolled his eyes. "*Yolki-palki,* please let it be a boy. We have our hands full with all these beautiful girl babies as it is. We will need a small army to keep the men away!"

As we exited the room, uncaring about the five million in gold bars still remaining on the table, Ivan placed his arm over my shoulder. "I hear you may need a place to stay for a bit."

I frowned. "How the fuck—?"

He gestured with his head over his shoulder. "The girls over *pelmeni* hinted that you may need to leave the Four Monks for a bit to placate your girl. You should use my penthouse off Michigan Avenue. It's been empty for months after Dylan and I bought that estate on the North Shore right before the baby."

I shouldered the door open as I considered his offer.

It was perfect.

I wouldn't be purchasing a new place and therefore Brynn would not feel obligated to help with the mortgage or rent.

We could move in there for a month or two while I accustomed her to the inescapable fact that she would be my wife and mother of my children.

"I accept your offer."

He pulled his key ring out of his pocket, slid two silver keys off the ring, and handed them to me. "Building doorman's name is Robert."

* * *

THE MOMENT the elevator doors opened, I was greeted with the scents and sounds of a home.

In the kitchen, I found a humming Brynn.

She looked up as I entered. "I hope you're hungry!"

"You cooked? For me?"

I couldn't recall a single woman since my mother who had ever cooked for me, outside of someone I was paying to do so.

She slipped two oven mitts on. "Don't get too excited. It's just Hot Dish."

I stepped up behind her and took the oven mitts off her hands as I placed them on my own, not wanting her to handle a hot pan, and pulled down the oven door. "What is Hot Dish?"

I surveyed the dubious-looking item in the oven.

She looked around my shoulder. "Tater Tot Casserole."

Grateful she could not see my face, I reached inside for the glass dish and pulled it out. In the time I had been living in America, I had successfully avoided the amalgamation of baked leftovers Americans affectionately called a *casserole*, probably by never being close enough to a woman to have her want to cook for me before.

I swung around and placed the dish on the marble counter as I stared down at the sizzling round orbs of greasy brown floating on top of what looked like ground beef soup. "What are Tater Tots? And is this what they are supposed to look like?"

Her mouth dropped open. "You can't be serious? You've never had a Tater Tot?"

She picked up one of the greasy brown orbs with her two fingers and juggled it a little as she said in a mock deep voice, "Open. Your. Mouth."

Raising an eyebrow, I gave her ass a playful spank, which was muted since I still had the damn oven mitt on. "Is that supposed to be me?"

She stuck out her tongue.

"Don't tease, unless you want me to take you up on that offer," I warned.

After a resigned sigh, I opened my mouth. She popped the still piping hot Tater Tot in my mouth.

I talked around it as the molten hot ball of grease

sizzled on my tongue. "Am I supposed to taste something other than salt and lard?"

"Hey, that's the taste of 'merica you're makin' fun of there, commie!" she teased in an exaggerated Southern accent.

As it cooled I slowly chewed. "It is not bad. It is like a latke but with less flavor."

She shoved my hip with hers as she cut the casserole with a spoon and dished it out onto two plates.

It didn't improve.

I swallowed as my stomach clenched, bracing for what was to come.

When she looked up at me, I smiled as I took the plates and brought them over to the table that was already set.

As I pulled out her chair for her, I asked, "What goes best with Hot Dish? A red or white wine?"

She tilted her head back to glare at me. "Stop being a prude."

I kissed her on the forehead. "Red it is."

I opened a bottle of Silver Oak Cabernet and poured us both a glass before joining her.

As we toasted, I said, "Thank you for making dinner. It was very nice coming home to a meal and a beautiful woman."

She took a sip and then laid her napkin on her lap. "Wait until you try it before you thank me."

I waited until she picked up her own fork before picking up mine.

After she took a bite, I judged it safe and did the same.

It wasn't bad.

She laughed. "Try not to look so surprised."

I wiped my mouth with a napkin. "You're right. I'm sorry. You have to admit. It didn't look like much."

"Fair point. We didn't have much growing up and Hot Dish was sort of a staple meal you could always make for cheap out of a can of soup, some hamburger meat, and a cheap bag of Tater Tots. Once my mom... well... once the drugs started to take hold, I learned to make it for myself, so I sort of survived on it for much of my childhood. It's pretty much the only thing I know how to make."

I covered her hand with mine. "Thank you for sharing it with me. I was not fortunate enough to have such memories with my mother. I think I would like to share yours if you'd let me."

Her eyes teared up. "I'd like that. I've avoided talking about her for so long. It'd be nice to start reminding myself about all the good stuff and really there was a lot of good stuff ... before the bad."

I held up a forkful of Tater Tots and mystery stew. "Starting with Hot Dish."

She laughed. "You don't have to eat it. We could call down to the restaurant or I could scramble some eggs."

I chewed and scraped my fork against the plate

for another bite. "Are you crazy? This is better than the foie gras of chicken with cèpes mushrooms at the Turandot Restaurant in Moscow and that is a high compliment."

"You're a terrible liar."

I winked at her. "I'll have you know I've made billions of dollars with this poker face."

She rested her chin on her hand. "Then they were all fools. Apparently all it takes to short wire you is a bad meal."

I leaned over and kissed her forehead.

We continued to eat in companionable silence for a few minutes.

It was nice.

Domestic.

Cozy.

I looked up and smiled at her as I forced myself to swallow another large bite of the actually fairly awful Hot Dish. It was just a salt bomb of grease and meat, but for her, I would eat every fucking bite and like it because I wanted to show her that we made sense as a couple.

As husband and wife.

That we could sit down and have a civil meal together.

A civil conversation.

That we could actually go a full twenty minutes without fighting or fucking.

After I had taken another bite, I remembered the

penthouse keys to Ivan's place and pulled them out of my pocket. "As to our agreement, I've arranged for us to stay at a friend's place."

She stared at the keys on the table between our plates. "So you … just arranged it? Without thinking that maybe I might have an opinion or want to see it first?"

Crap.

She put her fork to the side.

I slowly put my fork to the side as well.

Weapons down.

Her beautiful eyes iced over as her gaze narrowed.

I raised one eyebrow as I spoke slowly and deliberately. "You have a choice to make … Fight? Or fuck?"

The space between my shoulders tensed as I waited and watched, gauging her reaction.

She placed both palms on the table and rose with a huff. "This time I stay on top the whole time," she declared as she stormed down the hallway.

I smirked.

We'd see about that.

CHAPTER 29

BRYNN

*A*s I looked out over the magnificent view of Lake Michigan through the panoramic windows, I shrugged. "It's nice, I suppose."

The place was freaking gorgeous, but I wasn't going to give him the satisfaction of saying so. Unlike the somber, almost medieval castle feel of Anton's home and the Four Monks, his friend's home was more open and breezier. With a soft palette of cobalt blue, white, and gray, and large windows overlooking the lake, the space was calm and relaxing.

Tossing the extra keys on the counter of the luxury penthouse, he crossed to the gas fireplace and turned the key to get the fire started. "So you think you'd be okay slumming it here for a few months?"

I wandered over to the kitchen and reached for the wine key and bottle he had brought. With a dramatic sigh, I said, "If I must…."

After the revelations of our fight, I realized I needed to stop overthinking things.

Walling myself off from the people who cared about me was no way to live.

Life should be about risk and danger and love and beauty and passion and pain and all those wonderful, ugly, fucked-up emotions.

If Anton was willing to fight for us.

Then I should be willing to at least stick it out on the battlefield.

And there were worse things than going into battle with a tall, handsome, sexy AF, uber-rich Russian badass who happened against all the odds to think I was worth fighting for.

He returned to my side and wrapped his arms around my middle from behind, kissing my neck. "I appreciate your *great sacrifice*."

I pushed out my lower lip. "Just remember this *great sacrifice* of mine next time I ask for something super minor and insignificant."

His gaze cast over the stacks of paperwork I had brought.

He had Dylan prepare real estate files on appropriate locations for my salon and rush them over for me to review while he was out tonight handling some business.

He turned me around in his arms and pinned me against the quartz kitchen island.

Placing his hands on either side of my hips, he commanded, "Out with it."

"I was talking with Dylan and I might be able to save money if—"

"No."

Dylan warned me he was never going to go for it.

She told me the men in their inner circle had come from nothing and had paid a hard and brutal price for every penny they now enjoyed. So unlike most rich men, they appreciated and never took for granted their wealth.

That being said, they were impossibly generous with it, to a fault, especially to the women in their lives.

She told me, no matter how sound my business argument may be, Anton would take it as an insult if I tried to *save him money*, when it came to me.

"You haven't even heard what I was going to say."

"The answer is no."

"You can't just say no."

"And yet I just did."

"This is supposed to be a business partnership. You agreed."

He tilted my head to the side, feigning innocent affront. "I did and it is."

Not fooled, I frowned. "Not if you say no."

He leaned in and kissed the corner of my mouth. "Fine, then give me a question I'll say yes to. I can think of one."

317

He pressed his hips against mine. The hard ridge of his cock pushed into my stomach.

I grasped the sides of his shirt. "That's not how business works."

He lifted me onto the counter and stepped between my open thighs as he wrapped his left hand around my neck and wrapped his right hand in the hair at the base of my skull. "It's how our business is going to work."

He pulled on my hair, forcing my head back as he claimed my mouth in a searing kiss. Sweeping his tongue between my lips, he tasted like coffee, mint, and arrogance.

I slipped my hand inside the collar of his shirt, teasing his chest hair with the tips of my fingers.

He groaned and pulled me against his hips just as a shrill buzzer rang.

I pulled back. "What the hell is that?"

He pressed his forehead against mine. "Fuck. It's the intercom."

With a resigned sigh, he moved away and into the hall.

"Sir, your car is here."

I had no idea what he had planned for this evening. I just knew he was tense and annoyed about it. And whatever it was, he didn't want to take his own car so he had arranged for a private car to pick him up here. I had learned from the days with my father not to ask too many questions.

At least I wasn't stupid enough to equate my father's bullshit drug dealing with Anton's business. My father was a lowlife mean thug who reveled in harming the vulnerable and weak, like me and my mother. Anton may not operate within the letter of the law but he was clearly no thug preying on the weak.

"I'll be right down."

The water on Lake Michigan rolled in somnolent waves as ominous clouds clustered over the horizon. It was strange how you could forget it was just a lake and not the ocean. It seemed to go on forever.

He stroked my hair. "I hope I won't be too long. Have a glass of wine in front of the fire and look over the files Dylan sent while I'm gone. Let me know which ones you want to see tomorrow." He kissed the top of my head. "And no cheating!"

"Cheating?"

He tapped the tip of my nose before shrugging into his dark wool overcoat. "No picking only the cheap ones or I'll choose the location for you."

Still perched on the kitchen island, I leaned my palms back on the cool quartz. "Anyone ever tell you, you're a bully?" I teasingly called out as he turned to leave.

"Not until I met a brown-eyed, impertinent little thief who stole my heart," he teased back.

Whoa ... did Anton just admit he's in love with me too?

I mean, I kind of assumed he was with his insistence that we marry and all, but he hadn't actually said it yet.

Strictly speaking, neither had I.

Although if this were a contest, and pretty much everything between us seemed to be, I was the one who had come closest to saying it so far.

I thought....

Out of me saying I was *half in love with him* and him saying I had *stolen his heart*, it would depend on which one was the closest to saying *I love you*.

I jumped down from the island and raced down the hall to chase after him and ask but I was too late.

He was already gone.

I placed my hand against the closed door.

The scent of his cologne still lingered.

It was strange to already miss him.

Absurdly so if I considered how accustomed I used to be to spending my evenings alone.

Now I didn't know how I would fill the hours without him. It was startling how quickly he had become such a powerful presence in my life but now that I was determined to face a true life and all its risks, not one sheltered and alone, I could finally admit how much fun I had around him.

There truly had not been a dull moment since meeting him.

Moving back into the kitchen, I poured myself a glass of wine and gathered the real estate files into my arms and headed into the living room. After arranging the files in neat stacks based on location on the coffee table, I grabbed a pen and paper, sat cross-legged in front of the fire, and got to work.

* * *

TWO HOURS PASSED when I heard the lock on the door.

My heart fluttered as I scrambled to rise, then bent in half to fluff my hair as I ran my tongue over my teeth and lips to make sure I didn't have any red wine stains on them as I prepared to greet Anton on his return.

My mouth dropped open when a frazzled and disheveled Heather blustered in.

"Heather? What the fuck? What are you doing here? How did you get in?"

As I talked she talked over me. "Brynn? What the fuck? What are you doing here? How did you get in?"

I threw my hands up. "Stop. Just stop!"

I looked at her.

Something was wrong.

Way wrong.

One thing about Heather, she always looked put together. The hair, the makeup, the nails. The style was a bit over the top and a bit much for me, but it worked for her.

Not tonight.

Her hair hung in a limp, lopsided bun that made

her makeup-free face that much more startling. Add in the oversized hoodie with what looked like a mustard stain down the front and it was downright alarming.

Before I could ask her any questions, she grabbed my upper arm. "You have to get out of here. Now."

"I'm not going anywhere until you tell me what the fuck is going on?"

"Brynn, you don't understand." She let go of my arm and turned in a circle. "Everything got fucked up tonight."

Latching on to her shoulders, I tried to get her to focus on me. "Heather. You're not making any sense. You need to calm down. This can't be good for the baby. What got fucked up? Why are you here? Did you know I was here? Did you come to find me for help?"

She stared at me with wide unfocused eyes. "No. No one is supposed to be here. It's been empty for months."

I frowned. If she wasn't here for me, then why the fuck was she at Anton's friend's penthouse?

Resisting the urge to slap her like they do in the movies, I gave her a small shake. "Heather. Heather! I need you to focus and tell me why you're here."

She broke free of me and paced. "This is where he's meeting me."

"Where who's meeting you?"

"I came before them because he said I need to hide the stash from him so he doesn't get all of it."

"What?"

"He said he can't get all of it or there will be none for the baby."

It sounded as if she were talking about two people, not one.

Heather lunged across the room for the bookcases by the fireplace and started to toss the books onto the floor.

As I ran to stop her, she turned with two tightly wrapped packages the size of bricks in her hands.

I backed away. "Tell me that isn't what I think it is?"

Drugs. Holy fuck.

She looked up at me, as if suddenly remembering I was in the room.

Without warning she launched at me, clawing at my neck. I stumbled backward several steps until I slammed into the window.

Heather bared her teeth. "You didn't see this. Do you understand?"

I nodded, afraid to speak.

Satisfied, she lurched away and moved to the kitchen counter where she removed one of the knives from the knife block.

The air seized in my lungs.

Placing the packages on the quartz island, she pierced the plastic with the knife point. A small poof of white powder rose as soon as the seal was broken. On the tip of the knife was more white powder. Cocaine.

In horror, I watched as Heather started to lift the knife edge to her nose.

Without thinking of my own safety, only of her unborn child's, I sprang across the room and knocked the knife out of her hand. Then, before she could stop me, I snatched the two odious packages off the island, ran to the fireplace, and pitched them into the flames.

There was another large puff of smoke as the plastic wrap melted, exposing the cocaine to the flames.

Heather fell to her knees screeching.

Where the fuck was my phone?

I needed to call Anton.

For once in my life, I wasn't going to try to be independent or handle something on my own.

I had a big, strong, powerful boyfriend and right now I needed him.

He picked up immediately. "Hey, babygirl, is everything okay? What is that noise?"

I ran my hand through my hair as I walked away from Heather's caterwauling. "I'm really sorry to do this. I know you're busy—"

"Baby, talk to me. What's going on over there?"

He was slightly out of breath so it was obvious he was already on the move.

"Heather just showed up. And she's freaking out. And she tried to do some drugs she had hidden here and I panicked and threw them in the fire and now she's *really* freaking out."

I could hear him talking Russian to someone nearby, then he asked, "Is Yuri with her?"

"No, she came alone, but she mentioned two men were on their way."

"Lock the door, baby. Don't let anyone in. I'm on my way."

With the phone pressed to my ear, I ran toward the front door. "Anton, she had a key, what if—"

Before I could finish that sentence, the front door swung open and Yuri stormed through with another man.

My eyes widened as the color drained from my face. "Dad?"

CHAPTER 30

ANTON

*T*he cellphone line went dead.

"Dammit."

Dimitri was already throwing the Range Rover into gear as I dove into the passenger seat. Ivan ran alongside as the car flew into reverse before hopping in the back.

I called out over my shoulder as I attempted to dial Brynn back, "The drop's at your penthouse. That motherfucking little bastard."

Ivan responded, "I'm already calling in reinforcements. All deals with Mac are off."

Dimitri and I exchanged a quick look.

This would hit Mac hard.

Blood was blood, but it had to be done.

Yuri had become too much of a liability.

Before Brynn's call, we had figured out the drug

deal location had been changed. We were in the process of running down sources when she called.

Ivan hung up the phone. "Everyone's on their way to the penthouse."

I tried Brynn again.

No answer.

My gut churned.

Dammit. I should have put a guard on her.

If I had thought for one fucking moment she wasn't safe, I would have.

I slammed my fist against the dashboard. "How the fuck did this happen?"

Ivan answered. "The piece of shit must have kept a key to the penthouse and kept using it. He must have bribed the staff in the building to keep quiet about it."

Whatever Yuri had paid them, it wasn't going to be worth it when we got through with them.

We took loyalty very seriously and betrayal even more so.

Dimitri pulled the Range Rover straight up onto the sidewalk, sending several pedestrians scattering.

We all jumped out, guns drawn.

Several of our men arrived at the same time.

After ordering them to surround the building and watch the elevators, we took the stairs, racing up the eight flights to Ivan's penthouse.

The door was ajar when we arrived.

Fuck.

Uncaring for what dangerous trap I might be walking into, I stormed over the threshold, intent on getting to Brynn.

The place was empty.

On the kitchen island, Brynn's cellphone, its screen cracked, rang.

I picked up. "Hurt her in any way and there isn't a hole on this fucking earth where you will be able to hide from me."

The voice on the other end chuckled. "Is that any way to speak to your future father-in-law?"

My jaw clenched. "Mark Davies."

"I hear you've been asking about me."

"Word travels fast."

"Especially when that word has a million-dollar bounty on it. Makes it difficult to conduct my usual business."

"Fine. You want to talk terms. We'll talk terms, but you deal with me, leave Brynn out of this."

"And ruin a long overdue father-daughter reunion?"

I tightened my grip on the phone. "I'm warning you, Moore. I'm not a man you want to piss off."

"Yeah, well, I'm the one holding all the cards so we're playing by my rules, not yours. I want ten million in cash. I'll call you in one hour with a drop-off location."

"I want proof of life."

I heard Brynn cry out in the background.

Then Moore, again. "You want proof of life? Here's your proof."

There was a gunshot and Brynn screamed.

Then the line went dead.

CHAPTER 31

BRYNN

I fell to my knees as I stared at Yuri's lifeless eyes.

Heather screamed incoherently as she fell over his body.

"Shut that stupid bitch up!"

I scrambled on the floor over to Heather.

Wrapping my arm over her shoulders, I hauled her away from Yuri's body and dragged her across the floor to lean against the kitchen island as I placed a hand over her mouth, urgently whispering into her ear, "Please, Heather. Please, stop crying. Please, for your baby. Think of your baby!"

I hugged her tight and rocked her back and forth as I glared at my father over her head. "Why are you doing this?"

"Is that any way to talk to your dear ol' dad?"

I pushed my lips between my teeth and bit down,

hoping the pain would ground me. There was no profit in antagonizing him. "I'm sorry."

"That's better." He wagged his gun in my direction. "This is all your fault, you know. You're fucking useless, just like your fucking useless mother."

I lowered my gaze, bracing for the torrent of cruel words.

He continued to wave his gun at me. "If that boyfriend of yours hadn't put a price on my head, I wouldn't have had to settle up with Yuri here and leave town. And then you had to go and trash one-hundred-and-fifty-grand worth of coke like the stupid dumb bitch you are."

He scratched the back of his head with the butt of his gun. "Fucking cunt. You should have killed yourself like your mother. Too bad you fucked that up too."

Tears stung my eyes as I squeezed a whimpering Heather tighter.

Don't listen to him.
Don't listen to him.
Don't listen to him.

He stormed over to me and rapped me on the head with the end of the gun. "Are you listening to me, *daughter*?"

I rubbed the top of my head. "Yes."

He sneered as he bent in half and placed his face close to mine. "What did I say?"

"That you're mad I destroyed the drugs you were counting on."

He rapped me on the head with the gun again. "No. I said you are a fuckup, a dumb cunt who couldn't even get killing herself right. You were a mistake, did you know that? You ruined your mother's life. That's why she killed herself."

He pointed the gun at me. "She couldn't take being burdened by a snot-nosed, stupid brat like you. She'd rather be dead than live with what a worthless disappointment her daughter became."

Don't listen to him.

Don't listen to him.

Don't listen to him.

He rubbed his belly. "I mean look at you. Most daughters are honoring, obeying, and taking care of their parents. Not you. The last time I visited I had to force you to do your duty by giving me a few measly thousand dollars."

He rapped me on the head with the gun yet again. "And now I find out you're fucking some gangster with millions and do you share with your loving father? No. You selfish cunt. You have him drive me out of town hoping I wouldn't find out about your good luck. Hoping I wouldn't take my cut. The cut I earned by raising you and feeding you and putting a roof over your head."

"You didn't raise me," I whispered under my breath.

He shuffled back up to me. "What was that?"

I pulled my arm away from Heather and rose, matching him eye to eye, no longer afraid of him.

It was stupid and rash and insane, especially since he had a gun, but I didn't care. I wasn't going to let this horrible man destroy my inner peace anymore.

Plus, for the first time in my life, I had someone I could rely on … to save me.

I knew, with absolute certainty, that Anton was coming for me.

It was a strange sort of empowering rush to know there was someone out there in the world caring about you, fighting for you.

And I needed to buy him time.

"You didn't raise me. You've brought nothing but pain and trauma and disappointment into my life."

He raised his fist to his eye and twisted it. "There you go again, crying like a baby about your childhood. Wah! Wah! Wah! No wonder your stupid mother slit her wrists."

"My mother was a beautiful, amazing woman who lost her way because of an addiction you encouraged. My mother didn't kill herself. Addiction killed her. You killed her."

He snorted and rolled his glassy, bloodshot eyes.

And that's when I finally saw it.

His weakness.

It was like a lightbulb shattering from a brilliant burst of light.

When I was caught in an emotional spiral, words were not logical. They had no rational purpose. They were just words, letters piled upon letters. Meaningless. And it was so fucking frustrating because I wanted them to mean something, to form a comprehensive sentence, but it always seemed just out of reach, like a memory on the tip of my tongue.

One such word was *bully*.

Bullies only had the power you gave them. That was simple logic. Simple words.

Words out of reach when I was spiraling, closing myself off from my own emotions, refusing to let anyone in.

But Anton broke me out of that spiral, by sheer stubborn, arrogant force of will.

And love.

I saw it now, clearly, like words written on a blackboard in bold capital letters.

My father's words couldn't hurt me.

Nothing he said was true. Nothing he ever said was true. And if that was true, then he had no power over me. Over my life. Over the choices I made.

My chest expanded as I took a deep breath, feeling as if I had been released from chains.

"Heather and I are leaving."

He raised his gun to my chest. "The hell you are."

"Are you going to kill your only daughter?"

"You mean nothing to me. You're just the bait for

that gangster boyfriend of yours. So I can get what's coming to me."

I smiled.

"What are you smiling about?"

I tilted my head to the side as I looked at what a pathetically broken man he was. "I'm so glad you said that."

I then looked over my father's shoulder at Anton's reflection in the window as he silently entered the room. "Because you are about to get *precisely* what is coming to you."

Before my father had a chance to grab me and use me as a shield, I dropped to the floor, avoiding his grasp.

As Anton charged, my father got off one shot.

I screamed as Anton lurched backward from the impact but then righted himself and charged forward like a raging bull despite the blossoming crimson stain on his shoulder.

Anton knocked the gun out of my father's hand and twisted his fist in his shirt. Pulling back his arm, he slammed his fist into my father's jaw.

My father crashed into the window and then slowly slid down to the floor in a slumped-over sitting position, like a discarded doll.

I braced myself for more violence, but instead Anton turned away from my father's sprawled body to face me.

I cried out when I saw the blood from his shoulder. "Oh, my God!"

He snatched me to his chest and hugged me tightly. He then pulled back and cupped my jaw as he tilted my head back and looked deeply in my eyes. "It's a through and through. I'm fine. Are you hurt, babygirl? The gunshot?"

I shook my head. "He killed Yuri." I wrapped my arms around his middle and hugged him close again, only truly feeling safe when I felt his arms tighten around my back.

He kissed the top of my head as he stroked my hair. "I'm so sorry, baby. I should have had a guard on you. I'll never risk your safety like that again."

I leaned back. "This wasn't your fault. How could you have known Yuri was using Ivan's place as a stash house?"

He stroked my cheek. "We didn't learn he had a connection to Yuri until tonight. It's my fault your father got desperate for a way out of town. You were right. I should have talked to you before getting involved."

"Did you just say I was right?" My head pivoted to the chaos around us. "Is someone recording this? I need someone to record this."

"Shut up and kiss me."

He wrapped his arm around my middle as his other hand caressed my neck while his mouth claimed mine. It was the sweetest, most searing kiss yet, because this time there was nothing holding me back.

Breathless, I pulled back. "How did you find us so quickly?"

My father had known he wouldn't be able to get a hysterical and pregnant Heather out of the building. And as it had turned out, Ivan's place wasn't the only one Yuri had a key to and bragged about. After killing Yuri, he'd forced us only one floor down.

Anton smirked. "It was the gunshot. We were already in the building when he fired it. I didn't only hear it through the phone. After getting to Ivan's and realizing you weren't there, I knew you had to be close."

One of the men, I think his name was Dimitri, called out, "We have signs of life over here, Anton."

I turned to see my father stumbling to his feet.

Anton looked down at me. "I've told you before I would always be straight with you, babygirl."

My stomach tightened as I braced myself for what he was going to say next.

"He signed his death warrant for what he's done to you… but now he's threatened our organization. There is nothing I can do. We have rules. You understand that, don't you, baby?"

I swallowed. "Will you be the one to do it?"

He rubbed my back. "Not if you don't want me to."

"I know in the movies, Russians are known for—" I swallowed.

He finished for me. "It would be quick. We don't need any information from him."

No need to dwell on the fact he didn't deny the portrayal of Russian criminals in the movies.

His hand stroked my hair. "Did you want to say goodbye?"

Casting a glance over his shoulder, I stared at the stranger I once called father. "I've said everything that needed to be said."

It was a relief to feel nothing. My father brought this on himself. He made his choices. Just like my mother made hers. And now I was making mine.

Resting my head against the comforting strength of Anton's chest, I said, "Can we go home now?"

He wrapped an arm around my shoulders. "Yes, babygirl."

As he guided me past his men toward the door, there was a shout of alarm.

We both turned to see Heather standing in front of my father with his discarded gun, her arms outstretched.

My eyes widened as I moved to go to her.

Anton's arms restrained me.

Heather's hands shook. "This is for Yuri."

She fired three shots, hitting my father square in the chest.

His body slammed against the glass as the bullets

cracked it in a spiraling spider web pattern behind him. For one strange moment, he looked like a crushed spider before he fell lifeless to the floor.

Heather then cried out as water gushed between her legs. "Fuck, the baby!"

CHAPTER 32

BRYNN

 *wo months later*

THROWING my arms into the air, I shouted at the ceiling. "Absolutely fucking not!"

Anton crossed his arms over his chest. "You're just being stubborn because it's my idea."

Casting him a look over my shoulder, I gathered the painting sample books up in my arms as I made room for the lunch he brought. "No, I'm saying no because it's a stupid idea."

He adjusted the sawhorses and made sure my makeshift plywood desk was stable before unpacking the bottle of chilled champagne, blinis, caviar, fresh strawberries, Olivier salad, and a Medovik cake for dessert packed by the chef at the Four Monks' restaurant.

His lips quirked. "I knew agreeing to not being your silent partner was going to bite me in the ass."

I leaned up on my tiptoes and kissed him on the cheek. "*Agreeing* is a strong word. I don't recall giving you a choice."

He gave me a playful spank on the ass. "Brat."

Laughing, I pushed two chairs up as he set out plates and napkins.

It had been an amazing whirlwind of a two months filled with drama, sadness, love, and support. My newfound family had closed ranks around me the moment we'd returned to the Four Monks.

It was like they had sent up some kind of bat signal.

All the women were there, taking control. Anton was ushered into a back medical center and patched up while Emma and Dylan insisted that I take care of myself. They ran a hot bath and gave me the space to process what had just happened.

In the weeks that followed, I was introduced to a fireball named Mary and we became fast friends.

And that was when we hatched our plan.

The women loved it.

The men hated it.

Which meant it was perfect.

Instead of Anton investing in my new salon, all the women got together and invested in it.

We had all become like sisters over the last few weeks as the plans came together and now construction had finally started.

Anton wasn't thrilled at first, but he realized that it gave me the small measure of independence my fragile heart still needed. He really was amazing that way.

I couldn't believe I almost let him get away.

Hard to believe I actually ran away from this man. Multiple times!

Working the cork, he popped the champagne and poured us two glasses. "I don't think you gave the name much of a chance."

Despite insisting on four armed guards at all times when I was off premises, as well as only hiring his men for construction, Anton also showed up every day with lunch. It had become our little routine.

I raised an eyebrow. "I didn't have to. I'm not naming the salon *The Six Nuns*."

The clinking of the glasses sent a fresh cascade of bubbles rushing to the surface before we each took a sip.

Anton objected. "I think it is an exceptional name and will mark your affiliation with *The Four Monks*, which will only bring in more business."

"It sounds like a convent."

He took a bite of a fresh strawberry. "Hey, you don't have to sell me on the name. I already like it."

Reaching for my own strawberry, I shook my head. "I love you, but there is no way—"

He put down his glass and stared at me.

I broke off what I was saying. "What?"

His dark gray gaze turned intense. "Say it again."

I blinked. "Say what?"

He stood up so abruptly he turned over his chair. "You know what."

I staggered to my feet and backed up a step, at first confused. Then realization dawned.

I love you.

I said I love you.

It just slipped out.

I slapped my hand over my mouth.

He stalked toward me. "Say. It. Again," he growled. All laughter gone.

My back hit the wall.

He placed a forearm over my head, caging me in.

I tilted my head back as I swallowed past the sudden dryness in my mouth. "You say it."

He slowly shook his head. "Nice try. I've patiently been waiting months to hear those words from those pretty lips."

I rolled my eyes. "I'd hardly call you patient."

"Stop stalling. Say it again."

I played with the silver watch chain that dangled from his suit vest, suddenly nervous and self-conscious. "You promise to say it right after?"

"I promise."

I sighed. "Fine." I then said in a rush, "I love you. There, are you happy?"

"I love you, too, *moya ocharovatel'naya malen'kaya vorovka.*"

He placed his hand over mine and pulled on the watch chain. As the stylish pocket watch popped out of the pocket, something else slid along the chain as well.

It was a stunning engagement ring.

My mouth fell open. "Have you just been walking around with this?"

He unhooked the chain and slid the ring off.

Lifting up my left hand, he slid the ring onto my ring finger. "I wanted to be prepared for the very moment you were ready to say it, so that I could ask … Brynn Caitlin Moore, will you do me the honor of becoming my wife and *equal partner* in life?"

I stared up at him, hardly believing it was true.

Somehow. Someway. I was actually getting my fairy-tale ending with my very own Prince Charming.

He raised an eyebrow. "Well?"

"I'm thinking!"

That didn't mean I was going to make it easy for him.

His gaze narrowed.

Before I could object, he bent low and placed his shoulder in my middle, hoisting me high.

I cried out. "Wait! What are you doing?"

He carried me out the door to his waiting car. "Helping you make up your mind."

I propped myself up against his back and called over my shoulder, "This is not how a man gets an answer to his proposal in America!"

He gave me a spank on the ass. "No, but this is how a Russian man does."

EPILOGUE

MAC

I stared at the small blanket-wrapped bundle through the glass in awe.

Anton and Varlaam joined me on either side.

Varlaam nodded in approval. "He is getting stronger every day."

Placing a hand on his shoulder, I gestured toward my grandnephew. "He's a fighter. I'm naming him after my father, Stephan."

After Heather killed Brynn's father for killing Yuri, she went into premature labor. The stress of that evening coupled with her bad habits had made it a very difficult birth. The baby was born needing special care.

Within a week, Heather had checked herself out of the hospital and disappeared.

Abandoning her son.

I had made it clear to her that there would be no police or repercussions for her actions that evening, so I knew it wasn't any looming murder charge she was worried about.

Perhaps it was for the best.

Varlaam reached into his suit jacket and pulled out three cigars, handing one to each of us. He lit his and then passed the silver lighter around.

A nurse came rushing up. "You can't smoke these in here."

I reached into my pocket and pulled out my money clip. It was at least an inch thick. I gestured toward Stephan. "That little boy goes home with me today. We are celebrating. This is for you." And I gave her the whole clip.

What did I care for money?

Money hadn't saved my nephew.

But things would be different with Stephan.

The nurse looked around before taking the money. "Okay, but don't smoke the whole thing."

I winked. "Thank you."

We stood in silence as we watched Stephan sleep.

Anton took a long drag from his cigar and blew a blue ring of smoke before saying, "Guess you'll be needing a nanny now."

Varlaam knocked some ash into a discarded coffee cup. "Damn, I pity the poor girl who takes on that job."

· · ·

To be continued.

Sweet Severity
Ruthless Obsession Series, Book Seven
Macarius & Phoebe's Story

ABOUT ZOE BLAKE

Zoe Blake is the USA Today Bestselling Author of the romantic suspense saga The Cavalieri Billionaire Legacy inspired by her own heritage as well as her obsession with jewelry, travel, and the salacious gossip of history's most infamous families.

She delights in writing Dark Romance books filled with overly possessive billionaires, taboo scenes, and unexpected twists. She usually spends her ill-gotten gains on martinis, vacations, and red lipstick. Since she can barely boil water, she's lucky enough to be married to a sexy Chef.

librarian student.

She didn't belong in my world.

I would bring her only pain.

But it was too late…

She was mine and I was keeping her.

Sweet Depravity

Ruthless Obsession Series, Book Two

Vaska & Mary's story

The moment she opened those gorgeous red lips to tell me no, she was mine.

I was a powerful Russian arms dealer and she was an innocent schoolteacher.

If she had a choice, she'd run as far away from me as possible.

Unfortunately for her, I wasn't giving her one.

I wasn't just going to take her; I was going to take over her entire world.

Where she lived.

What she ate.

Where she worked.

All would be under my control.

Call it obsession.

Call it depravity.

I don't give a damn… as long as you call her mine.

Sweet Savagery

Ruthless Obsession Series, Book Three

Ivan & Dylan's Story

I was a savage bent on claiming her as punishment for her family's mistakes.

As a powerful Russian Arms dealer, no one steals from me and gets away with it.

She was an innocent pawn in a dangerous game.

She had no idea the package her uncle sent her from Russia contained my stolen money.

If I were a good man, I would let her return the money and leave.

If I were a gentleman, I might even let her keep some of it just for frightening her.

As I stared down at the beautiful living doll stretched out before me like a virgin sacrifice,

I thanked God for every sin and misdeed that had blackened my cold heart.

I was not a good man.

I sure as hell wasn't a gentleman… and I had no intention of letting her go.

She was mine now.

And no one takes what's mine.

Sweet Brutality

Ruthless Obsession Series, Book Four

Maxim & Carinna's story

The more she fights me, the more I want her.

It's that beautiful, sassy mouth of hers.

It makes me want to push her to her knees and dominate her, like the brutal savage I am.

As a Russian Arms dealer, I should not be ruthlessly pursuing an innocent college student like her, but that would not stop me.

A twist of fate may have brought us together, but it is my twisted obsession that will hold her captive as my own treasured possession.

She is mine now.

I dare you to try and take her from me.

Sweet Ferocity

Ruthless Obsession Series, Book Five

Luka & Katie's Story

I was a mafia mercenary only hired to find her, but now I'm going to keep her.

She is a Russian mafia princess, kidnapped to be used as a pawn in a dangerous territory war.

Saving her was my job. Keeping her safe had become my obsession.

Every move she makes, I am in the shadows, watching.

I was like a feral animal: cruel, violent, and selfishly out for my own needs. Until her.

Now, I will make her mine by any means necessary.

I am her protector, but no one is going to protect her from me.

Sweet Intensity

Ruthless Obsession Series, Book Six

Antonius & Brynn's Story

She couldn't have known the danger she faced when she dared to steal from me.

She was too young for a man my age, barely in her twenties.

Far too pure and untouched.

Unfortunately for her, that wasn't going to stop me.

The moment I laid eyes on her, I claimed her.

Determined to make her mine...by any means necessary.

I owned Chicago's most elite gambling club, a front for my role as a Russian Mafia crime boss.

And she was a fragile little bird, who had just flown straight into my open jaws.

Naïve and sweet, she was a temptation I couldn't resist biting.

My intense drive to dominate and control her had become an obsession.

I would ruthlessly use my superior strength and wealth to take over her life.

The harder she resisted, the more feral and savage I would become.

She needed to understand… she was mine now.

Mine.

Sweet Severity

Ruthless Obsession Series, Book Seven

Macarius & Phoebe's Story

Had she crashed into any other man's car, she could have walked away—but she hit mine.

Upon seeing the bruises on her wrist, I struggled to contain my rage.

Despite her objections, I refused to allow her to leave.

Whoever hurt this innocent beauty would pay dearly.

As a Russian Mafia crime boss who owns Chicago's most elite gambling club, I have very creative and painful methods of exacting revenge.

She seems too young and naive to be out on her own in such a dangerous world.

Needing a nanny, I decided to claim her for the role.

She might resist my severe, domineering discipline, but I won't give her a choice in the matter.

She needs a protector, and I'd be damned if it were anyone but me.

Resisting the urge to claim her will test all my restraint.

It's a battle I'm bound to lose.

With each day, my obsession and jealousy intensify.

It's only a matter of time before my control snaps…and I make her mine.

Mine.

Sweet Animosity

Ruthless Obsession, Book Eight

Varlaam & Amber's Story

I never asked for an assistant, and if I had, I sure as hell wouldn't have chosen her.

With her sharp tongue and lack of discipline, what she needs is a firm hand, not a job.

The more she tests my limits, the more tempted I am to bend her over my knee.

As a Russian Mafia boss and owner of Chicago's most elite gambling club, I can't afford distractions from her antics.

Or her secrets.

For I suspect, my innocent new assistant is hiding something.

And I know just how to get to the truth.

It's high time she understands who holds the power in our relationship.

To ensure I get what I desire, I'll keep her close, controlling her every move.

Except I am no longer after information—I want her mind, body and soul.

She underestimated the stakes of our dangerous game and

now owes a heavy price.

As payment I will take her freedom.

She's mine now.

Mine.

Sweet Jealousy

A Ruthless Obsession Vella

Serg & Maya's Story

Every day I watch her. She has no idea who I am or the power I wield.

To her I'm just the man who likes his coffee black and tips well.

She has no clue, I'm one of the most ruthless and dangerous Russian mafia crime bosses in the city.

That I'm the man who will dominate her, demanding her complete submission.

For soon, she will be mine.

For her own protection, I must keep to the shadows.

My enemies can never know of my obsession for her.

Of how I crave to possess her sweet innocence.

They cannot know how I jealousy guard over her, using my money and influence to control her life.

She can never know that the man who sits quietly at the end of her lunch counter each day...

is also the man who sneaks into her bedroom each night, ties her to the bed and makes her scream with pleasure.

She can quit her job, move apartments, even try to change her name.

It won't matter.

Come nightfall, when the shadows deepen.

I will find her and once again make her…

Mine.

-

<u>IVANOV CRIME FAMILY TRILOGY</u>

A Dark Mafia Romance

Savage Vow

Ivanov Crime Family, Book One

Gregor & Samara's story

I took her innocence as payment.

She was far too young and naïve to be betrothed to a monster like me.

I would bring only pain and darkness into her sheltered world.

That's why she ran.

I should've just let her go…

She never asked to marry into a powerful Russian mafia family.

None of this was her choice.

Unfortunately for her, I don't care.

I own her… and after three years of searching… I've found her.

My runaway bride was about to learn disobedience has consequences… punishing ones.

Having her in my arms and under my control had become an obsession.

Nothing was going to keep me from claiming her before the eyes of God and man.

She's finally mine… and I'm never letting her go.

Vicious Oath

Ivanov Crime Family, Book One

Damien & Yelena's story

When I give an order, I expect it to be obeyed.

She's too smart for her own good, and it's going to get her killed.

Against my better judgement, I put her under the protection of my powerful Russian mafia family.

So imagine my anger when the little minx ran.

For three long years I've been on her trail, always one step behind.

Finding and claiming her had become an obsession.

It was getting harder to rein in my driving need to possess her… to own her.

But now the chase is over.

I've found her.

Soon she will be mine.

And I plan to make it official, even if I have to drag her

kicking and screaming to the altar.

This time… there will be no escape from me.

Betrayed Honor

Ivanov Crime Family, Book One

Mikhail & Nadia's story

Her innocence was going to get her killed.

That was if I didn't get to her first.

She's the protected little sister of the powerful Ivanov Russian mafia family - the very definition of forbidden.

It's always been my job, as their Head of Security, to watch over her but never to touch.

That ends today.

She disobeyed me and put herself in danger.

It was time to take her in hand.

I'm the only one who can save her and I will fight anyone who tries to stop me, including her brothers.

Honor and loyalty be damned.

She's mine now.

CAVALIERI BILLIONAIRE LEGACY

A Dark Enemies to Lovers Romance

Scandals of the Father

Cavalieri Billionaire Legacy, Book One

Being attracted to her wasn't wrong… but acting on it would be.

As the patriarch of the powerful and wealthy Cavalieri family, my choices came with consequences for everyone around me.

The roots of my ancestral, billionaire-dollar winery stretch deep into the rich, Italian soil, as does our legacy for ruthlessness and scandal.

It wasn't the fact she was half my age that made her off limits.

Nothing was off limits for me.

A wounded bird, caught in a trap not of her own making, she posed no risk to me.

My obsessive desire to possess her was the real problem.

For both of us.

But now that I've seen her, tasted her lips, I can't let her go.

Whether she likes it or not, she needs my protection.

I'm doing this for her own good, yet she fights me at every turn.

Refusing the luxury I offer, desperately trying to escape my grasp.

I need to teach her to obey before the dark rumors of my past reach her.

Ruin her.

She cannot find out what I've done, not before I make her mine.

Sins of the Son

Cavalieri Billionaire Legacy, Book Two

She's hated me for years… now it's past time to give her a reason to.

When you are a son, and one of the heirs, to the legacy of the Cavalieri name, you need to be more vicious than your enemies.

And sometimes, the lines get blurred.

Years ago, they tried to use her as a pawn in a revenge scheme against me.

Even though I cared about her, I let them treat her as if she were nothing.

I was too arrogant and self-involved to protect her then.

But I'm here now. Ready to risk my life tracking down every single one of them.

They'll pay for what they've done as surely as I'll pay for my sins against her.

Too bad it won't be enough for her to let go of her hatred of me,

To get her to stop fighting me.

Because whether she likes it or not, I have the power, wealth, and connections to keep her by my side.

And every intention of ruthlessly using all three to make her mine.

Secrets of the Brother

Cavalieri Billionaire Legacy, Book Three

We were not meant to be together… then a dark twist of fate stepped in, and we're the ones who will pay for it.

As the eldest son and heir of the Cavalieri name, I inherit a great deal more than a billion-dollar empire.

I receive a legacy of secrets, lies, and scandal.

After enduring a childhood filled with malicious rumors about my father, I have fallen prey to his very same sin.

I married a woman I didn't love out of a false sense of family honor.

Now she has died under mysterious circumstances.

And I am left to play the widowed groom.

For no one can know the truth about my wife…

Especially her sister.

The only way to protect her from danger is to keep her close, and yet, her very nearness tortures me.

She is my sister in name only, but I have no right to desire her.

Not after what I have done.

It's too much to hope she would understand that it was all for her.

It's always been about her.

Only her.

I am, after all, my father's son.

And there is nothing on this earth more ruthless than a Cavalieri man in love.

Seduction of the Patriarch

Cavalieri Billionaire Legacy, Book Four

With a single gunshot, she brings the violent secrets of my buried past into the present.

She may not have pulled the trigger, but she still has blood on her hands.

And I know some very creative ways to make her pay for it.

Being as ruthless as my Cavalieri ancestors has earned me a reputation as a dangerous man to cross, but that hasn't stopped me from making enemies along the way. No fortune is built without spilling blood.

But while I may be brutal, I don't play loose with my family, which means staying in the shadows to protect them.

I find myself forced to hand over the mantle of patriarch to my brother and move to northern Italy…

…or risk the lives of those I love.

Until a vindictive mafia syndicate attacks my family.

Now all bets are off, and nothing will prevent me from seeking vengeance on those responsible.

I'm done protecting the innocent.

Now, I don't give a damn who I hurt in the process…

…including her.

Through seduction and the power of punishment, I shall bend her to my will.

She will be my rebellious accomplice, a vital pawn in my

quest for revenge.

And the more my defiant little vixen bares her sharp claws, the more she tempts me to tame her until she purrs with submission.

Scorn of the Betrothed

Cavalieri Billionaire Legacy, Book Five

A union forged in vengeance, bound by hate, and... beneath it all...a twisted game of power.

The true legacy of the Cavalieri family, my birthright, ties me to a woman I despise:

the daughter of the mafia boss who nearly ended my family.

Making her both my enemy...and my future wife.

The hatred is mutual; she has no desire for me to be her groom.

A prisoner to her families' ambitions, she's desperate for a way out.

My duty is to guard her, to ensure she doesn't escape her gilded cage.

But every moment spent with her, every spark of anger, adds fuel to the growing fire of desire between us.

We're trapped in a volatile duel of passion and fury.

Yet, the more I try to tame her, the more she fights me,

Our impending marriage becomes a dangerous game.

Now, as the wedding draws near, my suspicions grow.

My bride is not who she claims.

DARK OBSESSION SERIES

A Dark Romantic Suspense

Wicked Games: A Dark Romance

Dark Obsession Series, Book One

She's caught in my game… she just doesn't know it.

For weeks, I've been watching her. Stalking her.

Now it's time to start playing with my beautiful little pawn.

From the moment I first saw her from afar, I knew she would become my prized possession.

I will gaslight her into thinking she is my obedient ward, trapped in the Victorian era.

She is my unwilling captive, forced to play my sadistic game for her own survival.

She will have no choice but to bow to my rules and discipline.

In time, her memories of a modern life will fade.

If not, she will pay a painful price.

Her pretty mind is so caught up in my nightmare, she will never escape me.

The most wicked deception of all?

This isn't the first time we're playing this game.

Sinister Games: A Dark Romance

Dark Obsession Series, Book Two

She's trapped inside my twisted game.

And I am never letting her go.

I've started a new game. This one more sinister than the last.

Every time she tries to fight what we have, I just pull her deeper into my deception.

The slightest disobedience to my rules brings swift punishment.

I've pushed her to the edge.

She wants to kill me.

The only problem is… she loves me.

Against her will, she loves every punishing, controlling thing I've done to her mind and body.

She's caught in my web; the harder she struggles, the more entangled she becomes.

My beautiful girl will have no choice but to accept that I am her new reality.

She is just a pawn in my game.

Savage Games: A Dark Romance

Dark Obsession Series, Book Three

She broke the rules of our game… she ran.

Now she will pay.

When will my pretty pawn learn that I am the master of

this game?

And only I will be the victor.

She thinks she can hide from me.

She thinks she can escape my wrath.

She's wrong.

This time when I catch her, there will be no escape.

I no longer want her as just my beautiful captive.

She will now become my wife, even if I have to drag her down the aisle.

I want her under my complete control.

I want her every breath, her every movement, her every thought to be only of me.

This is no longer a game.

She changed the rules, but I will still win.

Cruel Games: A Dark Romance

Dark Obsession Series, Book Four

I'm not interested in love, it's the chase which intrigues me.

I saw her in the park, my pretty little prey.

I intend to make her mine, and the closer I get the more she will lose.

Her friends.

Her family.

Her freedom.

Each move will bring her more under my control until she

has nothing left... but me.

Am I playing a cruel game? Of course.

But I warned you: It's not love that I want.

Vicious Games: A Dark Romance

Dark Obsession Series, Book Five

I have taken everything from her.

She has no friends.

No money.

No one to turn to for help.

She's finally under my complete control, and yet, it's not enough.

I hold her body captive, but not her heart.

She knows I destroyed her life to possess her, so she fights me at every turn.

But she hasn't guessed the true purpose of my game.

She needs to understand that I will do anything to win. Anything.

She is my possession. Nothing, and no one, not even her, will keep us apart.

If she denies me much longer, she will learn just how vicious I can become when I don't get what I want.

And I want her... all of her.

For a list of All of Zoe Blake's Books Visit her Website!

www.zblakebooks.com

SWEET JEALOUSY BONUS

Introducing *Sweet Jealousy: A Dark Mafia Romance Vella.*
This Vella is part of USAT Bestselling Author Zoe Blake's Ruthless Obsession Dark Russian Mafia world. Side characters/couples who appear in this Vella appear in her Ruthless Obsession books, available in Kindle Unlimited.

Sweet Jealousy
A Ruthless Obsession Vella
Serg & Maya's Story, Episode One

Every day I watch her. She has no idea who I am or the power I wield.
To her, I'm just the man who likes his coffee black and tips well.
She has no clue I'm one of the most ruthless and dangerous Russian mafia crime bosses in the city.

That I'm the man who will dominate her, demanding her complete submission.

For soon, she will be mine.

For her own protection, I must keep to the shadows.

My enemies can never know of my obsession for her.

Of how I crave to possess her sweet innocence.

They cannot know how I jealousy guard over her, using my money and influence to control her life.

She can never know that the man who sits quietly at the end of her lunch counter each day…

is also the man who sneaks into her bedroom each night, ties her to the bed and makes her scream with pleasure.

She can quit her job, move apartments, even try to change her name.

It won't matter.

Come nightfall, when the shadows deepen.

I will find her and once again make her…

Mine.

Episode One

Serg

I flexed my fingers, hissing at the pain in my bruised and bloody knuckles, as I watched her every move.

My obsession with her consuming me.

She seemed so fresh and innocent, so pure — so

unlike the blood, filth and degradation which surrounded me on a daily basis.

The bright and clean Windy Delights Diner was a sanctuary of sorts, an escape from the life I had carved out for myself. The faint hum of the air conditioner and the soft murmur of conversations served as a soothing balm.

I savored each sip of black coffee, the bitter taste grounding me in the present moment.

My eyes were transfixed on Maya, her dark hair cascading down her back as she moved with grace between tables, taking orders and flashing warm smiles at customers.

As my gaze followed her, I saw her steal glances at the clock on the wall, counting down the minutes until her shift would end and her date would arrive.

Poor little one.

Her anticipation was all for nothing.

"Another cup of coffee, please," I murmured as she approached, keeping my voice low and measured. My heart raced as she poured the steaming liquid into my cup, our fingers brushing ever so slightly.

The electric connection between us sent a shock of awareness down my thigh, straight to my shaft, further solidifying my resolve.

The date she eagerly awaited would never come.

I had made certain of that, violently discouraging her would-be suitor earlier in the day.

It was a brutal reminder that no one would ever touch what was mine, not even in their fantasies.

As much as it pained me to see her disappointment when he failed to show, I couldn't...wouldn't... stand for another man stealing her away from me.

And so I watched her, knowing everything about her life, controlling her, from the shadows.

"Thank you," I said evenly, my eyes never leaving hers.

In that moment, our connection was undeniable, a tangle of desire and unspoken tension weaving between us. She offered me a hesitant smile before scurrying off to tend to her other customers.

I knew I made her nervous. Good. It kept her at arm's length. I couldn't have her asking any inconvenient questions... like my name.

As I sipped the black brew, my thoughts focused on Maya - the way her hips swayed when she walked, the sound of her laughter like music to my ears, the curve of her lips as she smiled. I knew I would never tire of her, my obsession only growing stronger with each passing day.

I also knew that this dance we shared couldn't last forever. Eventually, she would uncover the truth, and the world I had carefully built around myself would come crashing down. But for now, I indulged in the sweet torment of our secret connection, the mingling of darkness and light that simmered beneath the surface.

I reveled, knowing that I alone held the power to control her fate and the intoxicating thrill it brought me.

I watched from my usual spot at the counter, swirling the last of my coffee as Maya's delicate fingers fumbled with her necklace. The silver chain shimmered in the diner's light, reflecting the excitement in her eyes as she prepared for what she believed would be a night to remember.

"Can you believe it, Donna?" she gushed, glancing at her friend and co-worker while she continued to adjust the pendant. "I can't remember the last time I had a proper date."

She had changed out of her usual blue A-line uniform dress and white apron into a simple but elegant black cocktail dress with a plunging neckline.

The sight of her petite, yet curvy, body in the figure-hugging dress further justifying my beating the crap out of her date.

There was no fucking way another man was going to spend the night staring at her breasts on display like that.

"Maya," Donna whispered urgently, pulling her friend aside as she caught sight of the clock. "It's getting late, though. Shouldn't he be here by now?"

"I don't know," Maya replied, her voice barely audible over the clatter of dishes and idle chatter. "Maybe he got held up or something."

"Or maybe he just isn't coming," Donna suggested cautiously. "You know how guys can be sometimes."

"You think so?" Maya murmured, her face falling as she rolled her eyes. "Seriously, what is wrong with me?"

Nothing, babygirl. You're perfect.

She continued. "That's the third guy this month. Why do these guys keep asking me out and ditching? I mean, I'd get it if we had a boring first date, but I don't even get that far!"

Four. She didn't know about the guy who wanted to ask her out, but never got the chance.

I got to him first.

Donna shook her head. "Nothing is wrong with you. Guys just suck."

Maya's eyebrows rose. "Maybe something bad happened. Not like I'm hoping for that, but maybe he got in a car accident or a flat tire, or—"

I smirked as I lifted the coffee cup to my lips. Something bad had *definitely* happened to him.

Donna placed a hand on her hip as she replaced the coffee carafe. "—or his fish died, or his mommy got sick, or his car wouldn't start or the dog ate his homework. Even if any of those lame excuses were true, he still should have at least texted."

Maya let out a frustrated sigh as she kicked off her heels and pulled out her Ked sneakers from her backpack under the counter and slipped them on. "You're right. Screw him."

Despite her now being off the clock, she walked over to where I was sitting.

"Here's your check, sir," she whispered, her eyes never quite meeting mine as she slid the small piece of paper across the counter toward me.

As I reached for it, my fingers deliberately grazed against hers for the briefest of moments.

I was pleased to see the jolt of shock and desire flash across her sweet, chocolate brown eyes as they rose to clash with mine.

I rose, reached into my wallet, and pulled out several crisp bills. I placed them on the table under the coffee saucer with a steady hand, despite the turmoil raging within me.

Leaving a two-hundred-dollar tip on a cup of coffee and a plate of scrambled eggs and toast was a bit much but I wanted her to know that I had the means to provide for her, to protect her from the harsh realities of the world that sought to bring her down. But first, she needed to awaken to the truth of who I was — of what we could become together.

"Have a good night, sir," she whispered, her voice barely audible above the din of the diner.

I nodded in response.

As I walked away from the table, I could feel her eyes on me, burning into my soul like a brand. The weight of her gaze was both intoxicating and suffocating, pulling me deeper into the tangled web we were weaving together.

"Goodnight, babygirl," I thought as I pushed open the door and stepped out into the night. I felt a surge of adrenaline course through me.

Yes, something bad had happened to her date. He had dared to touch what was mine.

The darkness within me had been momentarily sated, but I knew it wouldn't be long before it came clawing its way back to the surface, hungry for more.

The night air was colder than I had expected, my breath visible in the dimly lit street. My thoughts were consumed by Maya, like a ravenous beast devouring every shred of my sanity.

It wasn't enough simply to watch her from afar; the need for control, possession, it festered within me, growing stronger with every stolen glimpse of her innocent beauty.

As I sauntered down the sidewalk, my hands buried deep in my pockets, I imagined how it would feel to have that petite body pressed against mine, to claim those lush lips as my own. The thought sent a shiver down my spine, followed closely by a surge of possessive jealousy.

She was mine, and I would not share her with anyone.

The very notion made my blood boil, my fists clenching in my pockets as I fought to control the rage that surged through me.

Maybe it was time I came out of the shadows….

Sweet Jealousy

A Ruthless Obsession Vella

Also Available on Radish, @ZBlake.

THANK YOU

Stormy Night Publications would like to thank you for your interest in our books.

If you liked this book (or even if you didn't), we would really appreciate you leaving a review on the site where you purchased it. Reviews provide useful feedback for us and our authors, and this feedback (both positive comments and constructive criticism) allows us to work even harder to make sure we provide the content our customers want to read.

Made in the USA
Middletown, DE
31 August 2024

60121291R00216